NADIA

NADIA

A NOVEL

Christine Evans

UNIVERSITY OF IOWA PRESS ∎ IOWA CITY

University of Iowa Press, Iowa City 52242
Copyright © 2023 by Christine Evans

uipress.uiowa.edu

Printed in the United States of America

ISBN 978-1-60938-909-3 (pbk)
ISBN 978-1-60938-910-9 (ebk)

Design and typesetting by April Leidig

Printed on acid-free paper

Music credits: "All Night Long (All Night)," is by Lionel Ritchie,
Can't Slow Down (Motown Records, 1983). "Lipe cvatu (Sve je isto k'o
i lani)" is by Goran Bregović, *Bijelo Dugme* (Diskoton, 1984). "I've Got
Those Teknicolor Eyes" and "Do Not" are by Dušan "Koja" Kojić,
I Think I See Myself on CCTV (Barbaroga Records, 1966).
"Večno V Zvezi" is by Laibach, *Laibach* (1985).

Cataloging-in-Publication data is on file
with the Library of Congress.

For Rosalba

and for my sisters, Jenny and Gail

and this is the dangerous summer
at the end of the century

in which we know these things
in which we were supposed to know these things

—Adrian Oktenberg, *The Bosnia Elegies*

NADIA

1

I live in the present these days. I type.

A million girls in dingy London offices are typing. Our nails clack on the keys. Data flows through our fingers. Waterfalls of numbers pour down the screen, disappear into files, memos, spreadsheets. *Click, click,* send. They come; they go. Every day is the same.

Two minutes . . . one . . . and then at exactly three thirty, Mrs. McGinley says what she always says:

"Nadia, pour the coffee, will you? There's a love."

"Okay, I do it." I always say this too.

Twelve steps to the coffee percolator. Five mugs: two white with one (Mrs. McGinley and Maudie); one black with three sugars for me; one black with sucralose, no biscuit (that's Priya, she watches her weight); one black with none for Roger. He is slim but his fitted shirts leave no room for cream. Last comes the nice cup with the saucer and teaspoon for Charles. Black with one. I leave the worker bees' mugs on the counter for them and knock, twice, on Charles's corner office door. He grunts, in that English way that is not rude exactly but says he is busy. I take in the cup, five steps, put it on the leather coaster on his desk. His window looks out over the little park with its iron fence and fountain and chestnut trees. From here, you can even glimpse the Thames.

Charles is the boss, but we are just a side business for him, *off the books,* says Roger, who knows everything. Mrs. McGinley actually runs the place. She tells us what to do, and sometimes brings in consultants with their slideshow displays and their strange English business words, like "innovate" and "motivate." I am not so motivated, but no one notices, because I am just the temp. The short-term girl. I tell them I am from Russia. I stay quiet. I enter data, make coffee, change the water filter.

Priya and Maudie are the long-term girls. No one knows what they do. They have cubicles with moving walls that conveniently screen their activities (*prying eyes*, says Maudie). Roger says they work together on an experiment to find out whether *all men really are shits*. They started it after *a complete shit* broke Priya's heart—he told her he was married, on the day his wife had their first baby.

"The day. The very day! And you know the worst thing?" Roger's gingery eyebrows go up into his hair, waiting for me to guess.

"What is this worst thing?" He thumps down his coffee cup.

"It was an IVF baby."

"A what?"

"In vitro. You know—fertility treatments, test tubes, Harley Street, all that."

"Why is that worst?"

"Not like he knocked his wife up by accident, is it?" says Roger. "And it's not cheap. Insult to injury." This IVF man never took Priya to nice places, only the dive bars where she and Maudie now do their men experiments after work.

"But why, they are still going to these dive bars?" I ask. "After this IVF man problem?"

"Ah," says Roger. "They don't want to look like pros, do they, sitting in the Hilton."

This is life in our office. It is the perfect job—or it was, until a snake slithered into the garden.

■ ■ ■

I was just ending my coffee and rinsing out my green flowery mug when Mrs. McGinley called me over.

"Nadia, this is Iggy," she says.

"How do you do," says the smooth young man without moving his face. The hairs on my arms stand; they know this accent from back home. I look at him as if down a long tunnel. Everything about him is slim-fitting, as if there was a tax on space. His hair is dark and slicked back, and his skin, though pale, will tan with ease. It is not that piggy-pink English skin that blushes and freckles. It's a dense cream that overlays the genetic memory of brown.

"He's from the same place as you," says Mrs. McGinley. How has she guessed this? From our accents? But the English have no clues about our accents, although they are like mosquitoes smelling blood when it comes to differences between their own. I must look shocked because she adds, as if speaking to a child, "From the *agency*, Nadia. Temp Angels."

Temp Angels. I try to smile but my cheeks have gone stiff. Inside my mouth is dry, because Temp Angels are extortionists. *Short-Term Solutions When You Need Them Most!* is their motto. They make short-term solutions with the shadow people, in exchange for a wicked slice of the paycheck. Refugees like me, with no work permit; people just out from jail; heroin girls from the rehab programs.

Mrs. McGinley is still talking. "Nadia. Nadia? Focus, please." I look up. "Iggy will be helping with accounts for the Baltic shipping deal, so do please make him welcome and show him how to log in."

Iggy. There's a roaring in my ears.

"How do you do," I say. My palms sweat. I scan the room, but there's only the one spare desk, and it's right next to mine. We'll be facing the brick wall outside my window, side by side. Reluctantly, I lead him to the empty chair. I look to see that no one is listening.

Then I say quietly, in our language, *When did you get here? Where are you from?* His face flickers, almost a smile—and then he glances around, and the smile shuts off.

"Sorry, I don't understand. I am Armenian."

A lie. Unless my mind is coming loose. While I stare, he sits quietly and waits for me to instruct him. He wastes no movement or word. He just waits. I stand behind him—I think he won't like that—then log him in and show him the accounts files. I get up for another coffee, trying to unclench my jaw. By the time I am back, those long, flexible fingers are already typing the numbers. He is very fast.

All that day, and then for the next week, we circle one another like stiff-legged dogs. He watches me when he thinks I don't see, but no matter how quickly I turn, his gaze has slid away.

Why did he lie? What does he hide?

I need a plan.

Mrs. McGinley tries to push us together. She calls us *you two* and gives us tasks that used to be mine alone (*Would you two change the water filter? Would you two pour the coffee? Would you two sort the mail when you get a sec?*). She mistakes our wariness for desire. She sees two quiet young people, a little too educated for temping, a little too exotic to be English, a little bit (but not too much) foreign—Iggy said he is Armenian. Naturally, with the administrator's talent, she wants to package us up. No untidy ends. She is always tucked in herself—the silky blouse over the steamship bosom, the chestnut hair lacquered into its French twist, the ugly English shoes that make the feet look like sausages. She is too nice to let herself finish the thought (*Such a shame . . .*) but if the foreigners would just couple up, the messy intrusion into the sex lives of the real English could be stopped in advance.

I am now one of the earliest here, and last to leave. When Maudie walks in to find me already here, she raises the eyebrow—as I said, I was not very motivated, and often a little bit late. But now I am always here before nine, like Mrs. McGinley. Unfortunately, so is Iggy. And every day we have a silent fight over who will leave the office last.

Mrs. McGinley must be regretting the *you two* plan. She sighs louder each day while Iggy and I each find one last little job to do as the office clock ticks past five o'clock . . . five ten . . . five fifteen. . . . On Friday at four forty-seven, she calls me over with the special frown of serious business.

"Nadia, I'm trusting you to lock up, since you two are always dillydallying—some of us have homes to go to!" She presses a key into my hand without letting it go. "But don't mention this to Charles, all right?"

"Yes, of course, Mrs. McGinley." She loosens her fingers from the key with difficulty. I imagine now she will wash her hands. As I pocket the key, I catch a little flicker in Iggy's eyes and risk a smile. Now he will have to leave before me. Now he cannot track me.

And indeed, come Monday, Iggy shuts down at the stroke of five like the others. At three minutes past, he walks out with them, laughing and joking. But when he says, "Good evening, Nadia," the lights go out in his face. Why? Who is he? None of the answers are good.

Our country is soaked in blood. Did Iggy run from the fighting, or was he part of it? But doing what? And where, and who with? The paramilitaries were the worst—they attacked everyone. Croats, Muslims, Serbs who stayed, mixed families. Even so, some Serbs fought beside us; he could tell me all this. But he pretends not to understand our language. So I fear the worst. And also, I am stuck.

I will have to do some spying.

On my third night with the key, I check his pockets and his desk for clues. He leaves his work jacket hung over his chair, like a dog who pisses on a lamppost to mark territory. I wait until everyone is gone, then count to a hundred. Clear the dirty coffee cups so I'll have an excuse—*cleaning up*—if anyone comes back. Then, hands sweating, I go through his desk drawers.

Chewing gum. A lottery ticket. A pack of child's birthday candles, probably left there by another temp. Some loose change. Some pens. A notepad with several phone numbers on it, and a doodle of a mandala. I copy the phone numbers down. I move on to his jacket pockets. An old lotto ticket, some tissues. More loose change—why do men always have this? I begin to feel foolish. Then I reach the last pocket, feel around, and find it. My fingertips prickle—they know this shape, this smooth, chilly texture. It's round on one side and flat underneath, like a mushroom.

I pull it out and stare at it. It pulses in my hand like a living thing.

It's an old-fashioned button, made of glass; inside is a yellow flower, as if frozen in an ice that will never melt. Sanja had an old cardigan from her grandmother with these buttons; I stole it from her and wore it nearly every day of the siege.

Suddenly I'm dizzy. Blood thuds in my ears.

Sanja's rubbing her hand through my hair to stop me pulling at it. Then she strokes the back of my neck, *shhh, shhh*. I can smell her bittersweet perfume. Her side's warm against mine; her cigarette smoke twines in lazy circles as we huddle together, staring out the window. *Look, Nadija. Jewels*, she says, and I see. The street glitters like a winter river. The dark holes where windows were, the burned-out buildings, fade into background as the sunset catches a million fragments of broken glass and turns them to diamonds.

My hand hurts. I open my eyes and see I'm squeezing the button in my fist. My hand jerks open. My palm is ice white, with deep red dots where the back of the button bit into my skin. It pulses in my hand like a toad, a curse from the past. Why does this Iggy have this button? *Focus, chick*, says Sanja from somewhere far away. I take a breath. *London, London*, I whisper. *Here, now*. I wipe the button with a tissue and carefully replace it in his pocket. Rub my hands together to bring the blood back and erase the pattern. Then I scuttle out of the office, as if I were the guilty thief.

■ ■ ■

I blame the summer for what happens next. For the next two weeks, I watch Iggy in every moment but he just comes to work, bares his teeth in a smile, types, leaves. Still, I am careful. Each day I find a new way to the Tube. Variation is harder to follow. I know routine can be deadly. But it is soothing too. Slowly the office days, each so like the next, loosen the fist in my belly, bring doubts: *Perhaps the English have these glass flower buttons also; perhaps it was left in the temp desk drawer and he just picked it up. . . .* Anyway, by my third week with the key I am settled in the new routine: lock up, plan my new way to the Tube, trip home, dinner. But then, the long, soft summer evenings, the whole city out for a drink—London lures me in. In a walking dream, I stitch together city pieces to make a new map of home.

I know the power of the map. Back home, the towns and villages were marked out, block by block, street by street, for ethnic cleansing. Jokey talk-radio wove together old grievances and new rage. By the time the paramilitaries came, the killing map was ready for them. This street: leave them be. That street: exterminate. Mixed households: a warning, then destruction.

As the war crept closer to Sarajevo, splintering areas, streets, even households, shutting my university and Sanja's photography classes, I clung tighter to my books. I barely looked up. But Sanja pulled me out. Even now, I hear the *click-click-click* of her camera as we swung through the city. She mocked the fashionistas, pointed out the gray-market vendors peddling fake Chanel perfume and handbags, CDs, whiskey, amphetamines, lingerie. She knew who was selling what, who was in trouble, what streets to avoid, where the underground parties were. Now the new city unfolds over the old one like an origami crane, each surface joining the next along the creases of story.

I miss the mountains all around, even though they became a death trap, hemming us in. London is different this way, so flat, and the Thames is sluggish, mud-gray, quiet. Yet when I walk these new streets, the cobblestoned alleys of Soho blur with the maze of the old town. The little parks with their iron fences could be the gardens, lined with cafés, along the rushing Miljacka river. The geranium window boxes, the birdsong chatter of girls on clicking heels, the bronze fairy statue in the little park—I store all these fragments for Sanja. She would make them into photos, *before* and *after* hovering just out of frame. The British gentleman on his bicycle (she'd laugh at that—his trouser clips exactly adjusted); the bright fashions in the windows of Top Shop and TK Maxx. Sometimes if I turn quickly, there she is beside me in the shiny shop window, before the image peels and through the glass, a mannequin copies her studied blankness.

I can't think of myself, yet, as alone. If I dropped a stone into that well, I would stand beside it forever, waiting to hear the splash.

But I get careless. Little patches, pictures, begin to stick, at first for Sanja and then for their own sake. Habit starts directing my steps. I have four or five routes, but most often I take the one past the wine bar with the flowerboxes, through the iron-railed garden where I surface into the roar of Charing Cross Road and dive into the belly of the Tube. On Friday, I sleepwalk to the Tube this way. I catch my train and sit down, unfolding my paper—but a cold feeling draws my eyes upward. Iggy sits opposite.

My hands sweat, my stomach convulses. He smiles fully, for the first time since I've met him. I force myself to breathe slowly. Little red spots dance in front of my eyes and bile rises in my throat. Suddenly I am floating, looking down on the carriage from above. I see myself, this mouse-girl, staring into the eyes of a cat.

Then the scene spirals and a thudding fills my ears. Sanja smiles at me, that secret sardonic smile that mostly involves an eyebrow, then turns back to her cigarette. I push away and spiral higher, above the town, its bakeries and bicycles, the main street where people still walk in defiance of the snipers in the hills who pick off a girl here, an old man there. I see the violinist, in his neatly pressed chocolate suit, playing in the street.

The thunder of mortars brings silence after it, a curtain of dust and silence, but if I lift the corner and listen, there is his violin. There are kids playing, the clank of the No. 3 tram, an old motorbike backfiring, the click of chess pieces, the chatter of people in cafés. Higher now, I float into the chilly mist around the mountain. I see a young sniper hiding. His face is hidden, but even from the back of his neck, I can tell he's fed up. His shoulders are hunched and his ears are pink with cold. A brown paper bag lies beside him as he squints down the sights of his rifle at our city, but his attention wanders. The bag, halfopen, reveals his lunch—a sandwich that in its neatness, with the little jar of pickles and an orange beside it, shows a mother's hand.

His spot is damp and cramped and I can see how he'd grow to hate that cave, the boredom and silence, the drip of rain from the leaves, and how restless his trigger finger might grow. It would be satisfying to watch faraway people fall over in the street. He puts his rifle down and looks at the sandwich—not time yet. Looks around a little—perhaps sensing me in the cloud—then furtively takes a magazine from under his shirt. His hand slides into his trousers. His face has an endearing expression of concentration, like a small boy with a toy car. He closes his eyes and as he does so, I feel myself falling. A sharp jolt brings me abruptly back to a disorienting pattern of shoes, a pain in my knee, and the cooing of English voices.

"You all right, love?" I'm on the floor of the train, looking at brown lace-up shoes and some leathery man's toes in flip-flops. Several faces peer down at me. A woman helps me back to my seat—in a panic I remember Iggy—I scan the carriage but can't see him. Was he even there?

"Where are we?"

"Euston," says a man. The round-faced Black woman who had helped me up adds, "Northern line."

Not even two stops have gone by. Yet Iggy is gone.

2

Red presses in on my eyelids. I squint back at it. A long finger of sun eases through the crack in the curtains. Sun on my face. Sun?

I sit up, fast. That means it's late. Very late. I reach for the alarm clock to punish it, and see two things that clench my stomach: first, I forgot to set it; second, it's now two seventeen p.m. Which means I have slept way, way late—past getting-up time, past getting-to-work time, past being late for work, close to having missed the entire day. I try to stand, but as I move, the sour adrenaline memory of Iggy on the Tube floods my mouth. I run for the bathroom and throw up.

Half an hour later I've brushed my teeth and got dressed, then somehow run out of steam. I'm curled up tightly at the end of the bed, trying to think. I don't know what to do. Go in to work? What if Iggy is there? What if he's not? How will I explain? I'll lose my job. I've probably lost my job already. I feel like a solitary crab on a beach full of seagulls. I can't sit in a cubicle this way, facing a window and a wall, open space to my back. And a possible sniper to my left, quietly entering data into the spreadsheets, drinking tea, wishing everyone a good morning.

Why is he in the office—of all the offices in London? Is he still hunting us down? Or does he want to lose his past, and I am the obstacle? Finally, finally I found this perfect office for myself with only the English workers. Until this Iggy came. What can I do? I will disappear—no. Not that again. I will take another job—how? Not possible. All right, I will tell Maudie and Priya I am afraid—no. Because I would have to say why.

The sun creeps across the wall, then across the bed, then to the other wall. I sit. I chew the inside of my mouth. Eventually I have to get up to pee. My legs are cramping and I scuttle, crablike, to the bathroom, hugging the wall. When I get back, I can think again. I need to call in sick. Everyone does in London, even temps. And then I need to go out and eat something. That will buy me time until to-morrow to figure out what to do.

I have to keep this job; it took me a year to find. A year of scrubbing dishes, serving coffee, babysitting, while I wait for my asylum case and the Home Office sits on my Yugoslav passport, a passport to the country that no longer exists. It could still be years, so many of us to process. All these horrid shadow jobs until Temp Angels saved me.

And now I am used to this nice life. To the kidney-grilling strong black tea, the endless typing of numbers, and the warm shallow bath of English conversation: The weather. The cricket. The shiny maga-zine stories: Britney, Alanis, poor Princess Diana. Whether the Y2K bug will end the world when this savage century rolls over into the new millennium.

But nobody talks about the real end of the world; they can't imagine it. About who got shot in the street yesterday getting bread and water. About who is a spy; whose daughter is selling herself for cheese and tomatoes; where to get cigarettes and aspirin and petrol. Whether the UN can buy anyone a way out and for what price. Such topics have a sepia tone; people here think back to World War II, not across to their blood-soaked neighbors. At twenty-three, I feel very old-fashioned. English men my own age do not see me; the older ones sometimes glance at me with alarmed longing, as if glimpsing a girl they once knew.

Focus, chick. Food—fuel up. Dress. Go out. Eat.

Once I pry myself out of this attic with its moldy pink-and-white wallpaper, which clamps me like an eyeball in its socket, it's nice to be outside. I start breathing again. It's early-shift return time, and all the people who got up at three and four a.m. to clean large houses in other parts of town or to weld machine parts in car factories are returning home with tired or sooty faces. Women in bright saris or all in black, a few with their faces hidden, drift past like rudderless ships. Some tow young children; some pull those little shopping carts full of groceries—dried fish, sambal, spices. I feel at home in this suburb, a pale bubble floating on a brown river. And you can get three samosas with peas (English peas are in everything) for £3.75 at the corner stall, and curry with chips everywhere.

I walk to the phone booth around the corner, but it's already filled with a large woman in a tight pink dress. She is banging the side of the phone—it must have swallowed her money, it does that—and there are two men lined up outside, waiting to make calls. One reads a newspaper, scowling and tapping his shiny-shoe foot very fast; the older one slumps inside layers of mossy clothes. Sad stubble peppers his face. He has a wet stain on his trousers.

I decide I will eat first and call in sick later. I buy a sticky bun and a cup of tea from the Happy Café, which is also an off-license betting shop and used-appliance store. Grimy signs for phone cards, bearing twenty or thirty different flags, adorn the window. Inside it's warm, with three chipped pink Formica tables and a TV behind the counter playing silent Bollywood movies. Mrs. K. brings me my tea and two buns, with butter. She is twice the size of her wizened husband. Over the years, all his color seems to have drained into her; he is small, grayly dressed and bespectacled, while Mrs. K. is a stately ship with brilliant-colored sails. She always frowns a little at me; I thought she disliked me, until she said one day, "You are so thin, girl. How will you ever find a man?" And then I realized her frown was one of professional challenge.

For £3.75 here, I always get more than I can eat. Today, though, I scrunch into a corner and refuse to look at Mrs. K., even when her plump bejeweled hand hovers with the tea and extra buns. She puts it down eventually with a clatter and leaves me to it. I munch slowly and try to think. But the tea thaws my ice-mind and my landmarks start slipping: the local chip shop, my peeling pink-and-white room, the two-word daily greeting with my landlord, Mr. Patel; the morning sticky bun at the Happy Café. The two-hundred-and-seventeen-step walk from my Tube stop to my bedsit. The geraniums and sex stores, pubs and cobblestones of Soho, the voices of the drunken English in the long summer evenings—all these things are placeholders. They form a frail web over the pit where home was, a web I spin and tend, in whose corners I hide. *But not well enough*— The shock of Iggy on the Tube, staring at me with that cat-cream smile, floods back. My hands clutch the warm cup for safety. My fingers tingle, remembering their blind crawl to find the button hidden deep in his jacket pocket. He too is a spider, waiting and hiding. We are the same.

At this horrid thought, I gulp in tea, burning my tongue. I jerk and hot liquid spills. My fingers can't hold on—they drop the cup and it shatters; the scalding liquid soaks my thighs. The air in my lungs rushes in and out and Mrs. K. hurries over, clucking her tongue, her motherly powers unleashed.

"Oh dear oh dear oh dear, what have we done here? You silly girl."

"I'm sorry, I broke your cup."

"Oh, it is nothing. Nothing at all. Let's get you out of this skin."

"Pardon?"

"Out of your tights. Come, come." She pulls me into the bathroom, still clucking, and makes me peel off, then whips an ice pack from the fridge for my leg. A large red lake is growing on my thigh. She leaves and returns with a blue silk cloth that she wraps around me, forming a loose tied-up skirt. She leads me into the lounge behind the café and says, "Now. Sit. And then tell me what is wrong with you today." I shake my head in frozen misery. She gives me a long look, then plops me down on the couch like a lost parcel.

Two hours later, I'm still here—engulfed in the middle of Mrs. K.'s sofa between Granny K. and a cat the size of a young puma. The back of the store, where I've never been before, is a comfy chaos. The floor is covered with scuffed gray and red lino, the couch could swallow small animals whole in its floral belly, and a couple of parakeets chatter in a swinging cage over the ironing board where mountainous piles of Mrs. K.'s side job as a laundress spill from a basket. Another large TV screen, muted with Hindi subtitles, oscillates between shampoo ads, where smiling women toss slow-swinging hair, and Bollywood dance routines, which look almost the same.

I am in some strange liquid state where I should feel afraid, should do something, but I can't. My feet are warm and I feel about five years old. I think I'll stay here forever. Mr. K. had unfolded from his little crab chair in the corner, frowning, when Mrs. K. brought me in—but she stopped whatever he was going to say with a thunderous look and he retreated back behind his paper. Now Granny K. and I are watching Bollywood and Mrs. K. is ironing and muttering about how the boys are late for dinner again.

She turns to me. "Nadia." I nod. "Boys are a bother, aren't they?" I say nothing to this. I haven't spoken for hours. "Come, help me with the dinner."

I lever myself out of the couch's whale belly and follow her. Here, everything comes into focus. The chaos of the lounge is gone in a neat, surgically clean and ordered steel kitchen. Mrs. K.'s pots and pans gleam and hang in precise order of size over a large stove. Spices line the maroon walls. She hands me a knife and a bumpy, pale green vegetable. "Cut. Keep the skin, but core the seeds. One-inch chunks, in this bowl."

I start cutting. Under the thick skin—what is this thing?—the flesh is pale, like a banana, but firmer. Somehow, I can tell it has no taste of its own; perhaps it soaks up flavors, like rice.

"Quick quick, Nadia. We want to eat before midnight, isn't it? The boys will be hungry and then Naveen has homework. Come on, finish the okra. Chop, chop."

I hate having to move, to focus. My hand starts to shake a little.

"I know you don't want to talk, girl. But you can't sit on the sofa all day and night. Life goes on. How is your leg?"

I'd forgotten about it, but as if on cue, the burned skin throbs. "It hurts," I say.

"So you can still talk. There's hope for you yet." Ridiculously, she nudges me hard in the ribs. I almost fall over, but the surprise makes me laugh. She laughs too, big rolling heaves, and I laugh harder, and harder, until I am crying. Big sobs shake my body and Mrs. K. engulfs me with her arms, pats my back. "Now. Will you tell me what is the matter, please?"

"I can't."

"Rubbish." She lets go and looks at me—a warm glare, if such a thing is possible. "Troubles are better shared."

"Mine are not. It's—something dangerous."

"You burned your leg because you were worrying. *That* is dangerous, Nadia."

"I mean—someone saw me. Someone who might be—might have been an enemy." She takes this in.

"Nadia. Do you mean . . . from here? From London?"

My tongue is glued to the roof of my mouth. Despite her abundant size and warmth, she is receding—or is it me?

"No," I whisper. "From before."

3

In the darkest part of the woods, down by the river, is a tree that bleeds. When the moon is waxing. When the owl hoots. Or whenever you were bad, or refused to do your homework. Then your mother would say, *I'll tie you to that tree and the headless man will come and split you in two with his black axe. Unless you finish your homework right now, before dinner.* You'd cry and beg, and she'd cock her head, considering it, then with a nod, you'd be reprieved: *Just this once . . . if you get it all done in time.* The fizzing relief soured, though, once you were old enough, because what boy wants to cry in front of a mother who's tricked him? Humiliating. Only babies believe in bleeding trees.

But tonight, there's a gibbous moon in the forest and you're down by the river. And there's a thin vertical line of shadow on a particular birch tree's trunk. It looks like a wound. A moon wound. *Huh*, you think, *that's how it*—but then there's a rustle behind you. You spin toward the prisoner who's trying to crawl away. You lift your rifle and hit him between the shoulders with the butt and he falls flat on his face. He groans a little. *Uh uh uh*, you say. You nudge him upright with your boot.

First assignment. It feels a bit unreal, like you're playing a bad guy in an American TV show. The prisoner's face is thin and grimy. He has a three-day stubble and his left eye is swollen shut. He's missing a tooth, and another two are capped with gold. Nonetheless he looks at you. No expression, but to look is to defy: *I see what you are.* You look back, giving nothing away, then get out a battered soft pack of cigarettes. You light one, ostentatiously drawing it in—*Aaah.* Hold it. Blow it out slowly. The pleasure, the light fizzy feeling of relief. Reprieved from the bleeding tree.

You think as you smoke. The woods are quiet, good for thinking. No sound carries from the village, but just through the trees, on the other side of this night, there's a barn full of men like this. Sometimes the wind brings their screams all the way to the village. Then the women shut the windows and everyone turns up the radio, which serves a cheery mix of war talk and techno-turbo-folk music. The farm-lads-turned-soldiers are busy. Everybody knows what's in the wind but no one admits it yet, even to themselves. Still, the village is excited. On edge.

It's your job to deliver this prisoner to the barn. You haven't thought further than that, but in the quiet of the woods, something rises in your gut, threatening to burn your throat. And you're angry now with this prisoner, for smiling a little with imagined pleasure at the smoke going into your lungs. Putting himself in your place, and forcing you, for a second—too long—to imagine his. For in that second, you think of the barn. You shut it out, but now it's there, waiting to be let in like a wet dog at the door. You offer the prisoner a drag. He takes it, inhaling with every cell in his body. Closes his eyes. Then as he hands it back, he looks you in the eye—and suddenly chest-butts you, knocking you flat. Then he runs.

Shit. You scramble to your feet and chase after him. Ten yards, twenty— He stumbles away, then zigzags behind a tree and disappears. Blood pumps hard in your ears but you force yourself to stop, listen, and wait. The years of hunting in these woods pay off now. A minute passes. Two. Your eyes adjust to the silvery darkness, and in the shadow behind a tree, you sense a darker shadow. And then a twig snaps. There he is! You're there in a second. In a hot rage, you swing the rifle butt, smashing his head. He grunts and lies still. Triumph pumps adrenaline through your body.

But after a moment, when he still hasn't moved, your legs wobble. You feel like throwing up. You've killed animals before, of course. Put down sick cows, lambs born with missing legs. But this—you're shivering. At least it was quick. What now? A huge uncharted wilderness unfolds where, seconds ago, there was just a short walk through the woods back up to the village where you've lived most your life. But now, just like that, you're not going back. Not with the barn, and—

You rifle through the dead man's pockets for ID. Nothing. Good. You untie his hands and push him into the bushes. Now he's not a botched capture; he's just an enemy who some sharp-eyed villager caught running away. Or so you hope.

You stand to go, but a movement catches your eye. The thin shadow on the silver birch is a flickering red line, trickling down the trunk. Optical illusion, you tell yourself, but the shadow moves like a living thing. One breath. Two. You start walking in the opposite direction from the village. One foot—another—just walk. Get away from that damn tree. It's all you can do not to run. And suddenly, something's moving right in front of you—your heart hammers, you raise your rifle—but then the bushes part, boots crunch on soil, and Stefan and Milan emerge. They're laughing in low voices. Stefan has a coil of rope over his shoulder.

"Iggy! What are you doing out here?" That's Stefan.

"Hey, man—you done already?" says Milan. Winks. "You're on delivery, right? Get the goods?"

They're grinning as they speak—you're all recent recruits, and across the chasm to the world-that-was just three minutes ago, you remember feeling clever too, saying "goods" and "delivery," in case anyone overheard. Like schoolboys playing Nazis and partisans in the woods. But now it's real. If they knew you'd tried to spare the prisoner interrogation—

"Had a bit of trouble with the delivery. Spilled the goods," you say casually.

They look at you. What does this mean? Stefan's boots are muddy, mixed with something else, a reddish stain. Milan has circles of sweat under his arms and he's breathing heavily. You see them with a telescopic clarity, these boys you've known all your life—the stubble, the shirts, the armbands. Stefan's already adopting the chetnik gear and attitude—bandana, leather waistcoat, ostentatious knife in the belt. Milan, a bit tubby, is trying to hide his chess-nerd softness behind a scowl and stubble. "Bastard tried to escape," you say. "Pissed me off."

"What?" says Stefan blankly. They look like cows, staring at you like that. And for the first time you feel it. That rush of danger that wakes your wits. So this is what war is for.

"I'll show you, but we'll have to figure out what to tell Aleks." Aleks is expecting you to show up with at least one prisoner. You turn and lead them back to the bush. Your heart hammers blood past your ears. Night vision sharpens enough to cut objects out from the dark. You glance at the silver birch and see clearly that the blood-shadow's just a trick of the light. Part the leaves with your boot, casually, as if the corpse were a spilled bag of wheat. As if killing him was nothing to you. Stefan bends, sucks his lips. Milan looks a little sick.

When they look back up at you, you realize you're now the leader.

On the way back to the village, you rehearse your stories. All of you were supposed to bring prisoners, in a surprise sweep of the next village: often people would creep back after an area had been cleansed, and the task was to make sure the job was complete. So you decide what to say: You found your prisoner on the edge of the woods and dragged him off, but another man had snuck up behind you and grabbed you. While you fought him off, the prisoner escaped and ran away toward your village. You couldn't let him find the barn, so to protect the operation, you had to put him down. Meanwhile, Milan and Stefan had swept the village, going from house to house, but there was an ambush in the second-last house. Three fully armed men had been hiding, then sprang out at them. They wanted to engage, but the cowards had quickly run away when they saw that the boys were armed and ready to shoot.

The first part of this was true. You'd hunted alone, finding your prisoner on the edge of the woods and promptly hauling him off; Milan and Stefan had gone on together to case the houses. They had indeed surprised two men, squatting in the gutted kitchen of a house, and nearly had them, but then Milan had slipped on a broken child's toy on the floor and fallen. In the confusion, the two men leaped out the window and ran. And then Stefan botched it. He shot at them through the window but missed, instead hitting a sheep that screamed like a human burning alive. Shutting up the sheep became the only thing that mattered. Once he stopped shooting it, the carcass resembled Swiss cheese, they had no bullets left, and there was not a soul to be seen around the village.

By the time you're nearly home, you're laughing, drunk on the stupidity of the night, the chances missed, the sheep, and the dead man in the bush.

"Fucking Muslims," you say as you climb up into the clearing, spitting toward the barn, which for now is quiet. The phrase has an iron ring to it, like a bell announcing a fire, a plague, an angel's landing. A great event. You feel stronger saying it, as if history were ringing through you, through the field. "Fucking Balijas," you say, and this time you mean it.

4

Wednesday. I'm wrapped up in a brown coat, brown shoes, brown beret—a human sparrow. I'm on the way into work, after some gluing back together by Mrs. K. followed by a couple of days where I just slept. I must have been more clenched up than I realized. Mrs. K. had made me drink sugary tea by the gallon and talked me down from the ledge of panic where seeing Iggy had left me. "Probably chance," she said. After all, everyone has to get home somehow. The turning point was her phone call to the office to explain for me that I was sick. She got Mrs. McGinley's voice mail. My mind whirled with possibilities—Iggy had killed her! The office was on fire!

But then Mrs. K. said, "You silly goose, you got me all worked up!" and waved the newspaper in my face. It was Saturday's paper. No one would have noticed me gone. Mrs. K. laughed and poked me in the ribs again, and I laughed to be polite, but then I could not stop till we were both howling and I was bent over my knees, gasping. When we could breathe again, I felt as though an angel had reached through the clouds and handed me an umbrella.

Mrs. K. told me not to worry, deeds in one country are often buried and left behind, and we all need to look forward. And anyway, there is no proof he did this killing in the war.

"Boys are followers, Nadia. They will take their cue from you, you see. So you wait and watch until you know more about him. Just ignore him for now with your pretend-English politeness, and nothing bad will happen."

It sounded so English sensible, and in the warmth of her kitchen my fears shrank. But now I wonder whether her advice on boys could stretch to managing a possible sniper in your office. But is he? Or is he simply waiting to "take the cue"? Well, I will give the cue. I will stiff my upper lip. I'll keep calm and carry on. I feel very mature and English in this plan.

I smell faintly of curry and rosewater. Mrs. K. has tucked a tiny paper Lakshmi goddess into my top pocket for protection, and I feel better than I have for months. Naveen is keen to beat Iggy up, but Mrs. K., Jamaal, and I think that is a bad idea: Mrs. K. for moral reasons, and Jamaal and me for practical ones. Jamaal is twenty-one and sensible, but Naveen is only fourteen. I don't want to find him bruised and bloody in a back alley. And also, with a night's sleep and an overfull belly, with the loud and cheerful swirl of Mrs. K.'s family in my ears, I feel far less sure than I did.

Perhaps Iggy is not stalking me. Perhaps it is just this coincidence that he is at my job. After all, how many agencies will deal with the shadow people? And for two weeks before the Tube event, I barely had a human conversation. I had stared into shop windows instead, trying to find glass buttons on the models' clothes, when I started seeing Sanja beside me, flickering along in pale parallel in the glass.

Maybe I'd just imagined a danger. I have made that mistake before.

It was before Iggy, in late spring. After a few weeks at the office, I'd decided I was ready for English leisure, for crowds. I thought I would try a walk along South Bank. There's a long stretch of cafés by the river there that feels a little like home. And the pavement is nice and wide. So this particular Sunday afternoon, there I am, floating along like a metal filing in oil, swirled by the crowds that bump you from café to stall to the next busker's performance. The sun is shining between little fluffy-sheep clouds, and I am almost happy. There are book stalls, people chatting over coffee, haggling for prices of comics, EP records, cassettes. Many voices, no Yugoslav accents.

I am browsing in the old-magazines stall when suddenly behind me comes a *rat-a-tat-tat*, very loud—and I'm running, zigzagging, thud-thud heart, past a statue-busker, thick clots of people watching, I push, they tangle, I trip, fall through a narrow break in the wall, slither down, I can't catch hold, down down, land in the river mud, crouch, make myself small, grab my breath, *shhh, shhh* my heart. Listen.

The *rat-tat-tat* has stopped. I hear only the soft lapping of the river, and the laughter of strangers floating above my head. Then it starts again, farther away— Oh, now I see. It's a jackhammer. But still my hands sweat and green spots pepper my vision. *Focus, chick.* What else do you see? Breathe.

A broken clay pipe lies next to a condom packet. The trace of a fish skeleton glows through the green-black slime of the high-tide mark. Farther to the right, a single silver high-heeled shoe bobs in a puddle. Between the mud and the high-water line is a world of lost things, revealed by the ebbing tide. Here, gone. Soon they will vanish again. In the sky, a purple balloon giraffe floats by, just out of reach. I wonder how long it will take to shrivel, die, and sink into the mud beside the shoe and the pipe. Then a child's yell interrupts—"'Scuse me, miss! Miss! My balloon—grab my balloon?"

Shocked, I leap for the string and catch it. Then I am slipping around in the mud, holding on to this purple floating animal. I turn and look up to see a small boy grinning at me, accompanied by a man in an old-fashioned, shabby suit.

"Thanks ever so much," says Shabby Man, extending his hand as I clamber up the wall. He looks down, and following his eyes I see that my new lime-green espadrilles are wrecked, covered in the mud that smears my legs. "Oh gosh, can I help? You're completely—"

"No, it is well— I am well," I say, already planning my escape. I notice that father and son have matching eyes—gentle, embarrassed eyes behind thick round glasses. I watch myself reflected in their lenses, growing smaller and smaller as I back away until, in the English way, they move on.

■ ■ ■

I ponder this muddy Sunday as my train rattles through the darkness. Nothing bad happened, except my ruined shoes. I look around. The carriage stinks of normality. It's crammed with the prosaic pink-lumpy English, with pale Russians, Poles, and ex-Yugoslavs like me, and the many brown and Black people who commute in to the center, all of them frowningly not-seeing one another or putting their noses deep into books or the paper. Not-seeing is an English art that I admire immensely. One day, I will be able to do this too. And my thoughts will flow into fluent English when I open my mouth.

We pull into my stop and I squeeze off. The faces of models that plaster the walls smile at me as I glide up the long escalator, and I smile back at them through the crush of coats and backs. My stomach-flu alibi for missing Monday and Tuesday has been accepted and the office is expecting me. I'll slide back into my seat like cream into coffee and after half an hour, no one will even remember I've been gone. I am even a little late, like the relaxed old days.

I climb the stairs, walk in, and say good morning to Priya and Maudie, whose competing hairdos seem even taller. Priya's is jet black, with a glossy green undertone, like a starling's wing in flight. Maudie's looks like the war baby of a bottle of red wine and a to-mato. It makes me nostalgic for the bold hair shades of Sarajevo. Only Priya turns around, her smile habitual. I walk toward my desk facing the brick wall, my fingers stroking the little Lakshmi goddess in my pocket. As I sit, I notice that the spider plant needs watering. But I will make it wait for the drink. I am the boss of this desk. Then, casually, I look to my left.

Iggy isn't there.

Just then, I hear footsteps and see him slide into the office in my wake—exactly twenty-seven minutes late. Maudie raises an eyebrow and snickers at Priya.

"How are you feeling, Iggy?" asks Maudie.

"Much better, thank you," he replied.

"Glad you got over it," says Priya. "You two must have caught the same bug."

"The love bug," snickers Maudie, elbowing Priya and setting her off. Roger rises like a ferret from his corner, sniffing scandal, and comes over.

"We've missed you both," he says.

"Fuck yes," says Maudie, to a stern look from Roger.

"*Very* bad luck," says Roger, "to both get sick for the same three days."

Iggy casts me a shadowless glance. "We are close," he says. His dark eyes reflect no light under the bony brow. His clothes are careful shades of gray. Roger, Priya, and Maudie are salivating with happiness.

Roger says, "And I'm sure these last few days off work have only brought you closer. Through adversity, of course."

"Our desks, I mean. They are close with each other. It is tricky to miss the infections," says Iggy, smooth as grease.

I think of the mystery vegetable I chopped for Mrs. K. with its bland, pale flesh. This man also could blend with many places and people. Unless you looked carefully. Unless you noticed the shirt tight around the biceps and shoulders, the graceful alertness to his movements. English office workers do not look like this.

"We must be late on the spreadsheets," he says. "I will start." And with that, he slithers into his chair and boots up.

"I'll make coffee," I squeak, making a panicked retreat to the loo instead. What could this mean? Is he just *winding me up*, as Roger does to Maudie? The ghost of that glass button pulses in my hand. What is it? A trophy? A keepsake? Where was Iggy for those three days, while I was hiding? Horrible answers sprout like mold in a dirty teacup. Maybe he's been staking out my neighborhood—my little flat, my café, my neighbors, my local Tube stop and the walk home. Why?

But there is never a why. Hate will hunt us everywhere. What is the saying? Fright or fight? I feel for the paper goddess in my pocket, but she is crushed.

The rest of the day at work passes in a fearful blur. I just concentrate on my desk and the spreadsheets. I speak when spoken to. But then toward four o'clock, the blur evaporates. A voice whispers in my mind, *If you can't run, fight. If you can't fight, look fierce.* And I suddenly see it: a bright, shiny, dangerous plan. It pushes me upright in my chair, pushes out my breath with a little snort. I turn it around, this way, that way. Yes. Time to act.

I saunter over to Priya's and Maudie's twin cubicles. I inhale and channel Sanja. My eyes narrow and I make a secret picture of myself with a cigarette and a tight, short skirt, eyeliner, lacy bra, attitude.

"Hey, ladies," I say. Both of them turn around to look at me—a first. "What goes on while I am . . . sick?"

"Same old, same old," says Maudie.

"We're more interested in your adventures," says Priya.

I lift an eyebrow, Sanja-style, and smirk. "I hope it is okay, that I come to you. It's nice to walk a little bit. I'm a bit too much sore to sit for long times."

Maudie actually blinks—this is the longest thing I'd said since joining the office, and the rudest.

"Nadia, you naughty girl!" Twin claws drag me into their fusty cubicle area. It is a secret nest of bower-birds. The woven walls groan with posters of Spain, pictures of Maudie with grinning sunburned women on a beach, coupons for beauty deals from Boots. Hand cream, magazines, and lipsticks litter the shelf over Maude's desk. Across the low barrier between them, Priya's mustard knitting pokes out of an enormous navy handbag.

"What's he like? Is he any good?" says Maudie.

"We thought he was gay."

"Bullshit. Roger swore—"

"And he'd know, after all—"

"Not always, sometimes they get it wrong—"

"Off topic! Nadia, dish."

"Well . . ." I say, lingering on my imaginary cigarette, "it's, how do you say—complicated. You are free after work? A quick drink?"

"Just a quick one, okay? Priya's got a new bloke lined up."

"Hag and Crow, five thirty." They smile at me like hungry eels. I wink, like a spy, and return to my desk.

"Five thirty," I say over my shoulder. If I tell the right story, the others will now watch Iggy and me like tracker dogs, sniffing for signs of the affair. And he will have no chance to stalk me unseen.

■ ■ ■

By seven fifteen, the walls of the Hag and Crow are pulsing. The wallpaper is purple, with flowery patterns, and feels furry to touch. The wood floor is sticky from spilled beer. It is cozy and dark here, like being inside a tree, except for the luminous bar with its huge mirror and display of liquors. Bottles, lit from behind, glow like magic potions. Men hover and buzz all along the bar, happy bees hunting nectar. A fat man swivels on his stool toward his friend, laughing; he bumps the woman behind him, who almost spills her drink. She backs away, rolling her eyes toward her friends.

Behind the barstools are more men waving money and calling to the barmaid. She ignores them; she makes a show of serving first the women, who struggle to push an arm through the throng. I like her for this. She is very fast but never looks in a hurry; she is a spiky-red-haired ballerina of beer. Fantastic snake and dragon tattoos ripple and flex along her arms as she works. I want to touch them and feel the muscles move underneath.

"That's Helen. Total bruiser," says Maudie, who has noticed me watching. She is sharp this way. Our table is in a corner, where I can put my back against the wall and still scan the room. I say barely four sentences about Iggy and me—mostly hints—and they make up the rest. So now we all think that Iggy and I hid in a hotel room in Brighton and had crazed sex for two days. I imply that I tired him out, and they hoot and howl at that thought because, as Maudie unkindly points out, I look like a twelve-year-old girl from a convent school.

Maudie used to work in a bar and she knows Helen well. With winks and shoves, our glasses keep getting refilled. Unfortunately, though, by the fourth drink or so, Priya is getting a little sad.

"Don't worry love, it's not you, it's her," says Maudie to me.

"It's not me, it's *him!*" says Priya. "I just don't understand how he could lie like that. How could he— It must have been that bitch black-mailing him into having a baby; he was terrified to say no to her."

. "Here we go," says Roger, sidling in late to our table. To me: "She's still getting over that complete shit who inseminated his wife while they were dating."

"Inseminated!" Maudie howls. "That's sexist! You make her sound like a cow."

"Effing cow, that's right," says Priya. "She had him by the balls."

"Stop right there, my love," says Maudie. "It's no good blaming the other woman."

"I *was* the other woman! I never would have touched him if I'd known he was married." Roger and Maudie exchange weary glances. I giggle.

"We've been through this, darling," says Roger. "The fact is, he was a complete piece of slime and he didn't have the balls to tell you he was married."

"He had the balls to you-know-what," sniffs Priya.

"Truth is, you were probably just too much woman for him," says Roger. "You wore him out, like Nadia did to poor Iggy." This cheers everyone up, and I feel daring and dangerous.

"You should make a hire to take him out," I say. "London is sniper's paradise. So much rooftops, so many targets." They look at me as if I'd spoken another language. Did I? "Joke!" I say. "I mean, only the idea—like when he doesn't expect, with a paint gun, or someone in a shop could spit in his face or so—so he'd never know what. Right?" Roger laughs and puts his arm around me. "Nadia, you are a wicked, wicked girl! Beneath that nice little button-up cardigan. I can't be-lieve we mistook you for a little mouse."

"Oh, I'm not really—I mean—no, I just think, people should make answers for their actions, you know?" I think I might have shouted that. Now they're all looking at me, quiet, waiting. Sanja in my mind says *Shut up right now*, but once I start talking, I can't stop. And my English comes out mangled by wine.

"People, you know they make terrible actions . . . see Priya, here are you, you're crying in the Hag and Crow and he is at home with baby and wife and it's—if the world is paper, he just made a big tear in it, he just ripped in your world a hole and home he goes, and he never must see it but you, you walk round that hole every day and what you see in it is darkness. He tore up paper of your life and left you with the little bit of darkness and now you know, now you know you're not safe, that people can do that any day. So maybe you can get someone to tear a hole in his day too. Give him the taste of that."

A long pause. They're still looking at me, Priya as though finally someone understands, the others with that glassy look I've come to understand means I've stepped too far. "I mean, could be fun to make him a fright, you know?" I say. "A joke."

"Ah, we went through all that months ago," says Maudie. "Revenge doesn't pay."

"Sod's not worth the effort," says Roger. "Is he, love?" to Priya. She smiles a damp, chin-up smile.

"Yeah, sod him."

"More fish in the sea," says Maudie.

"Mmm . . . like that one," says Roger, eyeing a navy-shirted specimen with tight pants. And the evening slides back onto its well-worn rails.

Finally, as we all stagger out, I feel brave enough to ask Roger to spot me for a cab home.

"I will be sick in the Tube," I say. He puts his arm round me—the last few days I've had more touch than in the previous three months—and bustles me into a cab with a tenner. With the machine part of my brain, I tick off, mission accomplished: a safe, hard-to-follow return home.

5

It's nearly dawn by the time the three of you straggle up into the village. Wisps of mist cradle the plum and apricot trees. A single star shivers in the slate-gray sky. The village is as peaceful as a landscape painting, and right now it seems as unreal to you. The houses nestle in clusters like small mammals, their backs to the forest, the dark, the fields. Cows munch grass quietly. The green fields are ready to harvest. The three of you pause and look over your home.

Only yesterday—could it be only then?—you'd been counting down the days till the military-training charade would release you to work the harvest. Idiotic stuff, the young men playing war games while the women and old men struggled along with all the farm work. It's been weeks of marching, shooting practice, running through fields, being yelled at by your superiors from the city who don't even try to hide their disdain for villagers; the army's dredging the bottom of the barrel now. You realize you've been holding your breath since it all started, waiting for it to pass, for real life to resume. But now it's the harvest, the houses, the cows that seem painted on the skin of some huge sleeping beast—and when it shudders and wakes up, they'll flake off and disappear into the void.

The village's oldest man, a veteran of two wars, had watched you bumble through daily training from the sunny spot outside his house. His dead gaze made you uneasy. But the three of you were a sight, all right—tubby, shortsighted Milan with a laugh like a wounded donkey; Stefan the loud party boy, who could shred a guitar solo like the devil—electric on stage, a loose cannon everywhere else. Always the one to get thrown out of pubs, yelled at by women;

now he's reborn as a bandana-wearing, rifle-toting badass. War suits him—it's as if he'd finally found the right clothes.

And you? Women are drawn to you, men are uneasy. There's something not quite manly about a graceful, long-fingered boy. And your black eyes, shaded by a bony brow and heavy lids, reflect no light, except when you pick up a guitar or bass. If Stefan's a screaming peacock on stage, Milan's an ox, plodding along on drums; you're a black cat, a hunter's shadow. You just meld with the instrument till it's time to attack. Somehow it all works, landing between alt-rock and New Wave—though the three of you could never agree on a name. But the band seems like a dream now, not just from another country but from another life that last night sliced clean away.

"Iggy! C'mon, let's go!" says Stefan. It's getting light—time to move. The three of you glance at each other—*Let's do this*—and stride forward into the new day.

■ ■ ■

Something's bothering your eyes. You squint them open—it's sunlight. Midmorning. You never sleep that late, but after last night, you'd crept back to bed, and now—you lurch out and find your aunt sweeping the floor.

"Ah, finally! Good afternoon, Iggy," she says, not looking up.

"Auntie," you say, yawning and tucking in your shirt. You pull milk from the fridge, look for bread, plum jam, cheese. There's nothing in the fridge. Or the cupboard.

"Where's all the food," you start to say, and then you notice how white your aunt's knuckles are, gripping the broom, her face turned away from you. She's still sweeping that same small patch of floor.

"Auntie?"

"They all took provisions."

"Who?"

"Your squad. Urgent mission, they said."

"What? They wouldn't—"

"Everyone's gone."

"Without us?"

She looks at you in that way that underlines the obvious. Her eyes are china-blue, opaque. She was pretty once; still would be, if she ever smiled.

In the silence, you notice how quiet it is. How very quiet. Even the cows are silent at pasture, and the barn . . . the sounds from the barn are gone too. You gulp down the rest of the milk and head out. What's missing? The cows look like trick cows, too innocent, decoys that say *Nothing to see here*. The sole tractor in the village is parked neatly beside the barn, instead of in front of its owner's house, where it usually sits to mark his wealth. It might as well be a flag, shoved into conquered land.

"Iggy!" Stefan stumbles out of his house, but stops, seeing you silent at the barn door. It swings slightly open, creaking in the breeze. It's empty. There are a few stains on the walls. Some rags lie in a corner. A rat scuttles across the clean, freshly hosed wet floor. The two of you look round silently. Stefan lets out a long, low whistle.

"Coming?" you say. Stefan is still, then shakes his head. But you have to know. You leave him in the shadow of the barn and walk east, down the little track to the river. It's a beautiful day, sun filtering through dense green leaves. Dark vines flex and twine their way upward. You turn left at the secret fork to the sheltered field, and there it is. Fresh-turned earth, about the size of a small back garden. Twenty feet by ten, about. A big digging job—must have been a team effort.

There are low mounds marking its perimeter. Soon time will cover the wound with grass, wildflowers, bracken. Only the strangely even little hills beside it, those mounds of surplus earth, will remain. It's a perfect place for a picnic. Secluded, but not hard to get to, if you know the way. Very hard to find if you don't.

In the corner of the fresh-dug earth, something glints. You draw closer to see what it is. It's a gold ring on a crooked finger, sticking up out of the furrow like a "fuck you" from hell. The nail is grimy and broken. The finger belongs to a barely covered hand, then an arm, which you see is bent at a bad angle under the tramped-in earth.

The scene spins. Black-and-red spots dance in front of your eyes. But your training must be working, because your mind gives an order. It says, as if to a dog: *Go home.*

When you get back home you see at once that your aunt knows. You don't meet each other's eyes. You walk straight past her to the larder and grab the plum brandy. You drink about a third of the bottle. Then while you can still walk, you make a straight line to your bedroom, close the door, pull the curtains, lie down.

6

It's that fading dark before dawn—the most beautiful sky of London. In this small pause between night and day, everything seems possible. The excesses of the night, as the drunken English stagger home at eleven, twelve, one, two o'clock, are put to bed. Sleep and death curl round each other, waiting for tomorrow's round in the ring. The stars are still out—merest pale dots in the blue-orange night sky. I'm huddled in the pink attic room at home watching them. One streaks past fast and I make a wish—but then realize its steady arc makes it a satellite. I just wished on an instrument of surveillance. Maybe that makes a grim kind of sense.

Since Iggy, normal life is gone. Every day is a thin piece of paper plastered over disaster. As this thought comes, another satellite streaks through the sky. I feel something harden in my chest and Sanja whispers *Yes*. I breathe in cigarette smoke and the mellow of her hair, and rage and pain and desire fills my lungs. It shuts off my fear like a switch.

I go over my plan for tomorrow: Sanja approves. Good. Calm at last, I turn out the light.

Saturday morning at Camden Lock is a bewildering crush of bodies, most my age or younger. I come out of the Tube and am instantly confused. There seem to be too many roads, five or six, all sprawling out from the one intersection. The World's End pub is in front of me, a reddish-brown barnacle between three streets. Beside the World's End, stalls are jammed, sprouting a mad jungle of punk and rock regalia, tourist shirts, and glittery, shiny toys that spin in the wind and pull at your eyes. The day is gray with that nasty cold dampness they call "raw" here, even though it's still summer. A skinny white boy in ripped black jeans shoves past me out the station and vomits into the gutter. A girl with blue hair and a leather jacket over a petticoat goes over to him—no one else seems to notice.

I push through the crowds, catching phrases in my own language in the mix—from a blonde with thin eyebrows and fake fur, arguing with her boyfriend; a hefty man selling bootleg CDs. The familiar sounds make my neck prickle. These Yugoslavs are just magnets for bad memories, best to avoid before they pull you in. And today, I have my tasks here.

Time for a new look. Since I can't disappear, I will stand out like the moth whose garish wings look like eyes. They scream *I'm watching you!* and *Poison!* to the hovering owl.

I can feel Sanja cooing in approval as I finger a tight black polyester skirt and fishnet stockings. This new Nadia will be sharper, sexier, more aggressive. A bored woman with a hard face and blonde hair— everyone in Camden is blonde, hairdresser red, or jet-black—hands me the skirt and shows me to a space behind a dirty calico curtain. I try it on. It fits snugly, too tight and too high for my taste. I frown at the mirror, but reflected behind me, Sanja drags on her cigarette appraisingly. She approves.

I hand the skirt to the woman, pretending to speak no English. I'm taking no chances here—everything about her, the too-tight skirt stretched over solid farmer's thighs, the leather jacket with padded shoulders over an industrial-built bosom—it's all too familiar from home. She tries to shortchange me, of course, and I just look at her, tapping the coins in my hand, until she relents and hands over the remaining change. I glance over my shoulder as I walk out and see that she is making the sign to ward off the evil eye. She must have sensed Sanja in my shadow.

I walk through more stalls, weaving back toward the main street. It is a maze of blue plastic covers and bright things. And loud! Like a gathering of birds. There are cries, coos, and caws in many voices, cheerful and raucous: English, Jamaican, Indian, Pakistani, Polish, Russian. The English sellers have the most beaten-weather faces. Most are wearing bright fake hair colors and tight jeans and big jackets. They are calling people "my love" and "ducks." I like this, the love built into the language of shopping.

There are whole shops with just one thing—boots; bags; underwear; T-shirts. A bright festival of umbrellas, all colors, some with animal patterns and ears. Many T-shirts with writing on them, and pictures of bands. Union Jacks everywhere, some a little bit distorted or with punk writing over the top. Leather belts, leather jackets, bags. Ah yes—the shoulder bag. I buy a cobalt-blue bag with big silver studs and a swinging fringe. I am very pleased with this—Sanja says a bag carries attitude. The swinging fringe says *I am free-wheeling*. The silver studs say *Get out of my way*. Boots . . . one more skirt . . . a little jacket.

By now I am tired from all these decisions. There are so many colors and styles, and all so bright. They all scream *Poison!* and grate against my old habits: *Hide, blend in, reflect no light*. Still, I need the new habits. And now the task is done. Time for coffee and recovery.

But then a chilly drizzle starts. Within a minute, the drops fatten into pouring rain. The sky is low, a metal bowl over our heads. People huddle into their leather jackets, press under the blue tarpaulins. Across the road, crowds are shoving into the pubs and cafés. A wind gusts. A corner of tarpaulin flutters loose, then lashes about and cracks like a gun. For a moment, I lose sight of the street as the umbrella stallholder dives for the tarpaulin. By the time it is tied down again, I have lost my bearings. The stalls are winding crooked streets of odd-angled tables, all jammed with stuff, and I begin to feel dizzy.

I turn past a band T-shirt stall—Nick Cave, Madonna, the Clash, the Bangles—and then someone bumps me and I am turned around again. I want to pull at my hair; the back of my neck is prickling. Somehow, I am back at the umbrella stall. They wave in my face like a field of deranged poppies. Thunder cracks, then blurs into other sounds. I shut my eyes for a second. *Stalls collapse in slow motion, a child shrieks, blood is on the road, a solitary cabbage rolls past* . . . I force my eyes open, to breathe, to stand. But the two worlds still shudder together, too close.

I am breathing too fast. I clutch at a stall table behind me.

"Steady on," says a voice, and a strong hand grips my elbow. "You all right, love?" I turn and my heart races, because in front of me is Sanja.

"London, London," I whisper, and squint my eyes. But she doesn't disappear. The hand on my arm is solid, even hurting a little. There is the gull-wing eyebrow, the quizzical look.

"Hello? Everything okay?" She is speaking English. The ground steadies a little. I force myself to look properly. Tall, fair woman. Tight gray T-shirt. Stovepipe jeans, big black belt. Red lips. Fake bullet earrings, blue head-kicking boots. Bullets—boots—here, where there is no war. Attitude—style—this is Sanja, almost. But this woman's lips are fuller, her skin has some English freckle. Her eyes are a darker blue. And she has a small tattoo, a green butterfly, between the collarbones, in the dip at the base of the throat—what a lovely neck she has; what is the name for this little thumbprint part of the body?

"I like this butterfly," I say idiotically. It is at my eye level, after all.

"Glad to hear it," she says. "I'll take it where I can get it." And that little whip of sarcasm in her voice, hiding a smile, this is exactly Sanja's way. "You all right now? Dizzy spell?"

"Yes, not so much now."

"Need to sit down for a bit? There's a stool out the back."

We look at each other, as if across a bridge with a hole in the middle. The moment stretches. I don't want to sit, but I do need to inhale her. As if seeing into my mind, she pulls out a battered softpack. "Smoke?"

"I don't," I say. "Well, not so much." She lights a cigarette, draws in, then blows it out slowly, as if deciding what to do with me. Then she hands it to me, I take a drag, and of course, this too is us. And then I am dizzy again.

"Come in," she says, gripping my arm again. She sits me on the stool. "Where are you from?" she asks, but then a plump girl with orange hair and a buzz-saw voice calls out from the front of the stall, *Excuse me!* and Sanja's twin goes to serve her. I watch her angular back, her swinging fair plait, the way she moves. She dismisses the top the girl chose and finds another.

"This one's more you," she says, and it is. The shiny purple with the orange hair—unexpected but perfect. As the girl leaves with her purchase, her cheeks pink with pleasure, Sanja's twin turns and grins at me with a quick eye roll. Again, I know this look. I am here, not there, but Sanja has stepped out of mirror-world into this English body, this life. I want to touch the green butterfly at her neck, feel it flutter with life. *No. Focus.* I dig my nails into my palms, hard, and Sanja fades. Now I see that this woman is more solid, with strong arms like a farmer's daughter. Different shoulders, not as tall—but then she grins, and there is Sanja again. I breathe in sharply, scowl, dig my nails. My palms are wet. Her grin fades; she looks at me warily. My brain flickers like a strobe light.

Suddenly I need the concrete under my feet, the cold drizzle— the reality of this London. So when she turns back toward the next customer, I creep out of the back tent flap and walk fast through the maze. This time I don't look up at the swinging colors, the faces of the stallholders, but down. I watch the mud, and the feet, and I follow where the most feet are walking. This brings me out, finally, to Camden High Street. I walk toward the Tube and see the familiar maroon Costa sign. I know Costa. Inside each one is exactly the same; what an excellent thing. I go in, as far toward the back as I can, and barricade myself in a corner with the soft plastic armor of my shopping bags.

The café is very full, and people glare at me for covering the chairs with my stuff, but I call on my native rudeness and lift my chin. They are too polite to insist; the glare is their only weapon. So I have one little corner of London for myself. I drink my coffee. People come and go. I see that I am the only person sitting alone. I try to regain the buoyant feeling of the other night in the pub with my coworkers, but I can't. My head throbs from shopping, and meeting Sanja's look-alike, and too much English language mixed with every other tongue, and I want to go home. Wherever that is.

This last thought threatens to open the Pit. I pinch myself hard, but the pain has the wrong effect today and I put my head down on my arms and cry quietly in the back of the café. Thankfully, everyone not-sees me. Finally, I sit up to finish my sandwich, but my elbow catches it, and the plate teeters, then slides to the floor. A shabby-looking man reaches down to pick it up—*No need, sir, I've got it.* The café worker glares at me and with a surly slowness cleans it up. Embarrassed, the man retreats. He looks familiar but I don't know why. He is clearly English; no one else could dress that badly, a tacit apology for taking up space in every crease and rumple. And I don't know any English people except for at work.

"Um—are you all right?" asks the man. And then we both remember—

"The purple giraffe!"

"The mud girl!"

Here is Shabby Man from the day I fell in the mud at South Bank, but in Camden. It is the first time I've banged into someone I know from London.

"How is your son?" I ask.

"Oh, very well, fine, thanks. The balloon's long expired, though." Too late, I realize he has made a weak joke.

"Hah. Well, boys last a more long while than balloons, I expect," I say. There is a pause.

"Shopping at the markets?" he asks. Since I have five loudly colored bags of shopping with me, this is a safe guess.

"Yes," I say brightly. Another pause. "How are you?" I ask. This seems to be too personal; he shrivels a little.

"Oh, can't complain, you know." I don't see why not—after all, he's English—but I don't say anything. "Chilly day," he offers.

"Yes." Another pause.

"Well, then. As long as you're all right, then . . . ?"

"Yes." I say. And with that he leaves, bumbling into various chairs, trailing a small wake of *Sorry* and *Oops* as an elderly woman glowers at him. It was not a successful chat, but I feel better. Perhaps the English just accept that life is awkward, and that any smooth interaction is a bonus, like those little chocolates that come with your espresso.

I think about this man's behavior, his shambling shyness. He is a sniper's dream; he has the abstracted, forgetful look of someone who runs on habit. He probably has a local pub where he orders the same pint of brown ale and reads the paper each evening. How easy it is to ignore the world when you are at home.

This thought burns up my spine, pushing me upright before I even form the question: How hard is it to hunt someone? I catch sight of his yellow-y coat through the crowd, and I slip in behind him. He walks slowly, ambling along, inside a cloud of thoughts that must hide other people from his view—he is constantly surprised by little bumps of elbows, shoulders. He turns left into Camden Road and then right and left again, along a quieter street. Now there are trees, and their shadows flicker past us as we walk. I must be more obvious here, and that makes me nervous, but soon I find my rhythm. There is a secret string between us; the trick is keeping it just taut enough, but not to tug and create suspicion. He is shamefully easy to follow.

We pass a black Labrador, happy to be out alone; a red postbox; a series of white houses with steps up to the front door and steps down to a basement. Some of them have pretty little gardens, geraniums in windowboxes. Others are just concrete or dusty grass. It is the kind of street where you notice the sky floating above the chimneys and treetops. I slow down a little, letting the string between us stretch. The quieter street, the rhythm of the passing trees, the slow fluffy-sheep clouds after the rain, all calm me. My own thoughts cloud around me, and when I look back, he is gone. I am adrift in the street like a plastic bag, deserted by the breeze. *My bags!* Oh, I am a fool—I have left all my hard-bought shopping in Costa!

I run back the way I came, swinging my new blue bag-with-the-attitude to help clear the path. I am in a panic, but when I stand in the café doorway, panting, no one even looks up. I push through to my table where my shopping is still stashed on the seats. I grab it, scuttle out, and, at the door, pause. On an impulse, I wave my arm slowly up and down. Nobody sees me! Hiding in the shadows has turned me into one.

Outside, the crowds seem louder, thicker, faster. Bodies push me along in no clear direction, until, too late, I see where my feet have taken me: I am back in the maze of stalls, at this Sanja-twin's tent. Well, if I am a shadow, perhaps I can look one more time and not be seen. She is packing up the stall, her movements tired and heavy, no longer performing for customers. Her back is to me. She thinks no one watches. Will she see me?

I stand ten yards back, my heart hammering in my neck. I imagine when her heart beats this hard, the butterfly in her throat trembles its wings. Then another woman comes out from behind the tent, holding a big plastic container. She is stocky, with short, spiky hair and a doglike focus on her task. Together they pack up the stall, not speaking but passing things, in the silence of those who know each other well. I see, with a little sting of disappointment, that she has the same bullet earrings as the Sanja-twin. Now I want to go. But my feet have grown roots and I can't stop watching, even though the fair woman looks nothing like Sanja now; she is just a weary market girl.

I tell myself to leave, but then the spiky-hair woman looks over and scowls. She says something to the blonde, who starts to turn, but by then I am half running up the alley, my face on fire, as if I had done a crime. I push my way through the thinning crowds toward the Tube, but once I reach the open street, I have to stop because the world is moving too fast. I hold on to a street sign and stare at the bus stop across the street to steady myself.

Focus, chick. What do you see? What do you hear? The blue-haired girl is now sitting on the curb outside the train station. She looks sad. A Black man in a conductor's uniform and a brown woman in a sari are laughing together at the bus stop. My eyes drift past them to the bulging group crammed into the bus shelter. Some old men with felt hats. A solid woman in a sacklike dress, shifting from foot to foot, ankles swelling over her shoes. A little girl in an orange tracksuit, tugging fretfully at her mother's hand. It could be the queue back home, waiting for the bus from the outdoor market. In summer, the fruit is divine.

Another whoosh of dizziness comes, bringing the scent of cherries, and the white paper cones they sell the fruit in. We gobble it right away, fingers sticky-black with juice, and hand the cones back for more. I smell Lake Ohrid and feel cool water on my toes. Sanja's long brown legs dangle in the water as we gorge ourselves on cherries—it's our first holiday away together. Later, she'll teach me how to draw smoke into my lungs by leaning over, pressing her mouth on mine and blowing it gently in.

The butterfly woman's face flickers back to my mind, alternating with Sanja's. I push it away. After meeting her, the day came undone. No more smoking for me.

■ ■ ■

Sunday is a strange, quiet day. Leaden sky. When I was shopping in Camden, the gear I bought looked ordinary alongside the Mohawks, tie-dye undergarments over leather, thigh-high boots, but now . . . I perch on the small wicker chair by the window and stare at the clothes I've neatly arranged on my bed. I recoil from their loudness. There's a tight little pink T-shirt with fake rhinestones round the neck, tarty ankle boots and frilly socks, the black skirt with the slit up the back. A white button-up shirt with tattoo-style hearts on its sleeves.

Their neatness, their flatness, makes me ill. They look like they've been collected from the street and laid out. My heart thuds and bile rises. *Mortar thumps. The stalls collapse. After the dust cloud, shards of glass glint among torn pieces of clothing, a pink backpack with its* Beauty and the Beast *cartoon, a single bloody sock.* Someone starts to wail softly. A sharp rap on the door pulls me out of it. The wailing stops.

"Who is it?" I call out.

The door opens. It's Mr. Patel, my landlord. Everything about him is shiny—his head, his gold-rimmed spectacles, his alligator-skin shoes, the silver buttons on his cardigan. But he is frowning.

"What is this moaning noise?"

"Oh, I'm sorry. I was . . . I was singing." My face must look strange, because his frown transforms to— What is this look? Now he wants to retreat. As if he had seen me in my undies. "Well, please, miss, keep it down. My daughter's baby just got to sleep. You know this is a quiet household."

"Yes. I'm sorry. I'll be quiet."

"Very good." With that, he casts a chilly eye over my shopping and shuts the door with a theatrically quiet *click*.

He does not know, but Mr. Patel just saved me from the Pit. I didn't use to be such a coward; I make myself sick. Other quiet girls went the other way, became more brazen. Alma had been even shyer than me, very awkward and skinny, but once the siege really showed its teeth, she became another person. She would go to the alleys for food, for medicines. She argued with the peacekeepers and even with the soldiers. Somehow her bravado protected her—it put people off their guard, made them laugh. As if fear were a currency that she just refused to deal in.

I don't know what happened to her. One day, her whole family just wasn't there—mother, little sisters and brothers, grandmother—all gone. Her father had been shot the month before. Another family took over their apartment within a week. All their furniture and clothes were still there. Perhaps they made it out.

One day, we see her in action. It all happens right outside, under our window. Alma walks straight up to a peacekeeper who's about to light a cigarette, plucks it from his fingers and stands there like Marlene Dietrich, waiting for him to light it for her instead. A frozen second—will he smash her to the ground? Shoot her? But she winks and grins and he can't help laughing and lighting her cigarette. By now, Sanja is wasting her last precious roll of film. She leans out the window with her Nikon, very dangerous—*click click click*. Soon Alma and the soldier are chatting, and moving around the corner together. That night her family will have canned sardines and some white cheese and fresh tomatoes.

I ruffle up the clothes on the bed—what an idiot I was to lay them out like corpses—and think of Alma in the tight skirt, the saucy little ankle boots. Clothes for whoring. But Sanja and I can't stop watching for her. Sanja's hand is in my hair to stop me pulling at it. Her fingers soothe the back of my neck. We shouldn't be at the window where we're easy targets, but we're both hypnotized by Alma, even though we argue about her and I hate that.

—*Shameful*, I say. *Selling herself for cheese.*

—*Could be worth it.*

—*That's disgusting!*

—*Not if he takes her to Amsterdam . . .*

—*He never will!*

—*Some of them do! I've heard of it. And then she can have cheese every day. Lots of cheese. And chocolate. And tulips.*

—*Sanja! You don't mean this!* But she just laughs at me. She loves to provoke.

—*You're such a little granny. Got to work with what you've got.* This is one of her annoying fashion sayings. After the war, she is going to open a boutique and move to Paris or New York. Or she will be a fashion photographer for Italian *Vogue*. Her creations look fantastic on her, but then Sanja would look glamorous in a sack. Most people could not wear them, but then perhaps that is the point of fashion.

We still both had families then.

■ ■ ■

There's a huge mirror in my room. It's oval, set on one of those ancient, low-slung dark wood dressers, from the days when ladies would sit and do their face and hair for hours in padded satin dressing gowns. Mr. Patel jammed it up here, I suspect, because it takes up so much room—I have to walk sideways to get past it to the door. The good side is that from my bed, I can see sky and chimney tops reflected in it. It amplifies everything. On a gray day, it feels like it's raining in my room, but when the sun's out, I love watching the reflections of shadows on the roofs and the bustling pigeon society that lives in the attic of the man next door. Now they are all out for the day, of course, except for a single stubborn bird who has come home early and is tapping on the window with its beak to be let in. I wonder if it's confused by its own reflection.

But now Sanja is hissing in my ear again, *Focus, chick.* So I turn reluctantly from the mirror, leaving the solitary pigeon to its vigil. Back to the plan. I undress. A thin, small body reflects back to me in the mirror. Not much to work with here. You can tell this body is not English, but not immediately why—until you see there is no piggy-pink, no freckles. The face is very pale. Otherwise, it's ordinary, except for the eyes, which are big and green, like sea-glass. The breasts are small and the nipples nut-brown. The hip bones stick out around a slightly rounded belly. Below that, the triangle of tangled black is the only extravagance. Sanja pushed me to get the Brazilian but I refused, I hate this chicken-flesh look, and in the end, she was glad.

I put on the new lacy push-up bra, which does two little miracles; then the shiny tights, the black skirt, ankle boots, pink rhinestone T-shirt. I fluff up my hair, which is now dyed a color called Magic Magenta. It makes my eyes look as green as a demon's. The color is perhaps a little intense—actually, it's purple. It was meant for the black hair of my neighbors, not my mouse-brown. Well, I am no longer a mouse but a creature with bright, dangerous wings. Maudie will approve, I hope. *Go get it*, says Sanja, grinning. *Gimme a break, chick*, I tell her. Surprised, she recedes and the room is quiet, except for the flutter of pigeon wings from the stubborn bird on the sill next door.

I step back to appraise the full result, and a smile creeps up on me. Yes. This girl has attitude. She is bright enough to be poison.

7

Your feet hurt. Your head hammers, a dull hangover that thumps in time with your steps. Milan's given up trying to talk to you—he needs his breath to keep up. You have no idea what you're going to do come nightfall, but now you're the leader, you can't let on. It's a discovery you file for later—sometimes leaders have no fucking clue what they're doing. Their followers push them onward like a twig down a waterfall.

Milan found you early this morning, lacing up your boots and strapping on your pack.

"Where are we going?"

"Getting out of this dump."

"Hang on! What about Stefan?" And he scurried off. A couple of minutes later there they were, your sorry band of brothers, Stefan scowling and hopping with unlaced boots.

"Give us some warning next time, you bastard," said Stefan, and then you were walking together down the dusty road heading south—to what or where, you've no idea. Fuck the village, fuck the army. All you know is you're not coming back.

You feel light-headed and a bit sick as you walk away from the place you grew up, jammed with the band in the barn—no, don't think about the barn—pruned fruit trees with your tata. Ran back through the fields at eleven with your lungs on fire after he fell from the ladder, breaking his neck. Moved in with Aunt Ilinka after that, the aunt who never much liked you, whose lips compressed when you ate, farted, took up space. And who now, after last night, won't meet your eyes.

That's the thing. When she looked away this morning, it hit you—

it will always be this. Not just Aunt Ilinka, but everyone. The whole village will be a plague site, cursed. Eyes will slide away from the memory of the barn till the forgetting is real. Until it becomes just another lie spread by the Muslims to prove their saintly victimhood. You think of that severed finger again, sticking it to the village. Cursing you all. You don't know what to think about the killing—even though everyone knew it was coming, it hadn't really seemed possible—but you know you can never go back.

By midday the sun's burned a hole in the mist. Milan's really puffing now and Stefan's scowling, kicking at stray pebbles. You call a halt and the three of you collapse in the shade of a tree by a stream—more of a ditch, with a trickle of brown water oozing along it. You peel your single orange, hand around segments. Some leader—you didn't even bring real food. Stefan pulls the cap off his water bottle and drinks, then shares it. Milan wipes his red face with a sleeve. He didn't see the barn empty; maybe he doesn't know. Stefan does, of course. If he'd been there, he'd have been one of the first to dig, to shoot. And if you were there?

"Where are we going, Iggy?" asks Milan. It's not the right question. You have no idea.

"Out of that dump," you say.

"Gonna get in on the action," says Stefan, squinting along his outstretched arm, then squeezing an imaginary trigger. "They're calling for help. They need professionals like us . . ." This is a stretch, considering the Swiss cheese he made of that sheep. "Not just fucking weekend warriors."

However, he does have a point. Sarajevo's been under siege for several months, but unevenly—people drive over from the villages, sometimes even as far as Belgrade, to shoot and loot, but they don't achieve much. They just want to get drunk and high, have a shooting party, then head back to their boring lives.

Milan brightens. "I love the city!" he says. (He's probably thinking of his preteen chess club triumphs. Pathetic.)

"We won't be in the city, mouse dick," says Stefan. "We'll be up in the hills, manning the siege." He stretches out his arm again, takes aim. He's starting to sound like the leader—you'd better cut that off.

"Three days' walk," you say, as if it had been your idea all along. "Let's move. We'll want to get to the next village by sundown."

"I don't know anyone there, do you?" says Milan.

"Not yet, but we will," says Stefan, with a wolf's grin. It pisses you off that he's right again. If someone didn't know the three of you, they wouldn't see three stumbling boys who'd barely trained and botched their first assignment. They'd see armed soldiers walking into the village. You won't have trouble getting a bed. They'll give you anything you want, most likely. Anything. You think of soft white skin. An oily, dark feeling, a mix of pleasure, desire, and rage, uncurls inside you. It's a new sensation, potent and thrilling. And for the second time in as many days, you think, *So this is what war is for.*

Your feet burn. Your head throbs. But in your new persona as hard man, leader, you stand up and look down on your men. "All right, let's go," you say. And the three of you set off again along the dusty dirt road, observed by incurious cows and two hawks circling lazily overhead, just in case you turn into meat on the road.

It's late afternoon by the time you get to the village. You're amped up for a fight, belly churning a bit, but the place looks deserted. The meadow is overgrown. A solitary cow moos, swaying to and fro. She tracks you with mournful dark eyes. As you pass you see that her udder is swollen with milk—so the village's been abandoned, and in a hurry. No farmer would leave a cow unmilked. You walk into a dusty square with houses facing in. Something smells bad. You go over to the well and see the stiff hind legs of a puppy sticking straight up. Someone threw it in the well. Milan looks like he's going to be sick, and your stomach churns too. You've done the training—no choice there, except to run away, and you didn't take it seriously enough for that, more fool you. Killing the prisoner, that was an accident. But killing a dog to poison the water . . . that's a different kind of war. And these are our guys.

You're on alert as you reach the village center, the three of you, for form's sake—circling back-to-back, rifles raised—but you won't be needing them. Doors hang half off their hinges. You approach the nearest house and step inside cautiously. It's been ripped apart. Clothes, mattresses, pictures are strewn violently all over the house. A smashed frame holds a picture of a smiling family, posing together. A man and woman with lined faces. Two tall sons. A little girl with a missing front tooth. An elderly woman in black. Drawers are open as if people grabbed things from them and left in haste. The kitchen's full of broken glasses and terra-cotta dishes and spoiled food. A sticky pool of honey on the floor is covered in ants.

"Welcome to the Hilton," drawls Stefan. With a weird flash of pre-knowledge, you know you'll all talk like this now. With jokey derision. It's the opposite of punk, where the anger is raw and real. This is like the nonstop synth-based turbo-folk that blares from every radio, broken up with war talk.

Stefan looks like he'll say more, but you cut him off: "All right. Let's find the least shitty place to sleep and see if there's some food stashed somewhere. Stefan—you take that side of the street. Milan—come with me." Stefan trots off like a well-trained dog. Milan looks relieved that he won't be on his own to face whatever's left, and the two of you work your way up the street. It's depressing, because all the houses have been worked over. Finally, you come to a small house, a little apart from the others. It's less wrecked; seems it was almost empty to begin with: just a table and rickety chairs and some thin-mattress beds.

You look in the cupboard and find some hard bread, a jar of aivar, some oil, a half-full bottle of rakija, and in the cooling safe, amazingly, a big hunk of cheese. Your mouth floods and you realize you're starving. Milan yells out to Stefan and the three of you perch like giants in a doll's house, guzzling the rakija and tearing the bread apart and dipping it in aivar and oil. It tastes divine. Half an hour later you're all asleep.

■ ■ ■

It must be a school day. Your mother's washing your face with a rough cloth, pulling you out of deep sleep. "One more minute," you groan, and roll over. But she persists. There's a humming noise—a buzzing? Something nips at your neck and you startle awake, flinging the tiny ginger kitten that's been licking your face across the room. It squalls and runs off. For a moment, you have no idea where you are. You look round for your mother but instead, the sleeping lumps of Stefan and Milan, the dirty floor, the smashed-up empty house, drag you back to the present. A huge ugly raw hole opens in your chest. Your mother will never wash your face again, or call your name. Fifteen years gone. Her death is a black hole that warps time-space.

The kitten mews, fear and starvation battling it out as it hovers by the door. In a foul temper, motherless and stuck in a stupid war, you fling your boot at it. It disappears and immediately you regret it, but now the kitten's gone and you've startled Milan and Stefan awake, they're reaching for their rifles—

"Relax, it's nothing," you say. "Just a stray cat." In the morning light, your companions look young and disoriented. Stefan's face is curiously blank, as if no one's home unless he's fighting. You realize he's always been like that.

Milan's hunched in on himself, gaze inward, shoulders up. If a human being could turn into a cave, then huddle in at the back of it, that's what he's done. He looks like he did at twelve, when he realized the bullying wasn't going to stop, so he just set up his chess board on the playground and weathered it out. Every lunchtime he'd frown at the pieces, studying moves while banana peels, spitballs, and sometimes even small rocks bounced off. Boys would tip the board over and steal the pieces; Milan would wait for them to finish, then patiently set up again, substituting pebbles for pieces as needed.

Eventually his implacability grew boring, and the other boys left him alone, like some shabby statue covered in pigeon shit that no one even sees any more.

"All right, men," you say. ("Men." They blink and look up at that.) "Time to pack up and get out of this shithole." They pack up—how strange, to have them obey—and the creaky three-legged animal you've become limps out to the road. A mile, then another, and a farmer gives you a ride in the back of a truck. You jolt along for an hour or two, till he turns off and dumps you back out, itching from the stray bits of hay under your shirt, where the dusty road joins the main road toward the city.

You're the only ones heading toward it, it seems. There's a stream of traffic the other way. The details stick in your eyes—an empty birdcage on top of a car roof. A child dragging a neon-pink teddy bear behind an exhausted-looking woman holding a baby. An older child with a helium balloon with Yogi Bear painted on. Whole families on foot, lugging bedrolls, backpacks, laden with tin. The inevitable Roma and their carts. A few sorry donkeys. On your side of the road, the occasional UN or army truck thunders by, kicking up gravel and dust.

You call a halt and stick out your thumb. It's still way too far to walk, and you don't want to watch the people going the other way. Finally, a battered-looking truck pulls up. You and Stefan pile in next to the driver; Milan squishes over into the back. The driver is a square-faced man with flinty gray eyes.

"Shooting party?" he grins.

"Nah, professional," says Stefan, before you can answer.

"Headed to Pale? The hills? Whose camp, the Tigers?" asks the driver. Silence. He looks you over and laughs, and you feel heat round your collar. "All right, little virgins, I'll take you to Bogdan's. He'll sort you out. You can practice your knife work on pigs—they all squeal like Turks when they're cut."

He turns up the radio. Turbo-folk again—traditional tunes layered over bloated, cheesy synth chords. War's soundtrack. The road spins by. Stefan's eyes gleam; he's finally woken up. Milan catches your eye but you look away; you don't want to acknowledge what he's known since sixth grade—the only way out is through. The trap is sprung. You're going to be stuck with your moron friends, carting a gun and listening to this crappy music, until the war opens its steel jaws and spits you out the other side.

Out the driver's-side window of the truck, the human river streams past, escaping the doomed city. You stare instead out the other window, where the radiant green countryside slides away behind you like the memory of childhood.

8

Monday morning comes. New week, new clothes, new plan of sorts. But first, I wait in my nightie for the pigeons. The flutter of bird wings begins, mixed with their cooing and Mr. Pigeon's voice. Mr. Pigeon buys lotto tickets and cigarettes from Mr. Patel's shop, always Camel unfiltered, and wears a cloth cap. He is unsmiling and gruff, but when he's with his birds, he looks like an elderly lovestruck child. His pigeons wear little metal bands around their legs. They take off every morning at six forty-five a.m. and return at dusk in a whoosh of wings.

I watch all this every day in my giant mirror, where everything is a little more odd and beautiful. Now the whooshing builds, and then through the window bursts a soft explosion of birds, like a blown dandelion head, spores scattering fast, then slowing as they separate. Mr. Pigeon's gnarly hands are in the window, opening out as the birds cannon out. His hands linger a moment after the birds fly out, cupped open, palms up and empty. Then they disappear, and a single hand with a newly lit cigarette returns to hover in the window frame.

Suddenly, I see it as Sanja would. I picture her, intent as a hunter, focusing her zoom lens out the window—*click, click*. It is exactly her kind of photo—you wonder what is hidden beyond the frame. The hand and cigarette vanish. Mr. Pigeon exhales a pale blue benediction after the birds—*whoosh*—then shuts the window so as to build up a decent fug in his lair.

I pull Sanja's battered Nikon out from under the bed. It is ridiculously heavy, the biggest thing I took with me, and I don't even know how to use it. A few documents and photos, my tata's Quran, a lace tablecloth of my mama's, and this camera—that was all I brought.

When you must run, it's hard to be practical. I had put the Nikon away with this small bag of things, out of sight and mind. But now I wonder, for the first time, if her photos are still hidden on film, inside the camera. I open the back of the camera and see that the film is completely rolled to one side. Does that mean it is empty of pictures, or full? Before I can think more about it, I slip the film out and into my bag. There is a Photo Lab near work; they can tell me. I'll take it at lunchtime.

I head out, a shapeless raincoat covering my Camden outfit. I tell myself it's because it might rain—the day is clouding over—but actually I do not want people staring at me on the Tube. My plan for the office is to give the impression of being knocked sideways by new lust, awakened to my own sexiness, et cetera. I bought several *Cosmopolitan*s for research; I've based my look on "Ten Things Guys Go Wild For" and "He'll Never Tell You He Wants THIS!" I'll get more attention, and I hope more invitations to drink with Priya and Maudie after work. Now, if I disappear, someone will notice and it will be harder for Iggy to get me alone.

The other part of my plan, which was really Sanja's genius touch, is that I'll flirt with this Iggy in front of the others, avoiding him as much as possible the rest of the time. I want everyone to be seduced by the soap opera, so they watch both of us when we're around. This should give me time to gather more information on this fake Armenian. Maybe he is just another piece of war trash washed up on London's shores—I still don't like this coincidence, that he turns up here. But if he is a war criminal, I could call in a tip, get him deported for the fake passport. Or frighten him enough so he will leave London. In any case, information is good. It is money in a secret bank for the emergency.

Eight forty-five a.m. I'm walking toward work from the Tube. I'm ready to shock Iggy with a rehearsed grin and a wink, and to entertain the office gossips. My hands are damp and my pulse is thudding in my ear. Up the rickety stairs. I take a deep breath and walk in, hang up my shabby raincoat, and turn. "Hi, everyone," I say. No one even turns around, though there are a few Monday morning grunts. But Iggy isn't there. This lateness is a new trick of his.

"Nadia, love, we're out of coffee. . . . Would you mind?" That's Priya, waving a tenner. "Okay, sure," I say. I linger for a moment, hoping she'll notice me. She glances at me, then back for a second look.

"Wow! Been shopping?" Her face opens into a beaming grin.

"A little bit," I say, as if I did it all the time.

"Cute outfit, Nads! The boys'll be lining up." I smile back. *So, it is working.* I wonder if other people will see a different girl today? Then I wonder why Iggy is not there yet, and my smiling stops.

I take the tenner and walk down the stairs; I wobble a bit in the heels, but soon I am used to the extra height. I just have to push my hips forward and my feet slightly turned out, like a ballerina. On the street, a fat man in a suit whistles; it takes a moment to realize it's at me. My shadow self really has vanished. Men's glances follow me along. It's as if they can't help it. Back home, Sanja was always pulling the eyes; I walked in her shadow, where I could watch the world unseen. But now . . . I hum under my breath. Some girls look at me too.

I see that Photo Lab is empty, so I slip in and give them Sanja's roll of film.

"Is it full?"

"Is it what?" says the woman behind the counter, peering at me over her glasses. They have a line across the middle; behind them, her large wet eyes swim like fish. She wears a white coat, like a doctor.

"With the pictures?" I say. She stares. "To make prints?" I say.

"Prints? Right. Thursday," she says. "After four." Her melancholy gaze follows me out the door.

Next, I buy the office coffee from Costa, where the Jamaican server winks at me; I wink back at her, then return to the office, collecting more glances. Is this what they mean by "string you along"? I could tug on the string of their looks with a little smile, a head toss, and people would come to me.

I'm on the way to the corner kitchenette to set up the coffee when I hear Iggy say, "Nice outfit, Nadia."

He could not possibly have come in while I was getting coffee—the building has only one door, steep stairs, and is in plain sight of Costa. I feel sweaty and trembling but I toss my hair back, in a manner I've always considered revoltingly cute, and say, "Thanks! How was your weekend, Iggy?"

Now it's his turn to be shocked; I see his eyelids flicker a tiny bit before he smiles back at me.

"There wasn't much to it," he says. "You?"

"Oh, you know. This and that," I say.

"Oh, you two!" That's Maudie, enjoying our attempts at disguising our hot affair in the office. "Go and do some . . . what do they call it?"

"Work?" suggests Priya, and they both crack up.

"Very good," says Iggy, gliding over to his desk. I'm surprised he doesn't leave a trail of slime behind. "And—oh, Nadia?" he says over his shoulder, booting up. "I take the coffee white, with sugar."

I saunter over to the coffee, practicing my new high-heels walk. I turn my head quickly when I get there and catch him looking at my bottom. *Good.* I have a string to pull. I make coffee for all and carry each mug over, one by one; now the whole office will see my new look. Mrs. McGinley receives her coffee without comment, but her nicely penciled eyebrows disappear into the top of her face and her lips press together until they vanish. Maudie takes hers with no change of expression, but then she whispers, "Bit easier to walk now you're in practice?" Roger grins at me, then flicks a meaningful glance back at Iggy. I lift my chin—*What about it?*—and he laughs out loud.

Last of all, I pour Iggy's coffee, black with no sugar, and deliver it with a smile. He looks at the coffee for a moment, then at me, then back to the coffee. His expression is blank; I keep smiling. Then he gets up smoothly to add the milk and sugar.

"Oh, Iggy?" I call out. "I'll take a cup now too. Black, three sugars."

He stops midwalk, as if hit by a pebble in the back. Then he pours two coffees, brings mine to me, puts it silently on my desk, and turns back to his screen.

"Just how you like," he says, not looking at me. "Enjoy while it is hot, it will be very soon cold." Is this a threat? I keep my face smooth, like his. Maybe my new bright spots do store poison. I stare past my screen at the mossy brick wall, still in shade this early in the day.

"Nadia? Earth to Nadia? Hello?" That's Roger. I shake myself and start my data entry. 25.9. 32.8. 407.2. I'm pretty fast by now. Usually it's soothing, like knitting, and takes up about as much of your mind. But today I feel wriggly and strange, like a cat settling into a new armchair. I observe myself, this new Nadia with the tarty pink-and-silver glitter fingernails as they tap-tap at the keyboard, the sighing, the theatrical tossing of purple hair. Gone are the meek English browns and grays, the camouflage. I can feel Sanja's amused, sardonic gaze as we look together at this creature, and then it strikes me—I've put on Sanja's attitude and outlook, along with my outfit. I'm wearing Sanja like a tight little sweater.

At that thought, the old Nadia starts to tear up. *No!* I say firmly. She recedes, and new Nadia stretches out her hands to look at her nails and her watch, with studied ennui. Iggy glances over, surprised and—is he smiling? I glance back, but his face is blank again. Somehow, he looks less dangerous.

Maybe he didn't even shoot; maybe he just drove a truck—still, he must have been part of the horror. Not possible to be neutral. His people ripped open all the old scars and made them bleed again. Overnight, we weren't just neighbors, fellow Yugoslavs—no, we Bosnians, who smoked and drank and partied and mostly ignored religion, like everyone else in our socialist country; who had intermarried for generations with Serbs and Croats and Slovenians and everyone else; who joked about being the world's worst Muslims— we suddenly became usurpers. Traitors. Turks. I wonder if Iggy used to spit at us in the street.

At work he is polite, but in private, a face can turn ugly fast. Well then, my face is now all public. People see me; I tug on their eyes with my sexy strings. It is hard to focus on the numbers, with this new power I have. And so I make my first mistake as new Nadia. I wonder aloud how long it is until lunch.

■ ■ ■

I am in the Sandwich Shoppe. It is jammed full today. I forgot this silly office game—the first to mention lunch must buy it. So now, here I am stuck with everyone's orders. I can barely see over the shoulder of the man in front of me, sweating in his mauve shirt. From the tightness of his clothes and his muttering, I peg him as what Maudie calls "a bit of lad." The counter girl is in a surly mood, she's making the African woman repeat her order loudly— "What'd you say? Eh? Speak up!"—then rolling her eyes (for our benefit) at the bad English. She'll probably do that to me too. I practice in my head. *Four cheese and ham, a burger with the lot, and a garden veggie special, please.* If you say "please" in England, you can be as rude as you like. The counter girl's now buttering the African woman's bread as slowly as possible. She reminds me of those buskers outside the Tube, unmoving and painted silver like statues.

"Get a move on," mutters Mauve Shirt. The smell of frying burgers mixed with sweat and onions is making me nauseous. I sense someone right behind me and wonder who's pressing on my space. The back of my neck prickles. *Who is this?* I feel them not moving away, like a stranger would, but it is not hostile. It is someone who can hold ground in a crowd, not fidgeting. Could it be—? I breathe in, and there is the scent of tobacco and a floral perfume, faintly discernible through the sweat and frying-fat fume. I look down and back and glimpse blue lace-up boots. *It's her.*

I look straight ahead. I don't want to be wrong. But then I can't stand it, and I turn. This is a mistake, because then I am jammed toward her, staring at this green butterfly tattoo, today a little shiny from sweat, and she pulls back glaring since I "got in her face" (a sin here). The arched eyebrow, the practiced chilly sneer, the slightly lifted chin that says *What?*—here is my Sanja, again.

"Oh! Hello! It's you," I say.

"Right," she says, humoring the idiot. Then her face clears, and she grins. "Ah, the dizzy girl," she says. "Get home all right?"

"Yes, all right," I say, like an echo. I try for another phrase. "Do you come here often?" I regret it the second I say it. A dozen light sayings of Roger's jump to my mind too late— *Thought the clock was broken* or *Looks like the zombie shift in here.*

"Not if I can help it," she says. "But we're stuck in Soho today. You?"

"No," I say, "it is very slow here." I wonder who is the *we* stuck in Soho. She and the woman with the matching bullet earrings? This conversation is going badly. I should ask another question. "Do you have the time?" I say. Mauve Shirt snickers. I barely care, though— I need to hear her voice. But her eyebrow arches up even further as, without a word, she points at the enormous clock we've all been watching on the back wall as our lunch breaks tick by. Now Mauve Shirt has turned to watch, sniffing blood.

"I, er, it's just—" I stammer.

Mauve Shirt says, "Want a hot date, sweetie, come with us."

His yellow-polyester-shirt mate nudges him and adds, "Yeah, and bring your friend."

"Girl on girl, we're flexible," adds Mauve Shirt.

"Bet she's flexible too," says Yellow Polyester, and they snort at their own wit.

"Your sandwich is ready, slimeball. Why don't you flex your gums around that?" spits Sanja's look-alike, and this is Sanja, too—always slapping down a creep. Then to me, "Dickhead hour. I dunno what hole they crawl out of."

Somehow, we're allies. I laugh. She smiles at me. Three more people shove in behind us, bringing more heat and some rancid musky perfume. And I am stuck in the middle, no wall to my back. I think I'm going to faint.

"This is hopeless. Let's try the Green Room," she says, and steers me out. And with that, she's already trotting down the street. I stagger along behind, off balance in my new cheap heels.

"Here," she says, doing a quick turn into a hole in the wall and we're in a little green nook where a blackboard lists smoothies and wheatgrass drinks and gluten-free wraps. I have no idea what most of these things are.

"Bit crunchy-granola but it's never crowded," says the woman. "What's your name?"

"Uh, I'm Nadia."

"Jody. Nice purple hair, Nadia." She smiles, shoots out a hand, and crunches my knuckles with a powerful grip, then turns back to the blackboard. Everything about her throws me off balance. "You like pickles?" she asks.

"Yes," I say.

"Right," she says, and orders two pickle-and-tofu gluten-free wraps.

"I can't stay," I tell her.

"Why not?" She actually seems annoyed.

"I'm getting the office sandwiches," I say.

"Okay then." And with that, she turns her back on me, leaving me to stare at the incomprehensible menu. I decide I will order random things. Iggy's lunch will be the seaweed salad with daikon. Jody's sandwiches arrive, she grabs them and heads out.

"Wait—Jody," I say, surprising myself.

"What?" And now this strange abrupt woman has pivoted toward me again. She waits. I don't know what to say. I have no small talk in my mind. But then my mouth speaks on its own.

"Will you like coffee?" A pause.

"What's your accent?" she asks.

"Russian. Where are you from?"

"Manchester. See you at Ruby's, maybe?"

"Where is Ruby's?"

"Grove Street, opposite the park. Music pub. Friends of mine play there once a month. So—next one's Thursday fortnight, nine o'clock. See you there, then." And she's off, the string beads of the shop swinging wildly behind her.

Two weeks. Grove Street. Okay. I will find in my *A–Z*.

My sandwiches are ready. I suspect Maudie won't like her gluten-free wrap with tofu mayonnaise, and Iggy will surely hate his seaweed salad; excellent. I gather the lunches and walk slowly back to the office. Sanja could also throw me off balance like this girl—she was sharper and faster than me, and her moods could change in a second. If I could have inhaled her like smoke, I'd still be holding my breath. Holding her safe.

I've slowed to a dawdle when I hear an "Oi!" above me. I look up. Roger's leaning out the office window: "Get a wriggle on, Nadia, we're starving up here!"

They do not know starving. Their lives are too much stomach and beer.

"All right! The place was very full!" I pick up my pace, adjust my face for battle, and let the office staircase swallow me whole.

I feel like a movie star as I enter the office. Hungry eyes swivel toward me.

"Lunch!" I announce, plopping the bag of mystery wrapped foods on the kitchenette table. Maudie, Priya, and Roger dive like cormorants to grab fish, but joy turns to puzzlement.

"What is this disgusting goo, Nadia?" asks Priya.

"It is very healthy," I say.

"Is this stuff supposed to be food?" says Roger.

"Oh no. Don't tell me you went to that bloody rabbit-food place," says Maudie.

"Oh God. Not the Green Room," says Priya. "Please tell me you didn't do that."

"The Sandwich Shoppe was jammed full," I say. "Worse than the rush-hour bus. What else should I do?"

"Anything but that," says Maudie. "Chip shop. Pastries. You know—food. Stuff you can eat."

Iggy walks over, and I hand him his seaweed salad. He opens the box, looks at it thoughtfully, then gets his jacket and walks out of the office, slipping the salad into the bin on the way.

"Well, that's a vote of confidence, Nads," says Maudie.

"God, Nadia. How could you botch lunch?" says Roger.

"Well, it is not my training," I say with a little sniff.

"And what *is* your training, Nadia?" asks Maudie. She is looking at me, really looking, now. She is good at the putting of two-and-two together, as Roger says. But I do not want her putting my twos together.

"Oh, not so much the office," I say. "I assisted with photography, in a fashion shop, those kinds of jobs." These were Sanja's jobs, of course; fashion confuses me. Anyway, what could I tell them? That I studied literature in translation, in a language from a murdered country; that I have no actual job skills at all? Maudie's eyes have narrowed. She is about to ask me more, but I stand up, mumble "Gotta go," and scuttle to the loo for some breaths. As I return, the heavenly scent of charred meat tells me Iggy is back.

"Lamb kebabs," he says, grinning, and hands them around to everyone but me. "I know you prefer the bird food, Nadia," he says. "Very healthy choice." The office clusters round him, clucking with happiness.

"Good man, Iggy!" says Roger.

"Saved the day, love," says Maudie. "Drinks on us tonight."

"Excellent," says Iggy. "I will enjoy. Nadia, you will enjoy with us, yes?"

"Oh, I dunno," says Roger. "Beer's not very healthy."

"'Course it is. It's vegan," says Priya.

"Like crisps," says Maudie. "I've seen her eating those."

I slink back to my desk chair, where I push the spider plant out of its sun. I make a show of enjoying my gluten-free tofu wrap, until the others are distracted enough by their kebabs for me to slip it into Iggy's wastebasket. When Iggy returns to the desk, he is smiling. I am not.

At last, the eternal afternoon relents, and time moves again. Four fifty-three . . . fifty-four . . . I am starved.

"Hag and Crow? Nads, Iggy?" says Roger. Maudie and Priya are of course already packed up and at the door.

"Okay," I say.

"Good plan," says Iggy. I don't want to be near him another second, but also, I do not want him drinking with the others when I am not there. And I need the crisps and peanuts to fill the hole of no lunch. So I am stuck. At the door, though, he pauses.

"You go ahead," he says. "I forget I must make the phone call."

"We have to lock up, though," says Roger.

"Ah . . ." Iggy pretends to think. "But Nadia has the key, no? You will lend me for a moment?" He smiles an eel smile, holding out his hand.

"I'm not allowed," I say. It sounds ridiculous, even to me.

"Come on, Nadia, it's just for five minutes," says Roger. "He'll give it straight back, won't you, Iggy?"

"Of course," says Iggy.

I am cornered. I force my smile and claw through my bag to find my keys. But as I try to remove the office key from the ring, Iggy says, "Don't take the trouble, Nadia," and reaches out to take the whole bunch. My hand clamps round them in a fist, and his hand closes around mine for a second.

"Don't be too long," I say, reluctantly letting go.

"He'll keep for later, love," says Maudie, with a wink. *Ugh.*

Iggy smiles and pockets my keys. And then the rest of us are tromping downstairs. My palms are sweaty. He has the keys to every door I can open in this world. He could easily drop in to the shoe repair place on the corner and get copies cut, then meet us at the pub. And then I will never be safe again.

We are at the corner when I say, "Oh, I have forgotten my purse! Go ahead, I will meet you."

I run back toward the office before they can tease about the pretend affair. I start up the stairs, but my wretched new shoes creak. I pause to take them off and then, shoes in hand, tiptoe up the stairs. At the top, I peer through the frosted-glass panel into the room. He is on the phone. I feel foolish; he is doing what he said. But then he hangs up and sits very still, staring out the window at the brick wall. He pulls open his desk drawer and takes something out—what? The glass blurs the picture. He holds it a moment, then seems to decide something. He stands and moves to my side of the desk. He opens my drawer. My pulse thuds sickly in my ears. I start to back away but bump the wall. He spins and sees me through the glass; in a second, he is at the door, opening it.

"Nadia," he says. "When did you get here?"

"I was just going to knock," I say, staring up. He is tall when I am in my bare feet. He looks at the shoes in my hand. "Sore feet," I mutter.

"Come in, then," he says. I walk inside, and he closes the door behind me.

"Do you have the pencils?" he says. "They are not in my desk, I looked." He is clever with this excuse for his spying.

"I have no pencils," I say. He is between me and the door now, and behind my back is empty space. My neck prickles. We look at each other through the buzzing air. His shirt has a subtle cross-stitch pattern in darker gray. His arms are relaxed and loose, but his shoulders look strong through the close fit of the shirt. His belly is flat. He could move quickly if he chose. I notice that his fingers are long, like a pianist's. I am close enough that I can smell a faint smoky scent from his skin. It reminds me of home. A vein in his neck pulses, very slowly. I remember hearing that snipers learn to slow their heart, to shoot between two heartbeats. He does not ask me why I am back; he simply waits. It is his most alarming skill.

"I forgot something," I say. "In the bathroom."

"I will wait," he says. "We can walk together." I pad to the bathroom, lock myself in, put my shoes back on and gather my breath. One—two—three. I am calm. Yes, I am calm.

We pause at the door as he locks it. I wait for him to give my keys, but he does not offer.

"After you," he says, and I walk down the stairs gripping the rail tightly, the back of my neck on fire. He is silent as a cat behind me. It would be very easy to push me down.

At the bottom of the stairs I say, "My keys."

"Of course," he says with a little smile, and gives them to me.

We walk toward the pub in silence. Late-afternoon sun glints from the window, and in our reflection, I see a shiny young couple, each quiet in their own thoughts. Strangely, for people of different height, their steps match easily—or is the man just adapting to her stride? For a second, they seem attached, like body and shadow, moving as one. Then, as they turn the corner, the sun is gone.

"How do you like this London?" says Iggy. "This new life." I look at him cautiously.

"The office is nice," I say. "How about you?"

"It is peaceful," he says. "Better than at home." And now I sense him waiting. Home looms between us.

"What is Armenia like?" I ask. Now he can keep up this strange lie, or tell me. He is quiet for a long moment.

"Very pretty country," he says. "Hard for finding the work, though. And there is still this problem from the Turkish killings."

My mouth is dry. "What is that?" I say.

"It is old history," he says. "A hundred years, nearly. Turks killed many Armenians. People do not forget."

After a pause, I say, "No one ever forgets."

"All this old poison," says Iggy. "London is better."

Is this an offer—put away the history? But then, the Turks were the murderers in his story. At home, only since war came, did anyone start calling us "Turks"—a new poison from this old Ottoman history. So, what is this? A trap, a trick to make me feel safe? A warning—I will always be this Turk, this enemy, to him? He slows and turns to face me, but I walk faster because we are nearly at the Hag and Crow. The purple door swings open as I push; the noise swirls around us and soon we are with the others. A few times, I catch Iggy looking at me as if we have more to say. But I hide inside the lovely nothing of pub chatter until it is time to leave.

I wait for Iggy to walk out in front of me, then when everyone is still saying goodbye, in the sticky way of groups, I jump into a taxi, slouching low in the seat until the others disappear from the rearview mirror. I do have some skills, no matter what Maudie thinks.

9

Three weeks later, after you've gotten through base camp, you're mostly just sick of the fog. It hangs over the streets below like a bad dream. Up in the hills, moisture condenses on leaves, then drips with a steady mournful plunk onto the plastic tarp that's propped out the front of the bombed-out cottage you've made your base. You look around—ouch, too fast—as the dull bass thump of your hangover kicks in. Stefan's spread-eagled on his bedroll, his long legs twitching a bit. Milan is curled up like a child, his thumb near his face. Last night's whiskey bottles are strewn around. One's knocked over an ashtray, strewing butts and ash over the cement floor.

Time for a piss. You pull on your pants and stagger outside. As you finish, there's a rustle behind you. You turn slowly to see a young buck. His dark eyes gleam, and his new nubby antlers are fuzzy. His forefoot is lifted—he's calculating whether to stay frozen or run. As you lock eyes, a shaft of sunlight beams through the clouds, lighting the deer, the rough lichen-coated trees with their shining wet leaves, in stripes of silver. Your heart squeezes like a fist. You remember Bogdan's advice: *Never look into the eyes of a target. The eyes are the mirror of the soul.* And then, just like that, the deer bounds off and the sun is gone, taking with it all the light in the world. The pain in your chest eases and something like hope, a little bubble of light, returns. You can barely remember when you last felt it.

You rub your eyes and stumble back to the cottage to take the first swig of the day and start the cycle again. Dull mornings. Drunken nights. There's a window of sharp numb clarity in the afternoon when you can engage. It's a bit challenging, because the city's pedestrians have learned to run in a zigzag, to take cover. They're all over the place. Stefan doesn't care—if it moves, he'll shoot it—but you're going for fighters, not civilians. That takes patience, discipline. Wait, aim, shoot. Repeat as needed. This is the best, calmest part of the day, when you're absorbed in the task at hand. Years later, when you recall the dreamlike blur of this time, it's the only part that's in color.

Sometimes in these hungover mornings, you think of making a run for it, but where to? And then who'd keep an eye out for Milan or rein in Stefan? He's grown into a full-scale war beast. He drinks and sings all night, shoots all afternoon, obsesses over his kill count. White powder pours in waves through the paramilitaries these days, funding the war; you got over that shit in your band days, but not Stefan. A fat stream of it goes up his nose. He's in a maniacally good mood most of the time, but when he's not, he's in a rage. It's up to you to dissuade him from (say) taking out a whole group of little kids. You pride yourself on only targeting military-age men.

Milan never hits anyone, not even a dog, though so far, he's shot a lamppost, a mailbox, a car, and several buildings. He pretends it's because he's a lousy shot, and truth is, he's not great, but you've seen him fudge the shot, moving the barrel by a hair, breathing in as he shoots. It's just not in him.

Two tasks: Getting Milan through. Letting a few more civilians survive. That's all you've got on the other side of the balance sheet. That's the hair-thin thread you'll follow out of the fog, the cave, the shooting, the numb days and drunken nights, into a future that on bad days, you barely believe in.

You feel something on the back of your neck. It's Stefan's gaze. He's awake, watching you with those empty yellow eyes. As soon as you turn, his mask snaps into place. "Man, my head feels like an elephant trod on it," he says. "Big night, huh?" He rolls up, scratches his balls, reaches for the bottle. "Fucking fog. No action today."

"It'll clear," you say.

"Oh yeah, you checked the weather report?" You don't bother to reply. Milan crawls out now, woken by voices.

"What's for breakfast, Iggy?"

"Caviar. Champagne. Buttered toast. What do you fucking think?" says Stefan. You cut up some sausage and cheese and put it on plastic plates. The three of you eat, passing the whiskey to wash the dry food down. After about half an hour, the fog lightens. Stefan's the first to pick up his rifle.

"People to do, things to see," he says, as he does every day. You smoke your cigarette down to the end, burning your fingers. Then you stub it out and take your place beside him.

By four o'clock you're all too drunk to shoot straight. It's been a pretty slow day—three, maybe four direct hits between you; a few injuries. You hate those; they're messy. Milan, as usual, fudged a few shots before you took pity on him and told him to clean up your hovel, then head down to the drop-off point to pick up supplies. Now he's back and—miracle—there are tomatoes along with the dried venison, the bland white cheese. They glow. You eat them whole and they burst in your mouth. Nothing has ever tasted so good.

Tonight, the routine is punctuated by a party; occasionally, Bogdan invites you up to the big house to drink and eat. He took it over a few months ago, after cleansing the family; they must have been well-off, because it's a beautiful house, a bit scarred by bullets, with a view of the mountain. Bogdan is a solid man with thick black eyebrows and graying hair. Even his expanding belly looks hard. He wears a uniform covered with medals that you're never sober enough to focus on, but he fought with the partisans—or his father did, it all blurs together after a while. As you stumble in, panting from the steep climb, it's his wife Tatjana who greets you. She's glamorous, a movie star and singer, with lacquered blonde hair and a tight dress. Her dark eyes are lined in black and she pouts air kisses—cheek, cheek—to you and Stefan. Milan is completely smitten and bumps noses with her because he's staring too hard to move his head. She laughs and waves you all in.

"My little Tanja is so clever," says Bogdan after you're all stuffed full of food, sitting around among the dirty dishes and ashtrays. "She's a brilliant shooter, did you know that?" He pats her thigh and she gives him a smoldering smile, mostly for the fun of watching Milan turn beetroot red.

"Now, darling, don't boast," says Tatjana. "I was better at real estate."

"Really?" says Milan.

"Yes, really. Though I do look pretty good in a uniform—" Milan blushes again, he is hopeless. "But I don't like violence," she continues.

"Nobody does," says Bogdan, leaning forward. "Those bastards have driven us to this. Dividing the country. But nobody will ever hurt us again, after this war."

"Relax, darling," says Tatjana, rolling her eyes at Milan. "We know."

"You sold houses?" asks Milan. Tatjana and Bogdan exchange grins.

"Not exactly," she says. "I reclaimed them. It was part of my war effort back home."

"So patriotic, my little pigeon," says Bogdan.

"Idiot," she says, squeezing his thigh. "Well, boys—I'm a small-town girl originally. You know how it is in those places—everyone knows everyone, all the dirty laundry. Who lives where, who owes what favors. So my brother and I used to dress up—uniforms, guns, the works—and just drop in on our neighbors. The stubborn ones—"

"—the stupid ones," adds Bogdan.

"—the ones who wouldn't leave. They'd offer us coffee; we'd stay and chat. Admire their kids' photos. Their furniture."

"See? My little songbird is brilliant!" says Bogdan.

"Who is telling this story?" She scowls.

"Sorry, angel." But Tatjana is still paused theatrically, eyebrows like lifted wings. Bogdan clutches her hand. "Sorry! Please go on and tell the boys your nice story."

"So we'd compliment a rug. A coffee table. An expensive vase. Then, the next week, the neighbor would drop that vase over to our place. As a gift. And we'd visit again. I'd bring cake. Flowers. Always the pleasant chat, it's better to be polite, don't you think?"

"Definitely," says Milan, nodding hard. "Always."

"Then on about the third visit, I'd admire their home, which by then would be pretty bare. The light. The lovely view. And I'd tell them about my friends, who also really admired their flat. My poor friends, who'd been struggling to get good jobs and nice houses, because you know how this town's rigged against us . . . then I'd tell them how happy I'd be to help them out—after all, wouldn't it be better if their place had people they knew in it?—and I could arrange travel for them—"

Bogdan is laughing now, in little snorts.

"—And voilà! My friends have a new flat, one more cockroach nest is cleaned out—"

"—without even wasting a bullet!" says Bogdan.

"Oh please," says Tatjana. "I wouldn't have hurt them. Our kids all went to the same schools." She looks down with a demure little smile. Her lacquered fingertips smooth the red-checkered tablecloth, brushing away imaginary crumbs until it lies completely flat.

10

My cousin Risto is—was—terrified of flying. Their family left early in the war; a cousin got them out to Canada. Risto was stoic about mortars, blood in the street, booby traps, going hungry, but the prospect of getting on a plane turned his skin gray with terror. After they landed, we spoke one more time; by crackling telephone, he told me he wasn't afraid anymore.

"What happened?" I asked.

"Well," he said, "after nine hours in the air, I just couldn't keep gripping both armrests. So I let go. And the plane still didn't fall down."

Iggy is still there. He has this glass button—why? He took my keys and looked in my desk drawer. He may even have killed people I know. But since my Camden makeover, I feel braver. More visible. Even a little bit dangerous, a bright bee with a sting. And Iggy now speaks with me a little, even if it is these lies about pencils and Armenia and Turkish killers. I still suspect the trap, and I do not know what his game is. But I cannot every day put war and the office into the same story. Which one is real? In any case, my terror has faded into wariness.

Is this dangerous? Without it, I just float over the days' surface, a compass needle that can't find north. I know fear is still there, tucked in the seat pocket in front of me. But for now, it's left a vacuum.

The days tick by. I go to work. I come home. The city is tired of summer—the grass is dusty; men's ties are loosened round sweaty collars on the bus. Tourists jam the streets. In my tarty plastic clothes, no longer trying to fit in, I have somehow become a Londoner. Like the rest of us, I snarl at people standing in the middle of the sidewalk unfolding maps. The glamour of the city has worn off but not the vertigo of sliding over its surface, a slippery place without history or depth. There are no high- and low-tide marks for me, nothing to remember here—just sudden memory-traps of other times, other streets, that other life. Meeting Jody has put fresh bait in these traps. Once again, I'm seeing Sanja everywhere, except now she might really be Jody. I'm on the lookout for two girls at once, one alive and the other— At night, I wake up in tears from dreams so black I can feel my mind slam shut as I wake, leaving no recall.

■ ■ ■

Wednesday evening . . . the mirror mocks me with the loveliness of the sky, its soft horse-tail swishing clouds. I pace the three steps from my bed to the door, back again. It's too early for sleeping, too late to start out somewhere. I lean out the window, as I did so often back home, in the days when they still had glass in them. This street, that street, blur and fuse as Sanja says, behind my ear, *I'm sick of this. Let's make a day of it.*

It's been weeks since we got outside, and it's a gorgeous Sunday. We are leaning on the sill together, staring out the window at the lovely sky, the sun dancing on flecks of broken glass in the street. Sanja looks at me through half-closed, lazy cat eyes. *Come on*, she says. So we tear apart the closet, laughing, and out we go. We march up the street in our tightest, shortest skirts and boots. *Look at us, you murderous fuckers—shoot if you dare.* I could be a sexy librarian, and Sanja, a foot taller than me, swaggers like a sailor's whore.

No one shoots. The slower we walk, the more we don't die. We're goddesses! Nothing can touch us. We give the finger to the snipers, hidden in the hills. Then Sanja pulls her skirt up, waggles her bare arse toward the hills, then, still bent forward, sucks on her finger like Lolita with her lollipop. *Come on, you pussies!* she yells. But nothing. She yells louder. She starts unbuttoning her shirt. I stop laughing. Grab her, shake her, keep us walking.

Right then, we hear a singing whistle. And the woman just in front of us, dashing past with an armload of bread, falls over in a spreading puddle of red. Then again—that whistle. And right behind us, a young girl skids, staggers, and falls in the middle of the road. The shots, the bodies, fall neatly before and behind us. A *fuck you too*, spelled out in bullets. *Your turn to watch.* The woman drags herself into the shadow of a shop awning, leaving a broad trail of red. The girl, Besima Terzić, dies right there in the street. It's nightfall before her body can be retrieved. I know this because her father runs out to her, crying *Besima, my little one*, and is felled five yards from her body. No one tries after that. We walk home. We don't run—that's all we can manage.

■ ■ ■

I taste blood on my tongue and realize I've bitten it again. Sanja laughs at me somewhere far away and pulls my hand out of my hair; I've started tugging it out in clumps. She used to tease me that I'd be a little bald granny before I'm thirty. Sanja. I would be a bald granny for you. Anything to have you back. Your smoky kiss, taking away the sting of blood on my tongue.

Smoke. Blood. Yellow fog. Running to get water. Running in zigzags to avoid getting shot. Running out of food. The constant hunger. The little tin-can stove we rigged up. The UNHCR plastic on our frozen, bombed-out windows. *God, we're pity cases now. In our own city*, drawls Sanja, refusing to get away from the open window. *Shoot me now, chetniks, there's no coffee left.* Without gas or electricity, we ran on jokes, coffee, cigarettes; Sanja is a genius at all three.

My father was best at cigarettes. My stepmother Maya was good at jokes. No one cared that she was Serbian. Until suddenly they did. My father was terrible at talking. When the paramilitaries took Grbavica and Sanja had to escape the suburb, I asked if she could stay with us, and he just said, *Okay.* That was it.

He was good at making things, fond of books, but would leave the room rather than argue. Before Sanja moved in, we would often both read all evening—novels for me, histories for him. He read every book there was on World War II; he was obsessed with planes. Days could go by without conversation. He hated the creeping disease that couldn't really be hidden, even with his hands shoved in pockets, so he took to hiding from public places. Tata wanted to fight, not dig a tunnel, but his hands shook too much to aim a gun—one of the many things we never talked about. Digging the tunnel under the airport was perfect: it was narrow, silent, dark, and only one person wide.

Once the siege started, my stepmother turned inward too, hunched and taciturn, and silence came to roost in our house. That was bad. When one parent is quiet, the other needs to chatter or the air goes dead in the house. One day she left, unannounced, taking my little stepbrother Milo with her on the very last bus out of the city. A year later, when we really were living like plague rats, some random mail got through. A bundle of cheery postcards arrived from Zurich, where some distant relatives of hers lived.

Dear Zuko and Nadija, she wrote, *Milo and I are well. It's been very chilly this year, but the city is beautiful in the snow.* As if we were distant people she once knew, our catastrophe something in a newspaper. *Give my best to Sanja.*

My father hid them, but I found them. *At least Milo's alive,* I said, waving them in his face. I wanted something from him—tears? Shouting? Even to hit me. Just something to prove we were still alive ourselves. Tata took them back without a word and fed them into the little burner he'd rigged up to heat water and soup. They barely flickered; the paper was damp. They blackened and shrank to ash without catching fire. Three days later, the library was bombed. It burned for three days: a spectacular, terrible burning. Tata should have waited and thrown them in—the postcards would have been sparks in seconds.

These things really happened, only a few years ago, but they seem preposterous, unreal. They form piles of events with no logic. Scenes from another life. Time itself has become disordered. Like dirty laundry, it just goes around and round in the wash. I am stuck in this churn cycle about Iggy. I go around and round and nowhere. On the Tube, at home, at work . . .

"What's up, Nadia, brain freeze?"

I jump! Roger has just banged the back of my chair. I've been staring at the wall, one hand suspended over my mouse like a little hawk, frozen in position. I haven't even nudged my rival, the spider plant, aside to get my five minutes of daily sun. Each day it fights me for that skinny sliver of light, and today it has won.

"Sorry, Roger, I was in elsewhere."

"Away with the fairies."

"What?"

"Miles away."

"Yes."

"Well, sharpen up, love. Charles is doing the rounds this afternoon. Big schmooze day for Charles. So we want to look lively."

"Okay! I do that!" I look around in a lively way.

Unusually busy typing clatter is coming from Priya's and Maudie's cubicles. Iggy has slipped silently into the chair beside me; I didn't even notice—ironic, since I was thinking about him. I wonder if he saw me frozen. He is carefully not-looking my way, so I don't-look back. He is frowning slightly at the screen. Mrs. McGinley has on a tight shiny purple dress and high heels, instead of her usual ugly duck shoes, and a ferociously lacquered hairstyle. She is telling Elsie off.

Elsie is a new receptionist this week; I suspect we just got one for this visit of the Baltic Bigwigs. She is very pale with black eyeliner and dark lipstick and punky hair. She wants to have attitude but exudes timidity and is wilting under Mrs. McGinley's tirade:

"You're the face of the office! The front line! Do you think people want to see a scowling, slumping girl?"

"What people?" mutters Elsie. She has a point.

"What did you say?"

"No."

"No, what?"

"No they don't, Mrs. McGinley!"

"Right! So put a smile on it and for God's sake, sit up straight."

Elsie half smiles, resentment and appeasement battling it out. Mrs. McGinley raises an eyebrow. Elsie smiles harder. "That's better," says Mrs. McGinley, and she sails off to check Priya's and Maudie's desks.

If I know those two, they'll be immaculate—the cards, photos, little plastic puzzles, cuddly bears, postcards, makeup samples, and so on will have been swept hastily into drawers. They're office soldiers—always on watch, even when they act like they're in their lounge room in pajamas.

I sidle over to the coffee maker, timing my arrival to coincide with Priya's.

"What is happening?" I say.

"Oh, Charles is wooing the Baltic Bigwigs in person, they're coming by this afternoon. Loads of cargo if he gets the deal—they're moving tons of stuff, I hear, and they need it done quick and without all the red tape." I wonder what *the red tape* is, but I decide not to ask in case I'm supposed to know already. Perhaps it is a special packing term for dangerous things.

I wonder what is in this cargo, then, but brush that aside when Priya says, "Might have to do some actual work for a few weeks! Better look lively, Nadia. We want to hang on to you." That's the second time this morning someone's told me to look lively. It makes me wonder how I am looking. Half dead? And then I see: Priya just said something nice. She wants me to stay.

"Oh, me also. To hang on to you too," I say. She looks at me, a bit surprised, and I realize I have grabbed her hands.

"Steady on, my love. Me and Maudie've got your back, don't you worry." She smiles, a rare and dazzling event. Maybe it was the "IVF stinker," as Roger calls him, that had changed her into a brooding, half-absent lump. And now here is Roger himself, in his new too-tight pink shirt.

"Come on, ladies, enough of the lovefest. Nadia—put the last quarter's reports in manila folders and bring them over. Oh, and don't forget drinks. Six p.m. at Wishbone's. Charles is bringing the new clients over."

Ugh. I'd forgotten about drinks. I can't face crowded rooms when I can't get my back to the wall. The English idea of office drinks is to cram into an ugly room with a low ceiling around a table full of wine and spirits and for everyone to drink as much as possible as quickly as they can. Then all the people who grunt twice-a-day greetings to each other can start talking, and before long things start to happen that everyone must agree to forget the next day.

I must have looked panicked, because Roger says, "Don't worry, they won't bite. Unless you want them to." Iggy by now is listening to this. His face doesn't change expression, but I can feel him coming alert, like a cat poised to spring. "Iggy's going, aren't you, Iggy?" says Roger.

"Of course," says Iggy.

"So why don't you two show up together and you can hide behind Iggy if they get too touchy-feely." Roger grins. "Sorted!"

"What a nice idea," says Iggy, a small smile on his face.

"But I have another plan," I squeak. "A friend's band. I promised."

"What time? Surely not six on a Thursday," says Roger.

"No, later, but I want to prepare," I say.

"No need, love," says Roger. "Drinks'll be done and dusted before eight. You two can head over together early. Give you a head start on the party spirit. Iggy'll look out for you."

We look at each other across the tiny space between our desks. The air buzzes with an unpleasant humming sound. I stop myself from clutching at my desk. Iggy is smiling widely now, but not with his eyes.

"It is my pleasure," says Iggy. "We will walk over together after the Bigwigs visit."

And just like that, the trap is sprung.

11

It's a precarious balance sheet you're keeping. You try to keep your shots clean and your targets legit. Men, at least. It's a safe bet that every man left in Sarajevo—Serb, Croat, Bosniak—is a combatant, fighting for the city, for this foolish multicultural dream—as if that could ever survive now. Or maybe by now, they're just fighting to keep themselves alive, since no one can get out. But your balance sheet is getting tattered around the edges. And yesterday, on one of your rare trips down into the city, you tore off a big ugly corner.

The three of you are holed up in a bombed building in the south of the city, along with Boris, one of Stefan's chetnik buddies. Stefan, of course, is playing it up—macho man on steroids. You'd headed down to hold the place while Bogdan's main militia headed off on a mission to some village. It was going to be a good time—partying, girls—but no. Your job is just to hold the suburb, like babysitters with guns. Shoot down Sniper's Alley, scare the locals, make it seem like the full force is still there.

At first, it's great to see actual buildings, trams, faces—anything but the cottage—but then it starts raining. Three days of solid rain, interspersed with thick fog make it impossible to shoot, or do anything much, and the regular unit still isn't back from the village. They're probably stuck in some muddy bog, pushing their jeeps past cows and corpses, and you're trapped here till they get back. No speed; Stefan was jumpy as hell so you scoured the place for liquor to settle him down and finally scored—a whole case of Johnnie Walker was hidden in the back of a wardrobe.

So you've all been drinking solidly for three days. Three days of Stefan and Boris's posturing and boasting and outdrinking each other. Their stories are so absurd that after a while, you just tune them out—sex motels stuffed full of young Bosnian girls who'll do anything you ask, do what you like with them afterward. Shoot them, throw them on the garbage dump, or drive them back home to their wailing families. It's a strange sort of verbal war porn. You know that rapes, even gang rapes, happen on both sides, but this— Stefan must be coming unhinged.

Finally, in the late afternoon on day three, the clouds part, the deluge stops, and a shaft of sun lights up the street, framing a woman combing her silver hair in a window. She probably thinks the clouds are still hiding her. "I can take that bitch," said Stefan. You look at the target, then him. It's quite far, an impossibly tight angle, a midlevel apartment in one of those shitty communist-era blocks—gray, faceless, already pockmarked by many bullets. A very long shot.

"Bullshit," you say. "Can't be done." Stefan puffs up, gets his rifle, and makes a big show of aiming. Pretends to shoot. *Bam!* Laughs, looks around, expects the room to laugh with him. But there's a hot blade in your gut and you say, quietly, "Scared you'll miss?"

Now the room is jittery-quiet. Stefan's eyes go white. He aims and fires, and of course he misses. Time warps and you see yourself in icy slow motion, moving to the window, aiming, taking the shot. It's a perfect hit, you know before you've even pulled the trigger. The window shatters. The woman disappears. Triumph over Stefan floods your body with a divine blue flame. But then it recedes, and something dark and ugly is waiting for you in the room. You turn. Milan is there, looking at you with a sick, heavy face. You want to punch him—idiot, fat boy, little prick—who is he to judge you? The room spins and you realize how drunk you are. You lurch outside into the rain that's now falling heavily again. You run up the hill until you're looking down on the city, above your infernal shooting-house. You just stand there getting drenched, half hoping someone will shoot you, and let the rain wash the sickness off you.

You hate this fucking siege. The irony is that you are really good at it. You know how to wait, to place your shots. You have patience.

You're at home with silence; you grew up in it. The charged silence of unspoken rage. The easy silence between friends. The deep, living silence of the woods, patterned by wind, bird cries, soft footfalls of deer. The tense silence before a kill. But now there's the silence of poisonous things. It drove you from the village. It's there between you and Milan now. He'll look at you, and you'll look away, even though you were just doing your job. *And what's that job? Terrorizing civilians.*

You crouch down and pull moss out of the ground, rub the earth on your fingers, smell it. You're homesick for a time when shooting was simple, when you could just vanish into the woods for days at a time. Hunt a deer, take it home, skin it, cook it, and eat it.

The rain eases up. You're cold now and a bit shaky. You walk back slowly to the bombed-out house; none of the others speak when you enter. You share cold baked beans and each of you retreats to your corner for the night. *Just live through this*, you think, *that's all you've got to do*, but as you fall into dreamless darkness you know it's a lie.

12

Four o'clock. The Baltic Bigwigs come in. They are not what I expected. "Bigwigs" made me think of English judges on TV, with their somber faces and white curls and black gowns. Or the puffed-up generals at home. Instead we get Oleg and Marta. Oleg is a short, round man with a shiny head and a few dark strands of hair plastered across the top. He pauses at the door, eyes darting quickly around to check the exits before entering with an oily grin. Marta trails him like a feather boa—she's at least six inches taller and half as wide. Her movements are jittery and her long fingers keep drifting up to her nose as if to pat the last remnants of white powder up it. Her hair looks like gilded straw that would break in your hand. Behind these two is a hard-faced Russian in a blue suit that bulges in the wrong places.

Charles bustles around them like a dinner party host. "Come in, come in! Oleg, Marta, and"—they nod nicely but don't introduce the Russian—"and welcome! Come in! This is our merry crew—"

Priya, Maudie, Elsie, and Mrs. McGinley smile like those beauty counter ladies at Selfridges. Oleg's grin expands without tilting up at the corners. I think of sharks. He clutches Charles's hand.

"Thank you, my good friend! Always a pleasure to be in your great city."

He moves toward Priya and Maudie, standing to attention like Beefeaters at their cubicles' entrance. "We love your London—and its blooming beauties." Did he actually say that? Yes, he did. And unbelievably, Priya is blushing and smiling.

Charles intervenes: "Come, Oleg, let me show you the view. And then we'll get to the inventory," he says as Oleg releases Priya's hand. Marta has drifted over to the window, her limbs a-twitch.

"Marta," says Oleg, a little whip-crack in his voice. Her empty blue eyes focus back to earth and she moves toward him. One more Oleg shark-smile at Priya, then Charles whisks the trio into his corner office.

"I think you'll be impressed with the efficiencies we can . . ." we hear, and then the door, which is always open, clicks decisively shut. I exhale and realize that Iggy and I have both made ourselves invisible. We are sitting still, folded in, eyes down—the Baltic Bigwigs barely registered us—but we are on throbbing high alert. We glance at each other at the same second. Yes. We know these types. Their enemies disappear. Then Priya's low laughter breaks the moment, and I shake off our odd moment of mind-meld.

The visit doesn't last long; Charles shepherds the Baltic Bigwigs out soon enough. They seem charged up in a hidden way, like school-boys planning a porn session, so I guess the deal is on. Oleg farewells Maudie and Priya and murmurs a hope that they will be at drinks at six. Marta is cheerful and hyperfocused, smiling directly into each person's eyes, after her short restorative trip to the loo to powder her nose.

"He's quite the charmer, Priya," says Maudie.

"Oh, I don't know." Priya's smiling down at her desk.

"You do so! He fancies you something rotten!"

"That's a bad sign, then—sure bet he's a creep."

"That attitude. Right there. That's the problem. Right, Rog?"

"Self-fulfilling prophecy, my love," says Roger, who's slid over to them like a paper clip to a magnet. "Not all men are complete tossers. Just need a bit of persistence." I don't have to look at Iggy—in fact I resist—to know that both of us have carefully blank faces. But then Iggy does something very unusual. He joins in the gossip.

"Oleg has good taste, Priya. But good taste is not always good intentions. We should leave for drinks now." In the odd silence that follows, Iggy starts cleaning his desk. And I realize this is a skill of his—he puts people off balance, then takes charge. To me he says, "I will walk with you now."

Again, that washing-machine feeling comes over me as my thoughts tumble and circle, going nowhere. I close my eyes for a moment. Then there's a hand on my shoulder. It's steady, calm, and I want it to stay. I don't want to open my eyes because it's Iggy's hand and then I will have to know that and start being afraid again. So I sit a moment longer, like a rabbit soothed by the shade of a hawk. One moment. Two. Between two heartbeats, I hold my breath and Iggy does too. Then I exhale and open my eyes and his hand is gone, as if I'd only imagined it.

Priya and Maudie, Roger bringing up the rear, clatter past and swirl us along.

"Come on, lovebirds, what is this, bloody yoga camp?" (that's Roger, of course). And for the first time, all five of us leave the building together.

Wishbone Tax Solutions, Inc. do our office taxes and other things called *optimization* and *gradient curve release product placement* and *incremental seizure something effects* and *international flow consignment planning*. And it's not just my English; no one else knows what those things are. But when I asked what Wishbone did, the replies didn't help:

"That stuff's all smoke and mirrors," says Roger. "That's why they're called 'Wishbone'—they're our go-to magicians."

"'Wishbone'—no, it's 'cause they're so bent they come back out their own arses," says Priya.

"Yeah, they're very obliging, just like you, Rog, they'll bend over backward to be of service," says Maudie, and she and Priya snort and chuckle.

"Minds in the gutter, girls! You've got it completely *arse* about," says Roger, to groans from Maudie and Priya. "It's magic, see! Crack a wishbone and poof! All your problems move to the Canary Islands."

English jokes are difficult. I feel like the slow girl at school, laughing three seconds late and probably at the wrong thing. What do I know—I just type in numbers. Iggy lopes and I have to trot a little to keep up. *My life used to be so much simpler,* I think crossly as we hurry along. Boring maybe, but simple. Get up. Tube to work. Nice enemy-free office. Data entry. Coffee. More data entry. Lunch. More data entry. Walk through London to the Tube home—this was my precious moment to let the day blossom, take unexpected shape— and look where that got me. Staring at this dangerous fake Armenian across a train carriage. Iggy, he has ruined everything.

"Slow down!" I tell him. He does, matching his stride to mine. That's worse, though, because the others slowly draw ahead. We walk in silence, our long sideways shadows tracking us along the pavement. They jump, leap, shrink, expand, as if in panicked retreat from light. They zoom in close as we pass a phone box, a tree, and finally dive into a long stretch of shop windows where our twin reflections replace them.

In shop-window-land, our silvery twins are happy. She's not very tall and has an air of elsewhere about her. She looks old-fashioned despite her strangely purple hair and tarty Camden clothes, like a librarian at a punk theme party. He is a human cat, graceful without trying, dark and smooth. Somehow, he absorbs the light. They go together like coffee and cream. In mirror-world there are only surfaces, beautiful surfaces, and I want so badly to live there. The blood and bile and the stain of death on the cat-man's fingers are all airbrushed away.

As we round the corner, the late sun bounces off the glass, stabbing my eyes. Suddenly, in the green throbbing afterglow, there are three of us in mirror-world—our silvery twins, and Sanja. Her face is pale, urgent. She reaches toward me. Iggy flicks his fingers, as if warding off a fly. Her likeness shatters into pieces of silver and vanishes. I stumble, let out a small yelp. Iggy waits, quietly—he never wastes a movement. Then, wordlessly, he takes my elbow and we continue. Again, his touch is calming. *Forgive me, Sanja*, I breathe. I should shake off his hand, and I can't. And now we are at the threshold.

"Drinks," he says sardonically. We take a deep breath and walk in.

An hour later, I don't know what I was worried about! I'm having quite a bit of fun. I've only had one drink but my glass seems to mysteriously refill itself—Mickey from Wishbone's has been very attentive. He has curly dark hair and very white teeth; he is the kind of person who would hate losing at tennis but never let it show. Many bodies are jammed in the gray room with its low ceiling and nasty fluorescent lights, but because I'm shorter than everyone else, I'm in a pleasantly flickering world of shadows and torsos. A table full of drinks is the centerpiece and people are plastered against it like swarming bees on a hive.

There's not much air. The men are in suits but their jackets are off and ties are loosened. Some have three shirt buttons undone, and little bits of chest hair poke through at my eye level. The women are in various mixtures of polyester and nylon and those astoundingly ugly office shoes that only the English could have designed. They are a copy of the queen's and make their wearers look like they have the feet of ducks. As for me, I've kicked my purple platforms off because it's a party! This makes me even shorter.

"Gosh, you're petite," says Mickey, as if I didn't know. "'Scuse me bending over to hear you," he continues, smiling down hopefully into my fake cleavage. "Cute accent! Where did you say you're from?" I mutter something. "What?"

Now he's really leaning in. He was funny a minute ago, but now—I look around for the others but I can only see Iggy. He's with Marta, who's standing much too close to him, the slut, patting his shirt and laughing with her arms pressed to show off her boobs. "Who needs boobs, they're overrated," I mutter under my breath.

"Sorry, it's deafening in here," says Mickey. "Tell you what," he says as he starts steering me away, "let's get somewhere quieter where we can hear ourselves think." But then somehow, we're in a corner, and he's murmuring something while his hand feels my bottom. "Mystery girl, are we? Strong silent type. I like that . . . can you tell?" Now he's guiding my hand toward his bulging fly.

"She's Russian," says Iggy, materializing somehow—I wish he'd stop doing that—and with his arm around me, he pivots me away. As we walk, I remember, "My shoes!" I try to turn back, but he holds up his left hand—he's got them—and without breaking stride we are out the door.

London streaks past, honking and blurring. I grip onto him while I try to put my shoes on, but they are too high. This strikes me as very funny and I get giggles. He waves for a taxi but they're all full. I laugh so hard I nearly fall over, but then a sharp crack to my face stops me. Iggy has hit me. *He's hit me!* I go to hit him back but he catches my arms. "No, no," he says. "Be steady."

What's your real name, you bastard? I say in our language.

In English, he says, "Igor. Iggy's my band name." He flashes a grin, gone almost before I see it. But in that flash—I see him and it's electrifying. He's the dancer, the risk taker, the one who doesn't fall off the edge while egging his mates on. Then a second later, he realizes he's given himself away. He knows my language.

Igor. What are you? Wolf or sheep? He flinches a little, then says, *A bit of both, like everyone. What about you, Nadija?* He says my name the way it sounds back home. *Na-DI-ja.* He strokes the back of my neck, like Sanja did.

Something is hurting. It's recognition, cracking my heart. I am so lonely for my country. I hate him. I cannot stop looking at his face. I want to wipe it from the face of the earth. I want to print it into my cells and never forget it. I never want to see our lost city again. I miss it like the beat of my heart. Maybe it's raining, my face is wet, the world is wobbling. I really want to put on my shoes.

"I hate that I am so short," I weep; somehow we're back in English.

"Let's get out of here," says Igor—no, Iggy. We say Igi for short—ah, I see this now. This stupid name he invents. He waves at another taxi, which stops.

"But the band!" I wail. "Igor—"

"Iggy—"

"—at Ruby's. I promised my friend!"

"Of course," he says, smooth as butter. "We can go by there."

He opens the door, we pile in, and that's the last thing I remember.

13

Still stuck in town. At least it's stopped raining. This Sunday, there are small white clouds in the sky and the river sparkles, chattering through the city. The city, if you squint past the mortar paw prints and blackened buildings, is picturesque. The air is clear—a perfect hunting day. You just want to vanish into the woods but instead, after a restorative slug of liquor, you take your place overlooking the main shopping street. A tram chugs along—the city, in folly and defiance, keeps riding the No. 3 tram. The passengers sit up stiffly by the windows. They know the risk. Maybe they've just stopped caring. A few people dash along the street, out for supplies, taking cover between short runs. You decide to wait till it gets a bit busier. A couple of shots, economically placed in a busy street, will have maximum effect and let them know your end of town is still active.

Then a couple of girls waltz out. The taller one is a skinny blonde. She spells trouble, even from here. She has attitude. The short one has darker hair and a bemused look, as if she isn't really part of this. They walk slowly down the center of the street. Shortie is a prim little thing, but Blondie wags her backside. Blondie does a three-sixty, and with a little thrill you realize she's signaling to you. To the anonymous shooters. Her arm swings up and gives you the middle finger. The little one is looking around as if she's lost in someone else's dream. Then Blondie gets more crazy and lewd, flipping up her skirt, mooning you.

You have to laugh—these two, giving the finger to the war, are the first funny thing, the first human thing that's happened for months. As Blondie bares her arse, though, the other one is a bit alarmed, pulling at her. You focus through your rifle sights to see them better.

From here, you can't really see faces. But you can pick up on their energy. Blondie has a dangerous edge—she's thin, jittery, a man magnet, for sure. Total contrast to the little one, who's much stiller. Zoom in a notch—closer, closer. Straight shot to the head. Doesn't she know she's in danger? Is she simple? Why is she just standing there?

But now Stefan has seen them too, and he has a score to settle with you.

"Come on, guys," you say, "pretty dead out there. Lunch break."

Stefan says, "One more," and squeezes the trigger. Your heart lurches, but it's not the girls. Far away in the street a bulky middle-aged woman falls over. Her string bag spills bread, some cans, an orange. People scatter, but not the dark-haired girl, who stands completely still, then turns to look your way. She looks right at you, like Medusa. *Never look in the eyes of a target.* They will curse you, stamp you for death. Ice slides down the back of your neck, even as you tell yourself she can't really see you. Then Blondie grabs her and she snaps to and they run.

Milan says, "Okay, lunch already!" You turn away but then hear one more shot. A child has fallen—she must be only about twelve. An older man runs out toward her, and Stefan shoots him too. Three great shots—now he's up two on you. The street is completely empty. And now it's Stefan who takes charge.

"All right, Iggy, we can knock it off. I've herded them back into the cracks for a while." Stefan and his chetnik buddy are laughing now, in a good mood. Milan is opening a packet of stale crackers, his face hidden. But you don't move yet. That girl's gaze— She saw you. The real you. Suddenly that cursed feeling shifts, turns into heat, life, sex, another world—there's the scream of guitar under your fingers, thumping bass, girls dancing, smiling sideways at you, shaking their butts—everyone mixed, like it was before all this war bullshit— You look out the window. You need to see her again, badly, but she and her friend are gone.

As you join the others, a single clear thought cuts through the three-day liquor haze. *There are still girls in this city.* At least two, maybe twenty, maybe fifty—who knows? They'll be the first item on the balance sheet. They'll be your bridge across this river of blood. You will stop Stefan from shooting these girls, you will keep at least some of them alive, you will shepherd Milan through.

1. *Girls, civilians*

2. *Milan*

And.... There's one more thing, there are always three impossible tasks in folk tales, what's the third? You look up for inspiration but you're so drunk again, you fall off your chair.

■ ■ ■

Back in the fucking cottage. The days grow shorter and the chill starts to bite, even through the whiskey. You spend more time each day collecting firewood from the forest. Then when that gets scarce, you raid the nearby abandoned houses for furniture, books, anything that will burn. You're all pretty surly with each other now. Milan sits with his back to you for hours, moving gray and white pebbles around on a makeshift chess board he's scratched out on a piece of wallboard. It's not supposed to happen, but sometimes you'll even arrange to meet the enemy in the woods to trade. Cigarettes, coffee, booze, drugs, sometimes cheese and sausage. You can't even think about how fucked up that is, but there it is.

Still, people keep going out in the street. You can't tell much about them from this distance, and you're trying to figure out how to get back down to the city. You want to see those girls again. The one that turned and stared—you can't shake the feeling that she saw you, impossible as that is. As for the rest, you've begun to hate them—those frightened, rushing ants. Somehow, it's become their fault that you're still here. Without people, there'd be no one to shoot at and you could just go home.

Many days now it's just you and Milan, now that Stefan's so tight with Bogdan, and sometimes you don't even shoot, but there's not much else to do, so usually you do it. Sometimes you hunt deer instead and these are the good days—the silence of the woods, the simplicity of tracking, bagging your quarry, bringing it home.

Stefan worships Bogdan and Tatjana, who grow more animated when he's at the house, and the three of them laugh together as if in on an endless private joke. Last time the three of you were there, he and Bogdan went off to the cellar together for supplies and stayed for a long time. They returned like guilty schoolboys, straightening their faces as they came back into the kitchen, where Tatjana was tormenting poor Milan again, stroking his arm, asking his opinion of her soup. Stefan's yellow eyes darted from Milan to you, and his lips clamped in a secret wolf grin.

Later that night, through the drunken blur of singing that now ends every party, there came a moment of quiet. In that moment, you heard the sound of a child's weeping, quickly stifled. Tatjana must have heard it too, because she leaped up to pour more liquor and start another song. Stefan's and Bogdan's eyes flickered toward each other, so fast you'd easily miss it. Unless you were a trained sniper. Unless you'd been a hunter since childhood.

Milan, of course, is oblivious. But in that moment, seeing Stefan's eyes shine and the relaxation of his body, you feel a hard stone of resolve forming. You store it beside the other two pebbles anchoring your sanity—shepherding Milan through the war, keeping at least some civilians alive. Stefan is no fool and he's watching you now, so you laugh and open the next bottle, a little more unsteadily than necessary.

"Another song, Tanja!" you say. She laughs, then grows pensive. She sings a sad song about a young girl who drowns—she really does have a beautiful voice, deep and husky—and the girl's lover who mourns forever by the Sava's bank. Milan's eyes are moist; he's never had a girlfriend. The evening winds down, and as the three of you weave home downhill, you're careful to joke, to clap Stefan on the shoulder, to act like everything's normal.

After that, Stefan is gone with Bogdan's crew more often than not, sometimes for days. You don't ask, he doesn't say, but one time, when he's been away for three days and Milan is off getting supplies, you go through his things. Among the grimy T-shirts and tattered porn magazines, you find a girl's broken earring. A child's pair of flimsy panties. A bloodstained hair ribbon. Trophies.

There have been rumors, of course. About making war babies. And Stefan's absurd boasts about hotels with special rooms in them, where soldiers are led to girls and told to do what they want. You've brushed it aside as bragging, until now. You stride into the forest, breaking the ironclad rule: someone must always keep watch in the daytime. You run uphill. The graying trees whip in your face as you pound on but you keep going through the pain in your side. You run to the high outcrop and look out, this time away from the cursed city and toward the beautiful slopes of the mountain, dusted with early snow.

You sit there for a long time, oblivious to the cold. By the time you turn back down, it's getting dark. And you've decided on the third task. *Stefan.*

14

Something smells bad. I lever myself upright in bed and glance round—oh, too fast. My head spins and nausea strikes. Take a breath. There's a pile of clothes on the floor; I think the smell is coming from them. I lie back down and stare at the ceiling, willing it not to move.

Flickering mental pictures return. The pub, the band. The taxi stopping at the pub where Jody's friends were playing. A red guitar, Jody climbing up to sing a song. Was Iggy still there? Did he come in? Jody's in tight black jeans, black top, red leather jacket. The woman would look good in a flour sack. Her legs are very long.

I remember saying *No, I don't smoke*, then her lighting me a cigarette anyway. Sometime later, I was yelling that I wanted to sing a song too. What song? I don't even know any songs. Oh no— it was "Time after Time." Did they let me? Is Jody singing on the chorus with me? No—she's sitting out front with a tall, muscular woman—I think it's a woman—with burgundy lips, dark skin, and shaved patterns in her head.

Then I am walking somewhere with these two. They tower over me. We head downstairs to somewhere loud and thumping. Light flickers and dances on gleaming bodies, a peacock's party of glitter and laughing and shiny muscles and tossing hair and shaved heads and chains. Shadows twine together in the corners, pushing urgently into each other. A fizzing, melting feeling rushes up my spine; lust is off the leash. Who are these creatures? Surely, they vanish in the daylight. Drinks. Dancing. More, more, more . . . I'm laughing and spinning and bouncing off an arm, a back, a wall. . . .

How did I get up all the stairs to my pink-eyeball attic? Was I noisy? I can't lose this place. It's all too much—I decide to return to bed for the morning, but something's wrong with my bed. It's crooked. There's a lump—I stretch out a toe, then jerk back as if burned. Flesh! The lump is a warm body! And on the other pillow is a shock of blonde hair, poking out from under the blankets. *It's her.*

I lie flat on my back, heart racing. Strobe-lit flashes return—bodies, of pressing and wetness, of slippery flesh and the clink of metal, Jody, her friend, and me entwined—what did we do? Where was I, who are they, who am I—excitement and sickness and terror spin together in my stomach.

I have to get out of here. To normal. I slide ever so carefully out. The lump stirs a little but doesn't wake up. Knickers . . . jeans . . . I dare not open a drawer in case it creaks, so I'm stuck with what's strewn around the room or in the dirty washing. Luckily, that's plenty. I pick out a crumpled London Calling T-shirt from my Camden shopping day, slip some coins into my jeans, and unhook the key from the door.

Down the creaky stairs. Through Mr. Patel's spice shop and out the door to gulps of beautiful, grimy London air and drizzle. I cross the road, which is almost beyond me, and collapse in the Happy Café at one of the pink Formica tables. I have to put my head down to recover. When I look up, there's Naveen.

"You got a hangover, Nadia? You go clubbing?" Naveen badly wishes he could go clubbing and get hangovers.

"Don't be absurd," I say. "Get me some tea and a bun, please. And take away that stupid smile."

"Mum!" he yells up the stairs. "Nadia's here again and she's not feeling very well." His grin broadens.

"Get me my tea, Naveen." He leaves. I watch my own front door. Nothing moves. Naveen returns with tea and a sticky bun. He's hovering, but I scowl so he slouches off. The tea helps. I jam the sticky bun into my mouth. The sugar helps too. I inhale the first cup of tea and pour a second. Still no one comes down my stairs and out of Mr. Patel's spice shop door.

Mrs. K. swirls out. "Nadia, you silly girl! You look like a garbage truck has eaten you up."

"I think it did eat me up," I say.

"And what are these clothes? You look cheap," she says, frowning. Mrs. K. is not very tactful. "And you are not smelling very good, Nadia. Personal hygiene matters, you know." I should have a comeback to this, but today wit is beyond me. I hunch down over my tea and bun instead. "And why are you staring like a snake at your house?"

"A cousin. We had a fight," I say, looking up. I hope she'll soften, but she frowns harder and too late, I remember having told her I have no family left. She's about to ask another question, but right then, the front door tinkles and Mr. Patel's daughter Reena, her husband, and their baby come in. Mr. K. emerges from the back room with Naveen, and they all admire the baby, in a clatter of bangles and laughter and chat. In that moment, my own front door swings open. It's hard to see through the cluster of people, but I glimpse a fair plait, a red jacket.

Thank God, now I can go back to bed. What a wonderful thought. I drain my tea, leave two pound coins, and sidle past the group. Back upstairs, still a little queasy, I open the door carefully. All clear. I pull off my T-shirt and jeans and roll back into bed, oh lovely bed, and fall asleep again to the sounds of soft rain, the cooing and clicking of the birds next door, and the crackly rise and fall of Mr. Pigeon's radio.

■ ■ ■

The boys in my neighborhood all wear hoodies. If you could wear them at work, that's what I'd be in today. A big gray one I could hide inside, hands shoved in the pockets. When I arrive at work on Friday afternoon (I pleaded a migraine in the morning, which no one believed), it seems I'm not the only one who feels that way. The whole place has a beaten, sheeplike feeling. There are still crumbs from snacks with the Baltic Bigwigs, and Maudie is looking a little gray.

Elsie has dark circles under her eyes, but it suits her; she's finally achieved a surly punk look.

Priya, on the other hand, is sparkling. She is humming under her breath. Her black hair is shiny, with a new green undertone, and she keeps trying to catch my eye. I'm guessing that drinks turned into a racy night for Priya and Oleg. And me? I shut out that thought and pull my imaginary hoodie over my bloodshot eyes. Then peek to my left, surreptitiously. No Iggy. I don't know if I'm relieved or disappointed. I am so tired of not knowing how to feel.

I type. Focus on the present. But the data has slowed and after the big push for the Bigwigs presentation, I'm not sure what I should be doing. Even Mrs. McGinley seems at a bit of a loss.

"Tidy up from yesterday, would you Nadia?" she says, leaving me unsure if I should wash coffee cups or file the presentation reports. She walks to the window and looks out, casts an eye toward Maudie and Priya, taps her fingers on the window ledge.

Then Iggy comes in. Half smiles at me and sits down to boot up. The sun comes out and our morning finger of sunlight strokes the desk. The spider plant twitches in anticipation. I push it away. *You can wait till tomorrow,* I tell it silently. *Today, I want that warmth on my face.* I think it bristles slightly. *Get used to it, spider plant; life is unfair.*

"Any words on the contract yet?" asks Iggy.

"I'm hopeful!" says Priya.

"Oh, shut up," says Maudie. Priya looks hurt.

"Sorry," says Maudie. "It's just—oh, you're always hopeful and usually—"

"Usually what?" Priya's bottom lip is sticking out. I hope she's not going to defend that human oil stain Oleg.

"Better to be realistic, that's all," says Maudie. "Less likely to stub your toe and bleed all over your stockings."

"What is realistic?" says Iggy. There's a small silence, as there often is when he joins in.

"Well, you get your hopes up too high, you get disappointed," says Maudie.

"Disappointed. That is nothing," says Iggy. We wait. But that seems to be all from our office oracle.

We're about to return to typing when Priya says, "I'm just sick of it. Sick of all this squash yourself into a box, yes sir, no sir, and if something goes wrong it just proves you shouldn't even try—"

"No, it proves you cocked up again," says Maudie.

"—you should bloody vegetate in front of the telly and eat takeaway and look after all your cousin's bloody kids and when your niece gets engaged pretend to be happy for the little sod and at weddings put up with being sat next to someone's fat widowed uncle from Bangalore who wants to take some woman back home to scrub the floors and cook three meals a day." Nobody says anything. "It's all very well for you, Maudie, you don't have a bloody octopus of a family all getting married and asking who you're seeing—"

"Yeah, it's just tops for me, Priya, mum in hospital and dad in bloody jail, it's great to be free of all that family—"

"This week, I felt like a queen! A queen! You have to dare to dream—"

"'Dare to dream'—listen to yourself! Did he make you swallow a self-help brochure?"

"How can your dreams possibly come true if you're too shit-scared even to have them? Maudie?"

"Dreams are very nice for sleeping," says Iggy.

"That's right!" says Priya, and then there is an odd silence.

"Does nobody have any work to do?" says Mrs. McGinley, pivoting from the window. We burrow back into our desks.

The day passes in an odd blur. Charles comes in and calls Mrs. McGinley into his private office. They close the door—a new and worrying habit. When Mrs. McGinley comes out, she seems shrunken somehow, like a big juicy apple that has been left out in a bowl for weeks. She glances around as if she isn't sure where she is, who we are, what is this strange office. She sways slightly.

"Well, then," she says, then stops as if she's run out of words. She tries again. "Well, have a nice afternoon."

She drifts over to the coat rack, collects her jacket and bag, and walks out, shutting the door with a quiet click. It might as well have been a gunshot: everyone is suddenly alert. Our heads swivel in unison to the closed door of Charles's office. After a few breaths, it opens and Charles strides out. His sunglasses are already on and he barrels out the door and down the stairs in Mrs. McGinley's wake. We are pool balls left to roll around on a table after the game.

After a moment's silence, Roger emerges from his ferret corner, swirling Iggy and me in to Maudie and Priya's nest in the office center.

"What the fuck was—" says Maudie.

"No idea," says Roger.

"She looked like she'd seen a ghost," says Priya.

"*Was* a ghost," says Roger.

"Or had a bloody awful shock," says Priya.

"Probably just got the sack," says Maudie. It doesn't seem possible.

"Maybe he propositioned her," says Priya. We snort, because that seems even less likely. Although, why not? People are mysterious.

"Maybe the Baltic Bigwigs deal's gone south, those two never fight," says Maudie, and the silence of the true thing follows.

"We're always the last to bloody know," says Priya. "Just little worker drones with no life."

"Actually, the drones have a very good life," says Iggy. "In the beehive they are just for sex and feeding."

"Nice work if you can get it, eh, Iggy?" says Roger.

Iggy looks at him thoughtfully and Roger blushes to his gingery roots. I am ruffled too. I feel like one of the hens circling a rooster, which I do not like at all. I want to be a hawk, or even a pigeon, like Mr. Pigeon's birds, carrying secret messages across London. Maybe Priya is such a bird—no, a raven, with that shimmer of green and magenta in her hair. I envy her beautiful hair. My natural color is dark mouse. Mice are snake food, science experiments, prey for birds, always afraid, always—

"Nadia?" Roger is snapping his fingers in my face. "Earth to Nadia?

Drinks?" Our common purpose is restored and with a sudden bustle, we pack up this very strange day, heading off toward the rich fug of the Hag and Crow.

The pub is unusually jammed today. Shiny-faced men in too-tight shirts yell for pints, jugs, refills. Our corner table is taken and we're scrunched around a standing table. It's almost at armpit height for me, and I keep getting elbowed by tall men. Also Maudie and Priya are spiky with each other. Priya's new love glow has upset the order of things. Iggy and Roger are squished together across the table from us. Iggy is calm, as always, but Roger is a little flustered. His cheeks are pink and he is doing strange things with his eyebrows. I feel like—what is the English, the odd duck out, here with these two scratchy couples who are not couples.

A male roar rocks the pub. Someone has kicked a goal on TV. My head hurts. I hate having my back to the room. A passing man wallops me between the shoulder blades. My beer shudders and spills on the table, and in the smoky pub light it looks red.

"I'm getting outside with some air," I mutter, and weave away through the forest of bodies. Outside is not much better, also really loud. The summer sunset is streaking red and gray. Taxis inch along the cobbled street, beeping at drunken pedestrians and cyclists with pizza boxes. Then there's the crack of a gun and I'm running, I don't know where, zigzagging through the crowd, finding an alley, then another. Some instinct pushes me downhill till finally—there's the river. A shabby little park abuts narrow stone steps and I run down them till I'm on a tiny beach of stones.

Grimy foam laps the pebbles, and a beer can and plastic bag bob at the shoreline. A dead seagull stares skyward with a lidless yellow eye. I curl up, knees to chest, back to the wall, and close my eyes till the red throbbing behind my eyelids calms. After a moment, I look out at the water. Even the river is busy, but it's slow and wide and brown and the red sky is softer in reflection. Two tugboats chug by, brave little things. A flat barge, laden with steel girders, follows them, leaving a creamy brown wake. Seagulls circle and caw.

Maybe the gunshot was a car backfiring. Or one of those motor-bikes with the long pipes. There are too many maybes and I am so tired. *It's the ones you don't hear that kill you,* my father would say. *If you can hear it, you're not dead yet.* Oh, my tata. What was the last thing you heard? The Pit threatens to open. I push my tata's voice away and focus on my toenails. They are orange. They clash with my magenta hair but look nice with the sunset on the river. I close my eyes. Then something warm wraps around me. An arm. I know without opening my eyes who it is. Why do I have to open my eyes, ever again?

We sit there a while—this is Iggy's gift, his stillness. It is a great talent for a sniper. Finally, I look.

"Iggy," I say.

"Nadija." There is a pause. He is not in a hurry but he is waiting for something. A cue. But I can't.

"Who did you kill, Iggy?" He really does have good control of his reflexes. His arm doesn't move, but I feel the life go out of it. Then he carefully slides it away.

"It was war."

"You could have refused."

"You don't know that." A pause. "You don't know what I did."

"You're a killer."

"So sure, Nadija?"

"Well. Aren't you?" Stalemate. Then he reaches in his pocket and takes out something. It's the glass button with the yellow flower in-side. And now I am truly afraid. Who is this man?

"What is this?" I whisper.

"My lucky charm." His face is in shadow, but his eyes gleam red in the sunset.

"How—how did you get it?"

"I found it in the street." So it's true. He was in the mountains, where they shot at us.

"A trophy? From us, from your shooting meat?"

"No, no, the opposite, I stopped them, they shot at girls, women. . . .
I kept this to—"

Now we are standing, staring at each other.

"What?"

"To remind me. People were living there," he says softly.

I take the button. Then looking into his eyes, I spit, and drop it
onto the pebbles.

"It's poisoned," I say. I start to climb back up the steps, but he
catches me. By now I don't care if I die here.

"Nadija, you have no idea—the girls, what they did—I tried to stop
it, to help, but it was—it was bad—and now I find one of you here,
alive—"

I look at him. It's impossible, but he's crying. My brother, my
neighbor, my killer. The terrible things hover between us, they are
everywhere, in the air and ground and world, this ugly broken world,
in him and in me, and we know this, only we two, the survivors of
this earthquake and finally, he is kissing me and we are clinging together like the damned.

■ ■ ■

At first, I don't know where I am. I look up, up, up—where's the ceiling? Pigeons circle way above. A pearly light diffuses the space—and
then I see there are steel rafters, maybe twenty meters up. There's a
rusty smell; a scent of oil. Concrete.

I'm on a mattress on the floor, in a corner. There's a makeshift
partition that looks like our office dividers—maybe it is one—it sep-
arates this corner from the huge emptiness of the space. A disused
railway station? A warehouse? Across from me are a few milk crates
with clothes in them. And a black Fender guitar, very scratched up.
Stacks of CDs.

Then with a little shock, I see something I recognize—a torn and
faded band poster, stuck on an oil drum. *Zabranjeno pušenje.* It's an
old one, before the bitter split; they're in flares, long-haired, they look

happy. Sweat, lights, dancing . . . that driving guitar riff, Sanja, Sanja dancing in the crowd, head flung back laughing in an orange dress and boots, dancing—No. I push this picture away. By the early nineties, honey had turned to poison and broke the original band in half, like everything else.

I close my eyes, push out the past. Warmth seeps in from the left. Beside me, curled like a sleeping cat, is Iggy. My body slides itself back in and presses against his back, drawn by the scent of him—of us. His skin is cream-smooth but not soft. There's hard farmer's muscle under there. I smell coffee, faintly; and rosewater, and something else, a smoky smell. Grilling peppers. Smells I've known all my life.

For the first time in months, I am not spinning in space. Longing floods my body with a painful gravity.

If there were no time.

If I never had to wake up.

If the war hadn't—

Then right now would be the first time, since coming to London, of feeling at home.

15

New year, same as the old. But in the mornings now, there's frost. Sometimes when you wake and look out, the beauty of the world catches in your throat, and the woods beckon—and then you remember. The cottage is sour and smelly, split into corners—yours and Stefan's. Milan is the go-between, as useless as a bow-tie on a pig—peacekeeper's a thankless task. The only times you all get along are at Bogdan and Tanja's house parties, which grow ever louder, drunker, more hectic.

There's a sense of end times coming—NATO's stepping up pressure, Belgrade might even get bombed—and the house parties have the giddy greed of a liquor store raid. Of course, the regular army's long gone; it's all bandits and paramilitaries like Bogdan's now. When the war's over, they'll just dissolve in the woods, keep working the black market in looted goods, drugs, and guns. Why waste the new supply lines? Keep making hay while the politicians shake hands and carve up the country.

And there is so much hay to make.

You laugh at Bogdan's jokes. You clap Stefan on the back. You drink to the turbo-folk songs that are always belting away at high volume—Stefan sings along. You clap him on the back and join in. In another life, he hated this patriotic fake-folk-music shit too—but the memory seems impossible, the band a fairy tale. You grab your share of the spoils—a nice revolver, a pair of Italian leather shoes, a belt, a hunting jacket. There is whiskey. Chivas Regal, Johnnie Walker Black Label. So much whiskey. And cheese, and cured meats. The loot just keeps pouring in now.

All over the country, across the border, up through the Krajina, the villages are cowering, and the Croats and Bosniaks are being rounded up into camps. So much to plunder. Of course Serb villages have suffered atrocities too, you tell each other, a bit too loudly, as the stash of stuff piles up. Everyone boasts of their victories. There are rumors about the camps, about what they do to the men. Terrible, savage things. Castration. Forced cannibalism. As for the women and girls . . .

You've entered a strange dead zone in your mind where real and unreal coexist, in a protective bubble around your true self. It first formed when you left your village, after the barn was emptied. What happened to those prisoners next is in deep freeze, inside a memory that will never now thaw. But occasionally, something pierces through. In tonight's stash, alongside the usual guns, boots, toasters, tools, silverware, and lace tablecloths, there's a pile of kids' things. Little T-shirts, ironed and folded. Coloring books and pens. A stuffed Pokémon. Some playing cards. Some sparkly birthday candles, a pack of balloons. You stroke the candles, put them in your pocket. Just to touch something innocent.

"What do you want for your birthday, little girl?" says Stefan. *Shit.* He saw.

"It's not his birthday yet," says Milan. Stefan brushes him off like an ant. You swallow bile and laugh.

"More ammo. A Fender Strat. Ticket to London."

"We can do that," says Stefan, and he moves toward the biggest TV in the pile. He confounds you. He had you by the throat, then moved away. And how stupid is he, really? There's no reception or electricity in the fucking cottage.

"Stefan, it won't work—" Milan starts, but you cut him off. Let Stefan figure it out in his own Neanderthal time. But Stefan says, "Duh. For later," sets the TV aside, and settles on a pair of boots and a wicked-looking hunting knife.

After dinner, Bogdan claps his hands for silence. He has that secret excited look. Everyone quiets down.

"Brothers. We'll be in town again next week. And we have a special party planned. Igor—Milan—Stefan—I know the cottage is not the Hilton, and you've been working very hard." There's something wrong with Stefan's face. His yellow eyes avoid yours, and his face—he's trying not to laugh. So this is a setup.

"So, I invite you to our special party! Thursday. We'll have it all ready for you."

Clapping. Cheering. Milan looks pleased, then bemused. You count your breaths. Steady your heart. Keep your eyes on the goal. There's no way out of this expedition, but perhaps a chink will open within it. You slug back your drink.

"Tanja, a song!" you yell. "Sing—sing—sing!" The table of men takes up the chant. Tatjana smiles, modest but pleased, until Bogdan holds up a hand for silence. Then she sings a beautiful old refrain. Of rivers and mountains and the dear lost homeland. Of the blood of our ancestors. And how one day we will avenge them, and take back what is ours. When she finishes, there's not a dry eye in the house. Not even yours.

■ ■ ■

Next week, you're back in the city. The special party seems to have evaporated, like most promises. You're holding down the fort again, shooting into Sniper's Alley every so often, watching the scenes unfold in the street. Sometimes there's the glint of a rifle in a window, or a shot from an apartment, and you target those, or pass on information about where to bomb. But often, it's dull. Like Milan now, you shoot to miss when you can. Stefan doesn't miss.

You can't stand being in the house with him, so whenever you can, you do the errands. Trading booze and cigarettes for food and soap with peacekeepers, those useless, stuffed soldier-dolls on corners. Still, they can get in and out. And they can get supplies. And report back to NATO. If you're on friendly terms, that helps. And secretly, you're hoping to see those girls again. Or any girls. Any other humans except the ones you're stuck with, but the girls never reappear. You start to feel there is no outside, and never will be, to this war.

Finally, after five empty days of staring through your rifle sights, you have a piece of luck—you see a girl hurry out of an apartment building and around the corner. Is it Blondie from the other week? Could be. You start watching the building. Turns out she has something going with a peacekeeper. They're careful; they move out of your sights fast, around a building, up an alley. Whenever she returns, she's carrying something. A bulging yellow string bag.

You watch. The moon wanes. The nights grow darker. Finally, the moon is dark. It's three a.m. You'd drunk little that day, avoided pissing Stefan off. Kept it calm. You're not wearing combat clothes but civilian gear—black jeans, black shirt. You've rubbed coffee grounds on your face. You carry nothing identifiable and once the others are asleep, sodden drunk as usual, you slip into the night like a black cat.

At first, you're on high alert, hugging walls and shadows. You circle carefully round to the corner where this girl meets her man. Look up—there's a battered door leading to stairs. You wait, slow your breathing. In the stillness, stars sparkle over the broken city, which now has no electric lights to dim them. They're so bright you cast a faint shadow. It's like being back home in the village. You breathe deeply, for the first time in months, and then you're walking, just to feel the soft night air on your face.

One block. Two. Your feet have taken you to Sniper's Alley. A quiet day—no dead for those remaining to pick up under cover of darkness. There's a stain on the road, dark on dark. You don't know what moves you to kneel, touch the bloodstain, but when you do the night darkens and the hate in your heart for Stefan twists like a rusty knife. Then your fingers find something. Something small and round. You pick it up. It glitters in the moonlight—glass, but too smooth to be a shard from all the broken windows. It's clear, with a flower inside, pressed neatly like a butterfly from a kill jar. The back side is brass, with tiny raised holes for a needle to pull through. A button, then. Old-fashioned, a grandma-style thing. Must have fallen off a jacket, a cardigan. You put it in your pocket, next to the candles. And at that exact moment, a faint light goes on at a window, back at the building the girl goes in and out of. You look over toward it. The hairs on your neck stand on end.

Because even from this distance, you can see it's a young woman. She must know how lethal it is to sit by a window, but here she is. Reading by candlelight. You can't see her face properly, but something about her—the dreamy pose, the cardigan, the disregard for danger—once again, there's that sensation of ice sliding down your neck. It's her; it has to be. The one who saw you. The girl from the street.

16

Coffee, not drinks. Neutral territory—this is Mrs. K.'s advice. *And somewhere busy. People around.*

So we are in Bloomsbury, a little walk away from the Soho office. Crosscurrents of people swirl in the doorways and patios of pubs, cafés, the rose-sodden parks. The Shiny Fork Café is busy. Dutch, American, and Japanese voices mix with the clatter and clang of cups and the espresso machine's hissing. Outside every table is full, in a lovely late afternoon of slanting sun. But we are not out in the sun. We are inside, in a dark corner. I have my back to the wall and although it is warm, I am buttoned to my neck in my most serious white shirt. My arms are crossed and I have my notebook and pencil.

Iggy jiggles a teaspoon against his cup, taps a rhythm. Looks up at me and smiles. This still unnerves me, this new smiling.

"Okay," he says. "What is the list?"

We are in English. Careful, public English. I take a breath, and start.

"How did you get here?" I say.

"Bus. Then walking."

"No, idiot, not that," I say, and he smiles because he has made me smile.

"Oh—London?"

"All of it. London. Temp Angels. Our office!"

"Oh—I had a friend. A bass player. He had an uncle."

"We all had an uncle," I say, a little sharply; my uncle died during the siege.

"No, I mean—this guy's uncle helped me get out," he says. "Sugar?" I shake my head. "Sweet enough already," he says, and tips five cubes into his espresso. I frown a little—*Get on with it*—so he explains that this man works the gray market, like most people during the war. But he is international. He got Iggy a passport and visa for the UK, a phone number for the warehouse to stay in for free, and a job.

"Very generous, this guy's uncle," I say. My eyebrows are walking up my face to my hair.

"Ah, no, it's not—the bass player owed me a favor. I filled in for the band a few times, no notice, helped with the tour—"

"All right. How did this bass player's uncle get you this job?" I ask. I have a feeling I am not asking the right questions.

"Temp Angels. He does some business with them." I think about this. *Plausible.* Temp Angels' business model is placing us shadow people in jobs for a fat slice of the paychecks. Classical old-country gray-market dealing.

"And what was the deal?"

"What deal?" But he knows.

"The deal with the bass player's uncle's friend," I say patiently. Because there is always a deal: the price of the free lunch, as Maudie says.

"Oh, it's easy. Live-in watchman. I just keep the eye out for his stuff, make sure no one is snooping, that the shipments come and go when they are supposed to. He travels a lot so it rescues him from paying someone to check the floor each few days, and I get a bed, plus the office job."

And of course, Iggy can defend himself. A useful guard for this uncle to have. I wonder if he has a gun.

"Okay," I say, and write a note to cover my unease. He is here, and I see how. The next question is harder. *Why?* "Your job is where I work. Not possible this is an accident. Did you hunt me?" Iggy stops jiggling and his eyes flash up.

"What? No! The agency sent me."

"You turn up one day, from the city where you shot at us! You watched the street every day, you watched us—"

"No! Of course, I saw some girls, but only—"

"—then here you are—"

"—from a distance—"

"—what should I be thinking?"

"I don't know! Not this, this hunting—"

"So you didn't know I was at the office? *Some girl* from home?" *Aha.* He looks down.

"Iggy?"

"Okay. I did see you in the Temp Angels files. When I looked at this job. And you looked like, maybe, one of these girls—and then your name—so I did wonder—maybe you are this—"

He stops. Scowls at his coffee cup.

"This what?"

"This girl, one of these girls I would see on the street. Maybe, a girl I kept Stefan from shooting."

Ah, the shooting. He did this too. Maybe people I know. The churn cycle starts, but this time it's not only my thoughts, but my stomach. Because now I ask questions, but two nights ago, we were—I feel burning in my cheeks. I push the thoughts away.

"The killing," I say. The light goes out of his eyes.

"There was no choice but to fight. You know that."

"Some chose to stay and defend the city!"

"But I'm from the village," he says.

"You don't seem like it," I say. He is not one of these lumpy farm boys who sing to their sheep.

"Well, I was in Belgrade for a while. Then Zagreb."

"When?"

"Oh, a few months here and there. For music."

"What music?" I know his eyebrows are rising but I won't look at him. I hold my pen firmly and stare at my notebook. He sighs and plays along.

"Punk, New Wave—sometimes local bands got lucky, got a support gig. We never did, but I filled in for a friend a few times when he—when he got busy."

"All right. The war. The village," I say.

"Really?" He is frowning a little. This game is too long for him. I lift my eyebrows, tap my pen. He rolls up his eyes, but continues: He was back home preparing for the harvest when they enlisted him and his friends. Then patrols, then they tried to run away but got caught, trained with these paramilitaries, sent to the city.

"And we were your shooting meat," I say.

"No," he says, slamming down his cup. "No. Not this. Milan and me—we stopped Stefan, from, from the girls, the women, from more killing—then I escaped. I tried to bring Milan out, but they killed him too."

Could this actually be true—he fought against the killing? Hope spreads its wings, fluttering my heart—I quash it. I frown and look at him, ready to ask more, but he is looking down. He is seeing the dead. I am close to him now, against my will. But still, I feel dirty. Confused.

"Iggy. All my family is dead, because of— Here, I have no Yugoslav friends. I never want them, the bad memories, everyone is so sad or crazy, or your people, they are hiding from their crimes. I want this new life, no war."

"Yes. Yes, me too."

"I think you're lying."

"Yes? Why?"

"If you really want this, then why look for this war? Why do you come to my office when you see my name? Maybe you like shooting 'Turks,' you want to fuck me up, you don't want me to have this new life, maybe you still like hunting, is that it?"

"No. No!" He is almost shouting. A vein is pulsing in his neck. "Nadija, I think—I think one day I saw you. Back in the siege. On the street. And then, one other night . . ." He shakes his head, looks down.

"What?"

"It sounds—I can't explain."

"You will try."

"I just— The night I find this button, with the flower in glass. On the street. Then in the same moment, I see this girl, in the window. Maybe you. Like a—"

"What."

"A flower in a glass," he mutters, and now his face is red. "So, I think, my lucky charm. This button, this girl. She survives, I survive. And now, here we are. New city, new life."

Soldiers are superstitious. I know that. But this— So ridiculous, it could be true. Or he is the best liar in the world. Truth, lies. Which is it? I stare at him. Flickers of light dance at the edge of my eyes. My palms sweat.

"I will go now," I say, and close my notebook.

"Nadija?"

"I have to think," I say, pushing my chair back. "On my own. At home."

"I'll walk you to the Tube."

"No."

"Yes," he says, shrugging on his jacket.

We gather our things in silence and walk through the darkening streets, a little apart. Bloomsbury is lively with lights, and laughing, but our feet make no sound on the pavement. In the twilight, we make no shadows. We are shades ourselves—our real selves still wander the ruined streets of home. I shiver, though the night is warm.

"Nadija."

"What?"

"Remember the war radio?"

How could I not; turbo-folk oozed from every soldier's truck, every radio station. I nod.

"Here is different. Different music, lots of stations." Why is he talking about this? "Here, we can choose."

He waves around us. Behind us, smooth jazz floats from a café. Greek bouzouki music pulses from tinny speakers up the block. A saxophonist with dreadlocks in a ripped miniskirt plays a fast tune at the next corner, a small crowd gathering round her. Buses thunder by, people chatter, and under us, around us, the subterranean thump of bass and the machine pulse of disco says night is coming.

"New soundtrack, new life," he says.

"What about the old one?" I say.

He smiles and flicks his fingers. An ice cube slides down the back of my shirt. It is the gesture he made when I saw Sanja walk beside us in mirror-world—and then she vanished. I cannot just flick my fingers. There are too many dead.

"My stop," I say, and walk away.

"Nadija!" he calls after me. "I don't mean you should forget."

I hurry away into the cluster of people swirling into the Tube stop. When I turn at the top of the stairs, he is still standing there watching.

Everyone jams onto the escalator and glides down into the veins and arteries of this big living beast, London. Where are they all going? Who are they? This tall, dark girl: A model? A killer? A home aide? That shabby man with the red nose. A drunkard on his way to bed, or a banker after a boozy meeting? These teenagers, pushing through the crowd. Students, or refugees? A gray-haired woman in a fur coat notices me as she glides upward on the other escalator. She gives me a little nod. It is a secret society, we who look around us.

I think of what Iggy said. So, what is the soundtrack of London? It is the clatter and hum of this giant body, its languages banging together and sliding off each other. It's *Mind the gap* and *Please take your luggage*. It is *Sorry*, and *Please*, and *Give us a pint*, and *Another round, love!* and *More bloody rain*, and *Can't complain*. Bus brakes in the rain and the shout of *Taxi!* Priya's refrain and Maudie and Roger's chorus, this Hag and Crow song of the married IVF stinker who broke Priya's heart. *Duckie* and *my love* in the shops.

And underneath this soundtrack, like a recorded-over cassette, are other scratches and hisses. I know them from my books, my lovely translations, now all gone. Fishwives shouting on the docks, crying babies of the gin-wrecked poor, the clop of horses and wooden wheels over cobblestones. Soapbox speeches and brass bands and crackly victory parades. The coughing of grubby sick bandits under river bridges, then the gurgle of their victims as the bandits cut their throats. The loud rhyming of players who strut the stage. The gasp, then roar of the crowd at a beheading. The whisper, then roar of flame as the old city burns to ash. It is all a muddle, and some parts are ugly, and yet, like Mrs. K.'s chicken korma, it is completely and only itself.

I think of this English term, "muddling through." My city was just this way: Serb, Bosnian, Croat—all mixed up together for many centuries. But killers hate this. They want clean, simple lines. So they murdered our beautiful muddle.

The Tube is jammed, airless and sweaty. Lots of people are reading, many of them frowning to concentrate, to keep the Tube world out. A sudden love fills me for these grumpy, not-seeing people, who take the liberty to stare, or read, or talk, simply because together they are a muddle, and nobody is sorting them out to live or die for an accent. For one way or another of saying "bread" or "shop." For church or mosque, city or village.

And yet, when my people were burning and dying, these English watched it every night on TV but did nothing at all. What would they do now? If Iggy has done war crimes, and I could prove it, would they deport him? Is that what I want? My crotch throbs, then so does my face.

I am still churning with all this, walking home fast at the other end of the Tube. If the sky were glass I would smash it, then crawl through the glass to the moon. Has it risen yet? I look up; no, not yet, the sky is still pinkish-gray. A couple of faint stars compete with the neon and the few working streetlights. My cobalt-blue bag-with-the-attitude bangs awkwardly against my leg, stiff-shaped from the large shiny white envelope of Sanja's photos I finally picked up today. Tonight, this bag does not say *Get out of my way.* Tonight, it is nagging at me instead: *Open up, open up. Look at me.* But I will not open this envelope tonight. One step by one step. *Soon,* I tell myself.

I turn the corner to my street, and a voice calls my name. It's Naveen, a little bit out of breath, as if he's run to catch up with me.

"You had dinner yet? Mum says you can eat with us if you'll cut up the onions." I smile at him and his face lights up, then he scowls, to hide it.

"Surely," I say. I am guessing Mrs. K. wants all the details of my Iggy interview. "But you should do the onions, Naveen; they make me cry. I'll do the spuds and okra instead. How is this plan?"

"Okay," he says, meek as a little sheep, and together we step into the pink fluorescent haven of the Happy Café, where the soundtrack is the cash register, the chatter of family and the clatter of cooking pots, muddled in with customers' voices and the TV songs of Bollywood.

17

A boot in the ribs jerks you awake. "Get up, Sleeping Beauty!" Stefan bellows. "Do you know what time it is?"

You stare up at him. "Time for you to fuck off," you say, and stumble toward the bathroom. But instead of abusing you, Stefan laughs.

"It's party time! Grand motel opening tonight!" He's hectic, bursting with glee. "You two little virgins have to stay here, Bogdan's orders. Keep the cockroaches in line. We'll be out there getting supplies. And at nine o'clock—you're coming over." He writes an address on a grimy piece of paper. "Think you can manage that?" You nod curtly. You don't look at him, it's too charged.

"Sure!" says Milan. You bet he's relieved. He won't even have to pretend to shoot people.

"Hold the fort, men of honor!" Stefan yells, like a maniac, and the door slams. You wonder how much speed he's doing these days.

You count to twenty, then say to Milan, "I think we've earned a day off, don't you?"

"What shall we do?"

"Play some chess?" This is a joke, but Milan's eyes gleam.

"What with?"

"Oh, I don't know. You'll think of something." Milan nods, relieved. He looks round the apartment, then gathers his nerve and goes outside. You wonder, briefly, how you got here. With a real-life Rambo and a guy wandering round a war zone looking for pebbles. The three of you used to be a band.

Nine o'clock comes around. Milan's absorbed in his makeshift chessboard. You take a deep breath and tell him it's time. Milan looks up. "Do we have to go?"

"We'll get so much shit if we don't," you say. Milan nods. He knows this unhappy calculus too well. He laces up his boots deliberately. "Milan," you say.

"What?"

"Be prepared, okay?"

"What do you mean, Iggy? For what?" But that's all you can safely say; Milan has no poker face. "Just—you're a soldier. Be ready."

"Of course," he says, a little annoyed.

Your boots crunch along the street. It's deserted, which is strange—your side owns this part of town and usually there are fighters, vehicles, noise, shoddy bars, and makeshift markets. Peacekeepers—none of those around either. It's too quiet. The hairs on your arm stand up again. You suspect Bogdan's paid them off. A few blocks later, you reach the address. It's a shabby blue building that was once a hotel. Now there's no glass in the windows and the inside bar is full of broken furniture and pigeon shit. A rat scuttles away as you enter, but there's light and party sounds upstairs.

You head up the stairs to a small lobby, packed with men in bandanas sporting bullet belts and hunting knives. The stench of sweat and whiskey is overwhelming. A boom box thumps out tinny turbofolk. Stefan and Bogdan are laughing at someone's joke. There are traces of white powder on the makeshift bar. There's a hectic, excited feeling, like your team just won the World Cup.

Bogdan comes over to you, clapping an arm round each of your shoulders. "Welcome to the party! We've got something really special for you today."

"Come on, man, they just got here. They can get in line," says one of the guys. His pupils are pinpricks and his eyes are too wide open. At that moment, another guy swaggers back from the corridor leading off from the lobby.

"All yours," he says to Pin-Eyes. "Room seven is ready for your visit." He tosses a key to Pin-Eyes, who catches it with a flourish and heads up the corridor.

"Stefan!" calls Bogdan. Stefan comes over, grinning.

"The Three Musketeers!" says Bogdan. "One for all and all for one, eh?" He hands Stefan a room key. "Number eleven."

"Round two for me," says Stefan.

"Saved you the best till last," says Bogdan. "Off you go."

"Come on, brothers," says Stefan, his peculiar wolf eyes staring straight at you. "Time to play."

You walk up the corridor together. Time slows. Everything is very clear and sharp. There are cracks in the ceiling and walls. The purple carpet has a flowery pattern that repeats at two-meter intervals. You pass several doors; from behind one you hear a sob, cut off abruptly. Your feet sink without sound into the carpet and you have the strange sensation of walking on water. You've been here in dreams; you've been walking along this corridor all your life.

You reach door eleven, the last on the left. Stefan unlocks it and presses you inside. It's dark. Plywood over the window. A single bare lightbulb flickers in and out, casting nightmare shadows on the walls. Something red throbs in a corner—it's tomatoes, pulsing with life, in a bright string bag slung over a chair. In the center of the room is a single bed with iron railings. Tied to it, spread-eagled, gagged, is a woman.

Fair. Long legs. Impossible to say how old. Her clothes have been torn off, except for the underwear. Her face is bruised and bloody, with one eye swollen shut, but the other eye stares at you with unflinching hate.

"So. Who's first? We kept this one fresh for you," says Stefan.

Milan has turned doughy gray. He looks like he's going to be sick. Stefan's eyes gleam; he's high as a kite.

"Go on, then," he says to Milan. He pushes him toward the bed. Milan looks to you for rescue, but you've turned to stone. Milan shakes his head. "Go on!" roars Stefan, but Milan won't move. He's reverted to his old schoolyard statue pose, head bowed. He will take whatever rains down on him, but he's not budging. "Pussy," spits Stefan. "Little fat girl. Get out of the men's way." And then he turns to you.

"After you, Iggy. Show us how it's done." His mad eyes shine. Again, that feeling that you've been here before. All roads lead here. If you do this, Stefan and Bogdan will own you.

Time stretches. You think. The woman stares at you with her one good eye.

She's a fighter. Can't untie her; too messy. You'd never get her out. Stefan would stop you. And there are men in the lobby, still pouring in. Only one exit here.

"Get ready for action, Milan," you say, grinning. You really hope he's listening. You memorize Stefan's position, then move away from him and the door. Toward the woman. You bend down toward her. Your hand moves toward your fly, then swerves.

"I'm sorry," you whisper to her, and shoot her in the head.

In the split second of shock afterward, as blood and brains spatter the wall, you spin. Shoot Stefan through the heart. You start running before he even hits the ground, shoving along Milan, whose mouth is hanging open. You figure you have about seven seconds.

"Run! Fuck you, run!" you yell, and race for the fire exit, bursting through the metal doors, and then you're scrambling down the concrete stairwell, Milan panting behind. Behind you, you hear running feet, a roar, and just as the door to the fire exit opens behind you again—you're outside. You run up the street at full tilt, weaving through the streets. You don't stop until you're winded, wet through with sweat, back up toward the hills where the suburb gives way to goat tracks. You bend over. Black and yellow spots heave before your eyes.

It's not till you stand up, able to draw breath again, that it hits you. Milan hasn't followed. You're alone. You sink down to the ground, fists balled, shove your face into the dirt, and scream.

Two hours later, you're sitting on a hill overlooking the suburb you fled. You've taken off your bandana, the identifying arm patch. Your face is dark brown, smeared with dirt and ash from the little fire you risked. You're hungry, but that can wait; at least you drank from the stream. You look through your rifle sights and wait. The lights are off in the shooting house you were in; from this angle, you can't see anything moving.

An hour passes. Another. Later, on the cusp of dawn, Bogdan and three of Stefan's chetnik buddies sneak up to the house you were in. They go in the back door—so they're trying not to be heard. After a minute, the lights go on. You still can't see much. You calculate, then run quickly down the hill to the next big tree. You peer round it and focus again. The men are standing in a circle in the middle of the kitchen. One of them swings a blow. As he pulls back, you can see they've got Milan, tied to a chair. He doesn't know where you've gone, or anything else—clueless Milan—but they're going to beat it out of him anyway. You see he's not wearing his glasses—they must have broken them—and this simple detail fills you with rage.

You think. Nothing to do from here. By the time you'd shot one, even two of them, Milan would be dead. It's grim to watch a friend take a beating, but you do. Finally, the chair falls over. Milan has fainted. One of them pulls a revolver, but Bogdan holds up his hand. Some sort of discussion. Then they leave. Why? Your best guess is, it's a trap for you. And Milan's the bait. Best not to rush it, then. You're going to need supplies for this one. It's a gamble to leave him with the wolves, but there are no options.

The next night, after a hard day in the woods, you're back. You have what you need from one of the paramilitaries, bunkered in above the town where they lob mortars from on high. It's more like throwing rocks than actual combat, so a lot of the fighters are high, or drunk, or asleep—or sneaking down behind enemy lines to trade cigarettes, whiskey, food. Even so, it's grueling work, stalking and stealing; takes patience.

You're relieved to see that Milan is still on the chair, but in a different position—at least they've let him piss, have some water, you surmise. So they haven't given up on him, or the trap—if they had, he'd be dead. You wait. There's no one in the house, you're pretty sure, except Milan and one bored-looking chetnik. At least he's not hitting him. You could take the guy from here but it's too dangerous—it would take at least five minutes to get to the house, and they might all be there by then, and Milan would be dead. So. Back to square one.

You creep down the hill. It takes two hours to cover half a mile. Finally, there's just a small stretch of flat open land between you and the back door. You sprint, praying it's unlocked, and luck is with you. You slip inside, catch your breath, listen. No sound. And you don't want to make any, either. You slip into the room. Milan's facing you; his guard's back is to you.

Milan's eyes widen. You put your finger to your lips. Then you run up behind his guard and slip the nylon around his neck. It's a brief, fierce struggle, and then he falls. You turn off the light and cut Milan's bonds, but you don't take the duct tape off his mouth—not yet. You put your finger to your lips again and get him standing. He falls over at first. It takes an agonizingly long time till he can balance and walk.

Time to go—but he's pointing, eyes bulging. It's his glasses, lying on the floor. You don't have time, but you grab them anyway, shove them on his nose, then push him before you—too late. Bogdan and two men run in the back door.

As they reach for their weapons you pull out your final card—a grenade. Everything slows down. Holding it in front of your face, you back out the front door. You push Milan away and for the second time yell, "Run!" He stumbles away. You hear the crack of gunfire as you throw the grenade through the door and run. The blast almost knocks you off your feet.

When the smoke clears, you look round for Milan. He is lying a yard beyond his broken glasses, facedown with a bullet in his back.

18

If my English were perfect, like it sounds in my head, I would translate it for them like this:

Imagine a heart. The heart has four chambers that pump together. Sometimes there are fatty clumps or plaques. Sometimes the heart aches because something sad or difficult happens to the body, but mostly things lurch along. Then one day, some red cells get together and make a plan. Why should they do all the work? It's them that bring all the energy to the body. The blue venous side just drains it all away. It's a parasite.

Red decides to seal off the membrane. At first, it's a large success. Blood stops going around the body, feeding it oxygen, and nothing reaches the other chambers. The venous side shrivels, starves, and starts to die. The left atrium and ventricle fatten and swell with triumph. But then with nowhere for all that blood to go—they burst, and those chambers die too. Soon, the body dies.

After a while, the looters and scavengers arrive. Beetles, worms, flies, and wasps lay their eggs. The body is a busy colony. But eventually the eggs hatch and the little insects fly or wriggle away. Then all the flesh and organs are gone. Wolves gnaw the thigh bones, the pelvis. Birds carry away the smaller bones to weave into nests. Tiny, shy creatures—field mice, voles—shelter in the hollow vertebrae.

Finally, only the skull is left. A huge bright bird, a bird the color of blood, flies down and carries it to the top of a dead pine tree, where it lodges. The bird sits in its bone throne and sings all day, mine mine mine.

"Nadia! Why so glum?" Priya's voice startles me. I look up, from where I've been grinding the point of a pencil into my yellow pad. I have been thinking of how to explain it all to my English friends.

Perhaps at the pub. But there is no point, they just mutter "Terrible," and "At least you got out, love," or more often, "One more round?"

"Nadia?" Priya is beaming. Ah, it's the Oleg love glow. She wants to chat all the time now.

"Oh, the fairies were away," I say.

"Away with the fairies," corrects Maudie, coming up behind. She and Priya are not getting along these days. Still, Maudie sniffs happiness and she doesn't want to be left out.

"Penny for your thoughts," says Priya. But my thoughts are not worth a penny. Even I don't want them.

"I was thinking of love," I say, and in a way, it's true. "Happy hearts and broken hearts."

"Which is yours, Nadia?" says Maudie. She's looking at me with slightly narrowed eyes.

"Mostly happy," I say. "How about you?" and I smile. She flinches a tiny bit.

"Can't complain," she says. "Better get those files finished. Priya?" Priya wants to linger but they retreat, awkwardly conjoined twins. Priya turns to wink at me, mouthing *Drinks later?* I nod. *Of course.* I am so English now.

I look out the window. The sun has gone from the mossy wall. It leaves earlier each day now as we tip into autumn. The trees are still green but they look tired, dry. The spider plant is drooping. I get up to water it, and there is Iggy, who's just got in, at the water cooler. "Hello, Iggy, how are you?" I say.

"Well. And you?"

"Very well." We smile at each other like polite strangers. Ridiculous. Then Iggy remembers we are supposed to have this office romance and pats me on the bottom. Roger, Priya, and Maudie are all suspicious now, wondering if we are fighting, because now that we have crossed that line once, our strongest impulse is to hide it. This is difficult, because everyone got used to our fake affair—our little smiles and touches. Having a fake affair which you pretend to hide, and then . . . this thing we are circling—this is difficult. Pretending the old fake affair is now more complicated.

I have scoured Mrs. K.'s stash of women's magazines for advice, but there is none for our situation. Things are hidden or seen, black or white—there is no gray-market advice. For Iggy and me, what is hidden is everything. In clear sight. In the eyes of London, our white skin, which is not even English-white, washes everything else away. I am the only one who knows his passport must be fake. What does he know about me? How I got here—I don't think so. That my work permission is fake? Maybe, if he has snooped around the Temp Angels files.

I think about Maudie's question. Happy or sad? I don't know. I crave Iggy's skin, his black eyes, his touch, the scent of home, but when I come close, fear and desire shake together into a poisonous cocktail. I want more of it but it makes me sick, too. But I need to keep him in my sights. Fear is my natural home; without it, I am lost, like a balloon with its string cut, floating into the sky.

It is strange for a man to be beautiful in the way of a cat. Me, I am more of a moth, wings bigger than my body. I feel in some way Iggy and I are one person, joined up like Maudie and Priya, but I do not like this person so much. Victim, killer—they smell of old blood. Smell, touch, the oldest senses. They open my skin-memory, like a knife through paper, to Sanja.

I never thought of us as *gay*, even as we twined in the secret dark of the bed, curtained off from the day. Kisses, girls—that was just play; it didn't count. Unless you were a real homosexual—and we didn't look like them, we didn't go to their bars. Those men, and women who dressed like men, braced themselves for the streets. Sometimes they were dragged into alleys and beaten up by the men with crew cuts. Here in London, though, or at least in Soho, there is *gay pride* and rainbows in the windows, and men walk along the streets holding hands. Sometimes, too, the women with short hair and leather jackets are looking at me on the street. Sometimes also the girls in skirts. Or is it me, staring at them?

And then there is Jody. Her friends, they look sideways at me. As if they were having some joke. I have drinks with Jody after work sometimes too, and we sit with our knees too close. Never at the Hag and Crow, of course; we go to Paradise Island, down the stairs to this island-dungeon of night smoke and peacocks and shiny creatures. We never talk about that other night—like so many English things, it goes under the label *drunk*, so it doesn't count. I keep Jody's world sealed off from my day-life, my day-thoughts. She makes me laugh, but also uncomfortable, and hot under my shirt. Just looking at her makes my heart thud, because in one angle she is Sanja, and the next—there is nothing alike. And the lights in Paradise Island are dim. So I look too hard, and she smiles at me, with the cat-cream pleasure that comes with the power to draw the eye. And in the corners, on the dance floor, there are shadows and beings that flicker and flame. But I am afraid to burn.

Over by the bar, more often than not, there is the woman from the market, Marla, hunching with a beer and not-looking at us. Is this why Jody plays with me, to torment this Marla? *Maybe.* I shrug. Marla's pain is not my problem. And I wonder, too: What would have happened with us, Sanja, if you had appeared in my office instead of Iggy?

This is the worst of happiness—it brings with it hope. I got out. Maya and Milo got out. Maybe she did too. These thoughts are like chewing a pebble; they yield nothing but pain. *Sanja, where are you?* But she just half smiles at me and turns away.

With all of these problems of Iggy and Sanja and Jody, I am glad I live far away. Many days I just watch TV after dinner at the Happy Café. I never take Iggy. We all pretend I am a real customer because I buy a cup of tea and stay in the café area with the pink Formica tables, but Naveen sneaks in to do his homework. He also watches me; I think the silly boy has a crush. Then if Jamaal is home, he joins us, because Mrs. K. wants Jamaal to watch Naveen around me, but then the café is too full and eventually Mrs. K. tells us to stop hogging all the tables for paying customers and we go back into the lounge, with the parakeet cage and enormous couch and Mr. K., and watch *True Crime*.

There are often missing girls on *True Crime*, and stories of long searches and white vans and garages where they are kept *right under our noses*, say the neighbors, and *he was always so quiet and polite*, about the kidnapper. Mostly the girls die. But sometimes they escape. Other times, and everyone says this is the worst, they are never found. Women weep on camera for their lost children and the fathers' faces dry up like drought-stricken fields of wheat. Hope remains, but just enough to poison everything else.

Sanja. I can't even bury her.

19

Humans bury their dead. But you are a wolf, a beast in the woods. And right now, you're panting hard enough to make yourself throw up. When that's done, you stand upright—bad idea—and collapse to the forest floor. Running flat-out up a mountain can't be sustained.

When your blood stops thumping in your ears, you look round. There's a little stream nearby and you realize you're ragingly thirsty. You drink, then dunk your whole head into the icy water for as long as you can. But it washes nothing away. Milan is still dead, discarded like a gutted pig on the ground.

You want to punch your own face—but then something rustles behind you. You spin. A deer. A doe this time, looking at you with the huge wary eyes of the hunted. Then she bounds away, followed by a spotted fawn.

It suddenly hits you that now everyone will want to shoot you, not just the Bosniaks, Croats, and various bandits. It's like one of those idiotic cowboy movies, or *The Terminator*, where the hero shoots his way out of hordes of faceless enemies coming from all directions. Before you can get a grip, you're convulsing, heaving with laughter. Trying to stifle it just makes it worse. Yet as you laugh, your old self wakes up from cold storage and crawls back into your skin—the alt-rock guitarist, the mosh-pit surfer, the party animal. Someone fun. No more fucking miserable cottage and shooting days and psycho Stefan and the oily Bogdan and his Tatjana, lording over you, all the while raping and pillaging like modern Vikings. The other Iggy's *Lust for Life* starts pounding in your head—an oldie but a goodie— blowing out six months' worth of shitty, saccharine turbo-folk.

Change soundtracks, change your life. Why else would the generals grab the radio stations?

And so the most wanted man in the Balkans, filthy, stateless, bereft, and set free, rocks out in the woods with a shredding air guitar solo to the music of a secret channel. And as you hit the chorus, your eyes close and just for a second, your band joins in too.

■ ■ ■

Face blackened, you're lying on the overhang above one of the militia's camps. Turns out you're a talented thief. You scope out supplies, and once it's dark, you creep down and relieve the drunken troops of a packet of biscuits, some hard cheese, a rope, duct tape, a balaclava. A knife. They're singing some patriotic song that no one knows the words to, passing the bottle. *Good for them.* No one hears a thing. Soon you're back at your little wolf den—barely a cave, more a hollow under a rock. But it's near a stream and hidden behind a thicket of brambles.

You eat, and think. The goal is simple: Cross the border. Get out of Bosnia. To Serbia, to Belgrade. It's a big enough city to fade into the walls, and you know some musicians there. Some of them can still travel—they might help you get out of this train wreck of a country. Start again. That's the *what*. The how. . . . You hit a wall on that one. Back up. Start with the basics. Eat. Don't get shot. Then, step three . . . step three. . . . And then it hits you. A huge, audacious plan blooms full-grown in your head. You yelp—then rein it in. Force yourself to go through it carefully, because it's just too perfect. But an hour later, it still looks solid. And lucky you—it's Friday today, so you can go tomorrow. Done. You crawl to the back of the hollow and fall into black, fathomless sleep.

By midday Saturday, you're exhausted, almost to the point of shaking. This creeping-around-like-prey shit is harder than it looks. You don't have far to go, but you're moving through woods and hills crawling with soldiers, paramilitaries, mercenaries from the Caucasus, drug traders, raiding parties, and the odd stubborn shepherd still trying to keep his flock fed. And every twig underfoot could go off like a firecracker. Plus, you need one more thing.

Finally, through the trees, there it is: the remains of a village. You watch for a while. No animals, no movement, no smoke. You slip through the forest to the edge of the clearing, then run to the nearest house. The window is smashed in, the door swings open. In the bedroom, the mattress is torn, ornaments are smashed, but there are some clothes half out of the dresser, strewn across the floor. Nothing your size, but close enough—you find some men's jeans and a belt, a shirt, a crappy woodman's jacket. Civilian shit. Shove them in your kit and head on out, up the hill, back through the woods. Only an hour or so to go.

At one point, you tread on something soft, rotten, hidden under the thin carpet of leaves, and almost fall. You recoil, and when you look back, you see you've disturbed a barely covered tarp. It's squishy. The sweet reek of death rises up round you. The edge of a woman's scarf protrudes from under the blue tarpaulin, partly hiding a small child's foot, wearing a grimy sock but no shoe. You push the sight and stench out of your mind and move on.

You come over a rise, lift your head slowly—and there it is, just below you. Your target. It's a wide stone plateau with a low wall; before the war, it was a favorite viewing spot for the tourist buses. The view is peerless—Sarajevo is laid out before you like a pinned butterfly, its red roofs, silvery mosque towers, and ancient churches all on display.

The city is bisected by a narrow river and surrounded on all sides by mountains—a perfect setup for the siege. No way in, no way out except through those deadly mountains, glittering in the sun with rifles, guns, rocket launchers. Smoke spirals lazily up from buildings where mortars have landed, and if you squint, you can see the blackened holes in some. You wouldn't be able to see faces, but through telescopic sights you could make out bodies, cars, crowds. A shooter's paradise.

Your gamble's paid off—there's a party. It's the weekend warriors from the villages—maybe even some from as far as Belgrade. Men with beer bellies and loud colored shirts are drinking, laughing, and shooting. From where you are, you can see the bald spot on the back of one man's head. There are maybe seven men, two women, and a couple of teenagers. Easy meat—you force yourself to look carefully, to take them seriously. Overconfidence is death.

One boy with a crew cut, who looks barely fourteen, seems alert and handles his weapon with respect and familiarity. A boom box plays turbo-folk, the infernal soundtrack of the war. Beer cans and spent bullets litter the place, reflecting sun and rolling about. Careless—but why wouldn't they be? This is uncontested territory. The man with the bald spot has a real gun, a Kalashnikov, and the others take a break to cluster around and admire it.

There's a parking area about fifty meters behind the shooting party's lookout. You calculate distances and times. First you get ready—change into the clothes you took; scrape the worst of the dirt from your face. Shove your stinking old clothes in your kit bag, along with the duct tape and rope. Then you settle in to wait. You want to make your move before sunset, but not until they're too wrecked to shoot straight. You'll be walking out in the open for about two minutes. With any luck, they won't even see you, but if they do, you want them to miss.

The afternoon wears on. The men grow louder, more unsteady. They shoot in sporadic bursts, not even taking aim by now. The sun creeps lower. The shots peter out: time just for drinking now. Someone turns up the boom box, and the party gets going. Guns are left propped haphazardly against the wall—total amateurs. But you make yourself check the teenager who can handle a gun—yes, good. His gun's down. He's drinking now too.

You creep behind the group toward the parking area. There they are: three SUVs, a couple of motorbikes, two shabby little Yugos. You pray one of them's unlocked. After all the creeping and raids, you have to force yourself to stroll out into the open parking area like a civilian, to look like you know what you're doing. You go to the nearest little red Yugo, parked in the shadow of a towering SUV. You reach for the handle, heart hammering—

"Hey! Hey, what are you doing?"

You spin. He's bespectacled, early forties, pale city skin—probably just left the shooting party for a piss. Swaying a bit. Drunk.

"Hey, that's Neša's car!" He's running toward you. The shouting is a problem. You wait, then lunge, trip him, kneel on his legs, press your hands over his mouth. His glasses fall off, eyes roll like a frightened horse. It's too easy. Suddenly enraged, you press harder, hands on his throat—but Milan's reproachful face intrudes. *Dammit, Milan!* You pull back, scoop up the man's glasses; he coughs and sputters.

You pull out your revolver and snarl, in your best Tarantino villain voice, *Not a sound or you're dead. Up. Walk.* You push him in front of you back to the trees. Then you take the filthy shirt out of your kit bag and gag him with it. Tape it shut. Tape his ankles and wrists and head for the car park—but there's Milan's face again—*all right!* You run back and shove the man's glasses on top of his head. His eyes bulge, he's trying to talk, but you're running back to the car park. He'll be okay for an hour or so. But if the others come looking for him now, you're dead.

Out in the open, you make yourself slow down, breathe in. Then you walk over to the little red Yugo, no big deal, like you were just going to the corner shop for milk. Back when people did that. You rub the glass button in your pocket hard, for luck. Then you pull the car door open. The keys are on the floor; you don't even have to hot-wire it. Relief floods you so hard, you start shaking. This might actually work.

You jump as loud turbo-folk floods the car. You stall the car, slam the radio off. You start it again, then pause. Amid the trash, the front seat is strewn with cassettes. Slim pickings—but you turn the volume down, shove one in the cassette player. Middle-of-the-road rock—of course. You go to flick it off—then let it play, because at least it's not fucking turbo-folk. Then, with Lionel Richie crooning *All night long . . . All night long . . .* you crank up the volume and drive out of Bosnia, leaving the old Iggy behind along with his reeking clothes.

20

Maybe I've missed something. Maybe I can find where she went if I look hard enough. Here we are now, the only ones left in my home. We are shivering, we can't get warm; our hands are rough and raw. The picture is strangely sharp, like through a zoom lens. I replay it for clues: This is me, in the corner; now I'm pulling at my hair. She is fiddling with her camera, then pointing at me, *click click click*. This annoys me and I shout, *What are you doing, you think this is the time for that?* —Come on, sugarplum, couple more, she says.

I walk over; she's still pointing at me, *that's good*, but when I get up to her face, I knock the Nikon from her hands. She dives and catches it just before it hits the ground. There's blood on her knuckles and knees, but she saved the camera. I swear it's her first love. More than me. She's still for a moment, hands and knees on the floor, then she stands up and says, *You little Turkish bitch*, and slaps my face really hard. I look at her then I cry and I can't stop, she's holding me and we're both howling, she's murmuring *little baldie* into my hair where I've pulled it out, and then *What a stupid way to die*. I say, *Yes, typical Tata*—and then we are laughing and laughing and can't stop. Because my tata just dropped dead in the tunnel he helped to build— not from guns, not from bombs. From a stupid asthma attack—he'd run out of Ventolin, and we couldn't get more. He turned blue and died five yards from the entrance on our side.

And he ruined my nails, she says, and it's true: we still have dirt under our nails from burying him. We'd had to wait for five nights until the men from the tunnel could come to help. Everyone was panting, in a hurry, shovel-digs ringing loud as gunshots as they struck the frozen ground beside the Olympic stadium. Then quick whispered farewells before we scuttled off again to hide in the city's cracks.

Finally, Sanja says, *What shall we have for dinner? The steak or the chicken?* And then we stop laughing because there is no steak, no chicken, no nothing. Some rice, which we cannot cook with no fuel. Some powdered milk that the weevils got into. That's it. *Champagne it is*, she says, and gets us both a cup of water from the spout my tata rigged up that catches the rainwater off the roof. We drink it. We drink more. It helps. The sun goes down, slowly, and we curl up soon afterward. It's hard to sleep through the night, but also to stay awake in the day. The town is getting pounded night and day now with mortars and guns; we feel there's an end coming. But we don't know what kind.

Time gets blurry, sleeping these odd hours—was it the next day, or the day after? Anyway, at some point Emir drops round some stale biscuits and some cigarettes. He's a hard little man, caked in dust like a miner. Emir says he is sorry, but he can't come by again this week—too dangerous. Enemy soldiers watch all around the tunnel now. If they find the entrance, the whole town will starve because, as it is, the enemy steals most of our Red Cross and UN air-drop supplies at gunpoint. *And the peacekeepers do nothing, fucking useless*, he says. He goes to spit, then remembers he is indoors.

Sanja smokes. We eat the biscuits. Then I fall asleep and when I wake up, she's gone. I try not to panic, maybe she's at the market for gas, or a few weevilly vegetables. It's the one place they haven't bombed yet. I'm too anxious to sleep—but no, I must have dozed off again because a heavenly smell wakes me. Then in she comes, grinning, with her yellow string bag full of divine tomatoes, white cheese, fresh coffee, crackers, oranges, tins of tuna. It's a miracle!

Feast time! she says. We make a meal, dive in and devour it like stray dogs. It's amazing how high you get from food when you're that hungry. You feel the body sucking in the nutrients, shuffling them round to organs, skin, brain. Booting them up again. So it isn't till we've finished ... quite a while afterward ... that I wonder where she got these things. But I shove that thought aside. We both fall asleep, right where we sit.

The next day there are oranges for breakfast, and tinned tuna, and I can think again. I gear up to ask her where . . . but she's gone again. Still no note, nothing! This time for hours. When she comes back, the yellow bag is full again. Of course, her bag is this stylish color; everyone else has only plastic bags by now, or grimy gray string. I swear this woman will be buried in high heels and lipstick.

She flops theatrically into an armchair. She has a small bruise on her neck.

Sanja, where did you get this stuff? I say. *Forget it, chick, just be glad we can eat.* —Come on. *No secrets,* I say, but she bats it back, drawling like a spy in a movie: *The less you know, the safer it is.* This annoys me. I forget we both play this spy game, and snap, *I'm not your dog, Sanja. I need to know.* A pause. *Work it out,* she says. *You're smart.*

Of course I know, I just want to make her say it. She is doing what Alma did. With the Dutch peacekeeper on the corner. He is large and red-haired and shiny-skinned, like a slab of uncooked meat. I can't help seeing her on her knees, the man's guiding hand on her head—ugh—*How could you do that!* —Want to starve, bitch? she snaps back. I hate it. I eat the food anyway. She tries to make up, with that amused smile, a reach of the hand. But I won't look at her or let her touch me. All day. All night. It makes her crazy.

Remembering this is like swallowing live coals—everything burns, then goes numb. But it is done. So here we are, in silence. Then fighting. She gets in my face and shakes me. Then we scream and fight. I say things I don't even recognize. Things men say to women. She calls me a stuck-up snobby college bitch, a hypocrite, and finally— after, yes, I call her a whore, a liar, a collaborator—she calls me a dirty lesbian. That stops me.

You're always all over me with your eyes. So creepy. You're no different to Hans. You'll do anything for a feel, a fuck, a bit of tongue on your clit. At least he's honest about it.

I can't speak. Can't breathe. She was the one who started—
I thought she loved me.

But Sanja—

"But Sanja," she says, mocking me, in a whiny little voice. *Give me a fucking break.*

We retreat to the room's corners. Finally, it's dark, and she gets up to go out with her empty bag. Stares at me from the door. Waits. The moment hangs. If I'd smiled, or joked, or said anything— But I won't look at her. So she grinds her cigarette butt into our floor with her boot heel, goes out, and slams the door behind her.

She never comes back.

21

All day you're unhooking cow torsos to heave them into the freezer. Every time you open the freezer door, a blast of fog wreaths the room in white: it's a winter wonderland of death. Gray walls, gray men, purplish frozen cows. The only bright splash is your yellow boots and gloves. You wipe your bloody gloves on your coveralls and keep hefting. Heave, hook, shove. Heave, hook, shove. You can't feel your hands and feet. If you stop, you'll freeze in place, arms bent stiffly like a tin soldier.

Break time, you all share smokes and tips: Niki's friend's roommate scored a job in a pub, hauling barrels of beer in and out of the cellar. A girl they know is a nanny, but that's not a man's job—as if the English would let migrant men near their children anyway. And the girl says it's no picnic—the mother's wound up like an alarm clock and the dad gropes at her in the corridor.

"There's work on the docks," Julio says. "Better pay and you don't freeze your balls off."

Julio's from Spain, incongruously cheery next to this crew of Slavs and Romanians. Even in the pallor of the meat room, he glows with the memory of sun. The others look like ghosts beside him.

Niki shakes his head. "England is shit."

"Germany's worse," says Jan.

"Oh yeah? You been?"

"I hear Berlin is not bad for work."

"Good for music," you say. No one replies. It's like you spoke in a dead language. After a short pause they keep going. Rumors of better jobs, better rooms. Someone's cousin knows someone. A girl Julio says he's been seeing. Then the whistle blows and as one, you grind out your cigarettes, pull on the smeared gloves, and head back in.

By the end of the shift, you're frozen through, so stiff and sore you can't even face the pub. You shove down a meat pie on the way home, then crawl into the lower bunk of the crappy room you share. Shiver yourself asleep. You don't stir, not even when Niki slams in on a cloud of beer fumes, clambers over you into the top bunk, and snores all night.

Someone's shaking you.

"Get up, man. Iggy!"

"Fuck off, Stefan!"

You push him away as the dawn pokes through the cracked cottage window—but as you wake, the room shudders. For a second you're falling down, down through the layers of a video game where every time you fail to escape, the trap gets smaller and smaller until—

"Who's Stefan?"

"What? No one."

"Yeah well, get up. Bus leaves in ten. I made tea."

"I'll see you there."

"But—"

"I'll get another job." Niki stares at you like a cow. "Piss off!"

"Your funeral, dickhead." He shrugs and slams out the door.

You have no plan. But you can't put those bloodstained coveralls back on. You pull on your boots, head out, and your feet take over. They keep going uphill. Like an animal returning to its lair, you need the mountains.

Two hours later you're finally up above London. You look out over this washed-out city, the cramped chimney tops and old buildings dwarfed by shiny new ones clustered along the river. The Thames is an old, flat mud-snake, crawling out to sea to die. The sky is pale and watery blue, the clouds soft-edged. Nothing seems in focus. The longing for home hits you like a fist in the gut, folds you over. Crouched in the grass you see a worm sliding between clods of earth.

A tiny blue flower. A strip of gold plastic, the kind you pull to get the wrapper off a pack of smokes. You dig your fingers hard into the soil, driving dirt up under your nails. Lift your hands to your face and inhale. At least the dirt smells like home.

Eventually hunger drives you back down the hill. You find a phone box that isn't vandalized after a few blocks and try calling the friend's uncle for the hundredth time. The phone rings and rings, like it always does—but just as you're about to slam the receiver down, someone picks up.

"Yes? Who is this?"

You stammer your lines: new to London, friend of nephew, hard worker, help you out . . .

"Come over. I might have something."

He gives you the address. It's out by the docks. As you hang up, you have that falling feeling again from the video game, but this time you're falling upward. Toward escape.

By the time you get out there, the sun's slipped away. It's a lot farther out than you'd thought—the place isn't at the docklands on the map where the river curves back on itself. That's a dock in name only now: all brash new offices and construction sites, flinging themselves up over the bones of the old river port. This place is out east, on the District line or a bus from the city. The bus is cheaper but you soon regret your penny-pinching—it takes forever. Then it's still a fair walk from the bus stop.

Although you're following directions, you can't shake the feeling you're going the wrong way as the residential streets give way to weedy empty lots encased in chain-link fences with NO TRESPASS-ING and BEWARE GUARD DOG signs, graffiti-covered tin buildings that could be anything. Prison barracks, storage places, torture rooms, abandoned community art centers. The sky has a bronze cast, girding itself against the night. Your neck prickles as you walk along, toward the silhouettes of huge cranes, black against the darkening sky. Eventually the road stops. You still can't see water, but there are the outlines of container ships, towering over the concrete expanse. A few trucks move between warehouses, small as toys. Seagulls wheel and caw. You smell the sea behind the industrial grime.

Third single warehouse on the left. Force yourself to walk across the open space, past forklift trucks, coal loaders, stacks of pallets, the car-parts warehouse complex with the huge Ford sign. The hairs on your neck are standing on end now. There are scores—hundreds—of hidden places to shoot from. As you approach the warehouse, you see that the huge sliding roller door is shut. You keep going, and around to the side is a small maroon door, graffiti-gray splattered. You knock, feeling like some spy in a B-grade movie. After a moment, it creaks open. A short, round man with a hard beer-barrel belly stares at you. Stubble-jaw, a glint of gold in his mouth. Thinning brown hair, polyester short-sleeved shirt. Crisscross plastic sandals. So familiar. You smile, you can't help it. He doesn't smile back.

"So. You are Igor. What can you do for me?"

"Goran. Do you have work?"

"That depends. What can you do?"

"Most things."

"Most things, huh?" He pulls out a cigarette, takes his time lighting it. Doesn't offer you one. Blows the smoke out slowly.

"I'm adaptable."

"Can you type?"

"What?"

And now he smiles.

"I know you can shoot. Guard a space, I see how you walk over here. Can you type too?"

You're about to laugh, he's fucking with you—but no, he's watching carefully. You decide to treat it like a real question, whatever bizarre test this is.

"A little. Two fingers, peck peck. And data entry. I kept the books for my aunt's farm, after—"

And now he's laughing, clapping you on the back.

"Come in, come in. I have an office job for you! Have a drink. And I will show you your room." You stand there, like Niki earlier that morning. Cow-dumb and gaping. "You do need a bed, don't you?" He turns, not waiting for an answer, and after a moment you follow him inside.

22

I have a system. Days are for work. Nights are for sleeping. But in between are the evenings, when shadows grow long. The Happy Café soaks up some of them. Other evenings are for the Hag and Crow, and if I am lucky, for Helen behind the bar. She smiles at me sometimes now, through the forest of men's arms pushing toward their beers.

Tuesday evenings are for Jody and Paradise Island. Here, hovering between day and night, I'm close enough to smell Jody's skin, feel her body warmth. Marla sometimes joins, but mostly hunches over the bar or plays pool with the dark-skinned twins, with their bleached buzz cuts and chains. These two don't say much, but everyone nods and makes a little air as they walk past. There is danger in their wake, an electric hush like the silence before a mortar lands. They smell like men. I don't think they are, but the word "women" slides off them like oil, it won't stick.

People like this could not exist in my ex-country, even before the war. These twins with their buzz-cut hair, their men smell, make me afraid, but I can't stop watching. I'm just a visitor, I tell myself, but this place whispers, it pulls at my edges. What would it be like to be this way, to break the rules, strut fearless into the daytime? I always leave before the twilight turns completely to night. And lately I don't go so often. Not since Iggy.

Iggy. I keep him for weekends. The closer he is to me, the less afraid I am, like the pilot fish that hides under the jaw of a shark.

■ ■ ■

On Saturday, we go to visit Karl Marx. The trees in the Highgate graveyard are very old, their branches hanging low over small gray stones. A cluster of shiny birds sit high up in the branches of the tallest tree; Iggy says they are starlings. As we come close, they all wheel skyward, a cloud of bird cinders from a long-dead fire. A few gravestones have dates still visible, some with only a handful of years between birth and death; there are so many dead children in the past. But most graves are beaten by weather into mossy, indecipherable humps.

Marx's grave is marked by a pedestal. On top of it is an enormous statue of his head, strangely square, glaring out over Highgate. Around this grave, planted like bulbs that will not bloom, are the many lesser luminaries of revolution. The African leaders. The Bloomsbury radicals. Tito's ghost, hovering somewhere in the trees. But now only Marx still surveys London from his stone eyes.

Iggy scowls; the air around him seems dark. He kicks some leaves.

"This bastard," he says.

"What?"

"Fuck these great men and their ideas. Look where they took us." I look at him instead. He is staring past the grand head, the stern gaze. Then with a chill, I see: he is looking at the grave of our country. After a moment, we walk silently out from the dark under the trees, away from Karl Marx and his faithful army of the dead.

Later, back down at water level, the shadow of the grave melts away. The Thames sparkles in the sunset, the waiter plops down a saucer of olives, Iggy pours me a second glass of Riesling. I glance at our silvery twins in the café window, and they are so close, so real, I could just reach out and slide into mirror-world and live there. They could even be home, before the war, if the river were narrower and chattered over stones—but the seagulls make up for that sound, and bright flakes of many languages swirl past us, like bits of tinsel in a London snow globe. Shake it up, put it down. Everything swirls, then settles again, contained in its unbreakable orb of glass. I laugh, I don't know why.

Iggy laughs too. It's like seeing the light come on in a ruined building. You can see who he was, could be again. . . . A breeze chills my neck. "It's getting cold, we should walk," I say. We finish the bottle and stroll. The sun is almost gone, but as it grazes the horizon, that old feeling of being followed returns. Yet Iggy is with me, so . . . ? I start glancing sideways, as I used to—but there we are still, in the windows of the shiny café. As I turn back, though, I catch a flicker behind us. I spin, but there's nothing.

A few hundred yards on, the feeling comes again. I turn. And this time I see. She's crouched by the water's edge, collar up, feeding seagulls. I am suddenly alert, wine washed away by adrenaline. It's sunset, but she has wraparound dark glasses. She has a tight jacket, high boots. A fair plait over one shoulder. In this city of money and tourists she has that rare thing, style. *Sanja.* My hands sweat.

"What," says Iggy.

"It's nothing. I just thought—I thought it was someone." He follows my gaze and sees her. I know it cannot be her but I can't look away. I can't. Iggy is still in that old way, a cat watching a bird. The woman stands. She straightens her spine and looks at us. It's Jody. *Of course.* I feel sick, as if punched in the stomach, and the memory of her in my bed rises unbidden—and now she looks straight at me. Then she slowly raises her sunglasses. She is seeing us, and I must see her too. Then she spins on her boot heel and walks away.

Iggy looks at me, too casually. "She's that girl from the band night, right?"

"Yes," I say. Then, after a pause. "We are friends. But I haven't been—I have neglected her, a bit."

"You do what you must," says Iggy, a bit too quickly. Suddenly I'm angry.

"And what's that?" I say. "Hurt people? Take their homes? Rape them, shoot them?"

His face shuts. "I didn't rape anyone."

"No, you just shot them. Us."

"I told you," he says, in a dangerously quiet voice. "We tried to escape. But they caught us—"

"Yeah, and trained you to shoot from the mountains, where—"

"—Where I tried to control Stefan, he turned into a fucking maniac—"

"And you killed us every day—"

"Soldiers! Who were shooting at us! I kept civilians, girls like you alive!"

"Really? Like Milan—you protected him, no?"

The sun has set now. Iggy goes very still. A breath. Another.

"What is this? You know I only shot fighters."

"We were all fighters! For our fucking lives!"

There is a silence. Then Iggy says, softly, "I know." If he had argued. Or anything. But this— My eyes fill.

"My friend, my . . . Sanja—we had a terrible—a big, terrible fight, then she just—she just left! And I never saw her—I don't know what happened to her! That's the worst, worst thing."

"Is it?"

"She might still be alive! She was . . . She knew a Dutch peacekeeper. Some of them helped people get out, I know they did, there was this girl Alma and her whole family. . . . So maybe Sanja escaped."

"Maybe." He is looking down. I can't read his voice.

"She could be in Amsterdam! She wouldn't know how to find me, why would I be in London? I could be anywhere."

Another silence. Then he says, "I'm sorry about your friend. I wish— I'm sorry." It sounds like one of those stupid cards you send when someone dies and you didn't know them. I turn to him, ready to fight again—but his face is full of pain and the words dry in my mouth.

We walk, a little apart, as the sun paints the brown river gold, then red.

"After they're gone—bar, bus, crossing the road—I know, you see them everywhere," he says. "All these ghosts. But this band girl—she really looks like her. I see why you get this shock."

Then he is kissing me and there is no more talking. So it isn't until later—much later, in the cavernous dark of the warehouse, that I jolt awake beside him. Something he said . . . *She really looks like her.*

How does he know how Sanja looks? He said he kept watch over civilians. . . . I wonder how he did this. With binoculars? Through his rifle sights, more likely. Did he watch her—us?

Far above us, the shuffle and whisper of wings begins as the pigeons sense dawn coming. Iggy mumbles and stirs. I am lying, very still now, against the long curve of his back. But the warmth doesn't soothe me. A cold snake uncoils in my belly. My eyes stare into the darkness, and I wonder if I know him at all.

23

What do people wear to office jobs here? The parts of London you've been in, where people haul boxes or carcasses, sit out the front of corner delis on milk crates, give no clue. You push through the mothball-and-dust op-shop smell, past the dreary polyester cardigan racks, the rakish boots and worn-out shoes, the fake-leather handbags and kid's T-shirts, the old-lady dresses that flap sadly as you brush by, hoping for a dance.

Down the back, you find a corner rack a little apart, with all this gear on it. Slim-fit suits, sharp shirts. It looks strangely new, like it got lifted from a single wardrobe. Someone your size, more or less.

You haven't worn a suit since your cousin's funeral. But you try on the first suit, a nice herringbone gray. It's a bit close-cut and straight for your taste but a decent fit. The changing cubicle's tiny, a curtain across a corner jammed with boxes overflowing with crap to sort out. Hats, purses, kid's T-shirts. The pockmarked, misty mirror's six inches from your face. As you glance at it, another's face and body stares back, midmemory: Coming home to a low red roof. Small windows squinted shut by net curtains. You step back sharply, stare at the mirror, white-faced and glaring, until the other man's memories evaporate. You're wearing a dead man's clothes. Again.

Suddenly, you have to get out of this shop. Two suits, four shirts, and a couple of ties—a decent haul. You draw the line at a dead man's shoes.

"Four pounds fifty," says the woman at the counter. She must be eighty at least, though her hair is a defiant red helmet. You pull out a handful of coins, drop them on the counter. She sorts and counts them slowly, like they're magic beans. One . . . two . . . three. . . . Her lime-green nails clack on the counter. Finally, she's done. As you grab your stuff to go, she glances up at you with sharp blue eyes.

"Wear 'em well, sonny. Wear 'em well."

You wonder if she's his grandmother.

The bus stop's right outside, but the bus could be hours. You wait, staring ahead—you can feel the old biddy's eyes boring into the back of your head through the shop window. You think about walking another stop, but that's a sure way to make the bus roar past you. When it finally arrives, you can't resist a quick glance backward. She's still there, staring at you, surrounded by the ghosts of cats. You spit in the gutter, climb the stairs, brace yourself at the huge window in the front seat. Nothing in front of you except sky and buildings, streaming past. Pull out the headphones and crank up the Walkman. Let London wash over and through you with the Clash. Be thankful you're not still hauling frozen cow carcasses.

■ ■ ■

The next day, nicely dressed in a haunted suit, you head out to find the job agency. It's not easy, despite Goran's directions—this part of town is full of twisty alleys once you get off the main roads that smash together at Charing Cross. Down one side road, turn, turn again and you're in a maze of sex shops, cheap hotels, hole-in-the-wall betting shops, and buildings with blank, bolted front doors and buzzers. You veer right and walk two blocks and suddenly the streets open. Here, everything and everyone's Chinese. There are lanterns and the smell of sizzling meat and spices. Groups of women chatter as they walk, stopping to check out shop windows. A lot of the decor seems to be red. Toy cats nod in the windows of shops that are selling nothing you recognize. Smoked fish and birds hang naked and whole in other storefronts. You want to ask for directions, but people's eyes slide off you and they walk quickly past. By now, despite the chill, there are half moons of sweat in the armpits of your new shirt. You're so lost, you can't even figure out where north is. You back out the way you came.

Back in the alley maze. Uncrumple Goran's hand-drawn map, re-orient. Even so, you walk past the place twice before you see the sign: *TEMP ANGELS: Short-Term Solutions When You Need Them Most!* It's sandwiched between a leather shop with a rainbow flag out front and a travel agency with a fake-plaster white wall and port-hole window sporting posters of the Aegean Islands. To be fair to your hunting skills, the sign is tiny: it's been photocopied and sticky-taped to the glass panel of a grimy door. You can't see into the place; the glass is covered with broken Venetian blinds. You half expect some homeless guy to be sleeping on the doorstep.

As you push the door open, a bell jingles and two cats leap off the front counter to disappear into the gloom. The man behind the counter doesn't look up. He could be Goran's twin brother, and you have that video-game-trapped feeling again. But as your eyes adjust, you see that this guy's bald, or almost: a couple of comb-over strands refuse to give up. Open shirt collar, gold chain, Orthodox cross. You're about to ask about office jobs, mention Goran, when the guy speaks.

"You are Igor."

"Iggy. And you?"

He ignores the question, hands you a packet.

"Please fill in. You start next week."

"Um, what—"

"Data entry. Is all in the packet."

And with that, he returns to his magazine.

Dismissed, you flick a glance round the space. There are stools at a table shoved against the wall. A few cheap pens secured by string—like anyone would steal them. You find one that works, eventually, and fill out the basics. *Name. Address.* . . . You don't know if the warehouse even has an address. You give your old one from the rooming house. *ID: Passport.* Armenian is a bullshit choice, but it's all they had left in Belgrade. You just hope there are no actual Armenians in this office you're going to. *Skills.* . . . You hover over that one. Hand it back to the guy.

"Nine o'clock Monday."

"What am I to do there?"

"Data entry." A pause. You try again.

"Did Goran say anything else? He said to keep the eye open. For what?"

Finally, the guy looks up at you through his bifocals.

"He will say if there is anything."

"The address . . . ?"

The guy shoves a card at you with an address on it. You're used to rude, but he's elevated the art form. When you don't move, he rummages in the drawer and pulls out a small, well-thumbed fat book.

"*London A–Z.* Three pounds. My last copy."

You almost laugh, but you do need one. You grab it.

"Take it out of my first paycheck."

And just to get up the guy's nose, you take your time leaving. Stretch, yawn. Wander over to peruse the job board, as if you might find a better job. It's a sorry selection, thumbtacked to the far wall. *Short-order cook. Cleaner. Deli counter attendant. Dishwasher. Cleaner. Cleaner. Night watchman. Office temp,* but out near the airport. Goran's done well for you, it seems, getting you an office job in Soho. There are some photos of temps the agency's placed, as if to prove it can happen. They look like prison mug shots or the faces you see on *Wanted: Reward* posters. Black, white, Arabic, Indian, Eastern European. A couple of the white guys have shaved heads and neck tattoos. No one is smiling. The girls look like they just got out of rehab or work as hookers: hair-thin eyebrows, massive eyelashes, that special scowl that's supposed to be sultry.

And then you see it. It's her.

You close your eyes to stop the dizziness, but when you open them, the picture's still there. You make yourself keep looking—and now you're really not sure any more. After all, you barely saw her. Couldn't say what color her eyes are.

You peer at the board. Nadia. Her name's Nadia. Bosniak last name. And now that video-game sensation is back, but you don't know if you've gone up a level or fallen to your death. Because she's working where you're about to start. Global Flow Solutions.

24

The loveliest thing about Iggy's place is the ceiling. It is corrugated plastic and very, very high up. Thick metal beams cross below it. The light is pearly and soft; it is like drifting inside a cloud. Today, though, I stare up into rain and gloomy gray. The place has begun its morning rumbling, as buses and trucks come to Monday life. There are many heavy machines parked in big concrete yards with wire fences, and acres of factories and warehouses. Soon he will have to shift his bed corner when they start loading in boxes, but this is the deal with the friend's uncle. *The free lunch.*

I watch him sleep, one arm flung out. His smell is on my skin. I look out into the vast gloom beyond our little corner. There are huge boxes stacked at the other end of the space. They are so far away they look small. The boxes come and go, other things stay. Ropes in coils, buckets, pulleys. Old machines of wood and metal. The machines look welded into the floor. I joked last night that the boxes are temps like us, but Iggy didn't laugh.

"Price of a place to stay. Better than drunk flatmates," he said.

I have been awake since four. Planning. I make Turkish coffee and let the scent wake Iggy. I bring the pot over and pour us two little cups, sweet and dark. We sit and sip while the rain drums the roof far above us. "Iggy," I say. "My friend, Jody."

"Yeah, what about her?"

"You said, *She really looks like her.*"

"Uh-huh," he says, but he is awake now. "A little bit, maybe. You think so?"

I look down into my cup. The coffee grounds have made the shape of a seahorse. Or question mark.

"How do you know?"

"Know what?"

Now I look at him. "What Sanja looked like."

He stops smiling. He puts his coffee cup down very carefully. "From your words. And this photo you show me."

"What photo?"

"Nadija, this picture in your purse! You have it always!"

My hands are damp. The coffee has made me nervous. This little photo lives in the inside of my wallet. I almost never take it out, I am afraid to crease it, to wear it out from looking too hard.

"I never showed you this!"

"Maybe you don't remember. It was after these drinks with Wishbone. This night you went to your friend's band. You said then, this Jody reminds you of Sanja."

Could this be true? I can't imagine saying this. But then, I was very drunk; what do I remember? I get up to make more coffee. Touch something real.

"Or maybe," I say, with my back to him. "Maybe you remember her from the siege. Did you watch us? Through your gun sights?"

Silence. I measure the coffee, the sugar, into the pot and add water. Stir. Put it on the little gas burner. Make myself breathe, slowly. Finally, I can't stand it and I turn. His face looks old and sad, but when he sees me, it snaps back to blank.

"It's possible," he says. "Maybe I saw you two, just this one day. But we were drinking. It was far. And there were many civilians, running around."

"Not anymore," I say, then clamp my jaw. I want to scream at him, to fight, but this will not get Sanja back. I let the silence settle back. "You say you're sorry, you wish the war—the war," I say. "But there was nothing you could do."

His face is wary. "Yes. So?"

"Now you can do something. You can go look for her. You know Amsterdam. We can copy this photo."

"Amsterdam? Why? This is crazy!"

"Because this peacekeeper Hans is from there! If he got her out—If she was there, he would know. Even if she had moved on. And then . . ."

"Nadija," says Iggy softly. "Come here." He stretches out his arm. I don't move.

"Next week," I say. "Or the one after. You can get Ryanair; they are very cheap. Roger will work it out, so you can take a few days."

"Why me? Why not you—or us?" he says.

"Because I have no fucking passport!" The Home Office holds my passport, to the country that does not exist anymore. I must report every time I change address while I wait in asylum limbo. I am not just a temp in my work but in my whole life. Unlike this fake Armenian.

Iggy looks at me. He is deciding something. I wait.

"What if she's not there?" he says. "Isn't it better to have hope?"

I can't believe he's saying this. "No! No! That's the poison! I have to know." His face is sad. He doesn't understand. "Don't you see, Iggy, I—We had a bad fight, I pushed her away, that was the last time I saw her! So—"

"It's not your fault," he says. "Whatever happened." But it is. "What was the fight about?" he asks.

"What does it matter?" I say.

"About Hans?"

"How could you say that! She would never do that!"

"Do what?" And there, I'm caught in my lie.

I take the coffee cups and bang them around in the huge concrete sink. After a moment, he follows me.

"Nadija. Listen. It was war. People do things they never would normally—"

"I know that! I was there too!"

"You have to shut those thoughts out," he says. "Or you go truly crazy." I am silent. Thinking about how I escaped. He's never asked, and I wonder if he has guessed.

"I just have to know," I say. "Go to Amsterdam. And then I will know."

There is a long pause. This is life with Iggy, long pauses.

"I don't think this plan will work," he says. "All over Europe now, so many refugees. Hundreds, thousands, from all parts. Not just Bosnia; Serbs and Croats lost their homes too—"

"I know!"

"—new names maybe, new identities, how can you ever find—"

"Coward! You said you were sorry, and now—"

"Sorry for you, that you lost this friend—"

"I ask you this, this one thing, and you refuse?"

"Nadija—"

"You have a passport! Not me! Killers get passports, the refugees get nothing. Nothing! We're nothing!"

At this, he snaps, "Is it that time of the month?"

"Fuck off," I say, and stomp off to get dressed. "We're late for work."

We walk to the bus stop and stand on the bus in angry, jiggling silence, hanging on to those leather straps and trying not to touch. It is difficult because the bus is jammed full. Someone gropes my bottom and without turning around, I deliver an elbow, hard, into a soft stomach. It is very satisfying to hear them go "Oof!" as my bottom is suddenly freed. I hope I left a bruise.

When we get off, we still don't talk, but barge along the street full of other bad-mood people pushing their way to work. Two blocks later, as we walk up the stairs, I say, "Ryanair is cheap. You know the city. You could go."

He doesn't reply. But I will find the way. Because this is not *True Crime*. She was not kidnapped in a white van. She is alive somewhere—or she is dead in a Sarajevo grave. I will find her or bury her, but I will not sit beside the TV and shrivel to dust, like those families whose daughters never come home.

25

You haven't changed. It's all her. You still come in, say good morning, get no response from the wall of ice you sit next to. Type in the fucking numbers. Outwardly you're calm, but your brain churns like a waterwheel. Why is she suddenly fixated on this shit? How could you find one lost girl from the war—who's probably dead—in a metropolis of dealers, drifters, tourists, hashish in every pub and corner? And how has it become your fault that her friend can't be found? Of course she can't. She knows what that last winter was like. It was—
And that door slams shut in your mind.

You glance over at her and for the first time, you wonder if she wants to punish you, or herself, or both. You walk over to get coffee, breaking the unwritten rule: Nadia makes the morning tea. Your action ripples through the office; everyone pauses. The three-headed beast of Roger-Priya-Maudie sits up and sniffs, hoping for scandal or at least distraction. After a pretend pause, the beast trots over.

"Everything okay, Iggy?" says Roger.

"It is nothing."

"Humph," says Maudie, flicking a glance back toward Nadia. She'd be a good soldier. Bad enemy. Keeping off Maudie's radar has become your main game, since your last chat with Goran.

Roger gets bold: "Drinks after work, Igster?"

You look at him for a moment too long, put him off balance. Sometimes you can even get him to blush.

"Sure. We will all go."

Nadia doesn't react, but the wall of ice around her thickens an inch or so. Good. You make sure to smile a few more moments, laugh at Roger's next joke, flirt a bit with Priya, who always appreciates the effort.

At five on the dot, you all leave, except for Nadia, who doesn't move. Seeing the set of her shoulders, you feel a pang—she looks small, alone.

"'Bye, Nadia," you say, knowing there'll be no response, and head for the Hag and Crow. Swallow that small ball of shame from hijacking her friends; wash it down with beer in the Hag and Crow, so very far from Den Haag, The Hague if you're English because they love their long words, Den Haag where right now your countrymen are facing inflated charges of genocide. But in this Hag, there's no judgment, death is banished, the bar girl is tough and funny, and the beer flows. Just for an hour or so you float in a bubble of light, as night pours in all around you with no one to check or even care who belongs and who must be cast out.

After the third round, though, the others start mumbling exit lines and edging toward their Friday nights: first Roger, to meet a man; then Priya and Maudie, off to some chicks' thing. You stand irresolute on the pavement as they head out. Fridays used to be for Nadia, before this Amsterdam bullshit. You don't want to go home, but you're not going to prop up the work bar alone.

You have a tip from one of Goran's guys about an East End session. You need something loud, louder than thinking. A thrash band somewhere with loud carpet sticky with beer, graffiti in the smashed-up loo. So far, you and Nadia have both avoided the expat scene (unless you count the warehouse). It's one thing you agree on—neither of you is going near it. They're a sorry, dangerous lot, especially your side—but the odds of anyone recognizing you, let alone ordering a hit on a deserter, are tiny—you weren't even regular army. A bit of danger will keep you sharp. Maybe you can sit in for a song or two, borrow a guitar.

■ ■ ■

The place is harder to find than Temp Angels—you can't even find the street in your *A–Z*. All the best stuff in London (minus the pubs) is hidden behind bland walls and buildings. The better the gig, the crappier the outside. It's like the whole city wants to be in a secret club.

Finally, you get lucky—a skinny bloke with a trumpet case crosses the street ahead of you and vanishes into a crack between a shop front and a boarded-up bank. You follow him along a cat-thin alley, round a corner, through a doorway, and down some precarious stairs. Before you see the room, the sound hits you in the chest—that bass. You know it like the thumping of your own blood in your ears. It's Koja, the legend. It can't be. But you glimpse the band over the heads of the crowd, and there he is—Black Tooth, bent over his bass fretboard on some impossible guitarlike riff over pounding drums. You stumble down the last stairs and you're swept into the sway of bodies, the thumping jungle trance of drum and bass. Eventually the solo ends and the song returns—*I've got those technicolor eyes—Money don't ever come to me—Easily*—over and over.

You know this song by heart, but the shock of it in English—like walking into your own bedroom and finding a llama— You're stock-still, people are bumping you—you shove your way to the stairs and climb up a couple of steps, trying to take in the scene. This familiar-strange thing, world upside-down. The three of you used to play this song, Stefan adding guitar because the bass line's impossible, unless you're Koja. *Ja imam šarene oči*— All of you bellowing the words, even Milan.

Through the smoke and dim lights, you see: the singer is a big African woman—or American? She sounds American. Her voice is strong and low, a trombone breadth to it, an edge of brass. And the drummer's great but he's some blonde guy, something about the way he sits, you just know he's not from home. He's too nice. It's all wrong. It's perfect. It's all wrong. You soak it in, staring, ears stretching, storing it for later, the future whispering to you, *Look, listen, here it is, here* . . . and then the set's over, the crowded tiny room is yelling and clapping and stamping. You give it a moment, then slip back toward the bar. A corner spot, where you can scope out the crowd.

You scan for anyone from home but come up blank. No other corner-dwellers, just a regular post-punk and drum-and-bass crowd. All kinds of shorn and long hair; more men than women. Piercings, torn T-shirts, lots of black clothing. Head-kicking boots, but they don't seem like head-kickers. A sprinkling of dark faces amid the pasty white ones. No sixth-sense danger alert. Which is why you startle, knocking over your whiskey, when a voice right next to your ear says, *Iggy*.

The guy is grinning at you like he knows you. Stubble, crew cut, sweaty under the arms. Missing a tooth. You stare for a moment, and then you're smiling back:

"No way! Novi Sad! Bibo!" You're thumping Bibo on the back and laughing, Novi Sad was incredible, both your bands were playing, nearly got electrocuted in the mud when the sky opened—

"What are you doing here, Iggy?"

"Oh, not so much. You?"

"Yeah, same."

A small silence. But then the band starts again and you're both back in there, heaving and yelling along with the English lyrics, which after three whiskeys sound normal, the language gap glued over by stitching, thumping bass:

Do not / Throw concrete blocks from the top of your house / 'Cause you can smash some limousines / Limousines and human beings / Do not / Do not /

Bibo's yelling in your ear, something about a band, a gig, a friend. What?

"—need a room, these council flats are shit, you can hear your neighbor fart, everyone's so polite but they all complain to the fucking cops and the landlord and then—"

"Come to my place! It's a palace!"

"Yeah?"

"Yeah! And leave the gear there! I've got a whole fucking warehouse to myself!"

And when the band winds up, you're still there, you and Bibo, cadging a biro from the cadaverous bar guy, drawing a map on a beer coaster of where you live. You stagger out into the street together, still singing, brothers in arms. Jam session your place, Saturday night. Bring your friends. Bring the whiskey. Bring the band.

26

I have been back in my pink eye-socket attic for five nights in a row. It seems very small and cramped after the soaring ceilings of the warehouse, but Amsterdam looms between Iggy and me; he refuses to go and he won't say why.

Just, *It won't help.* So we are fighting, it is Saturday, and I am alone. And hungry. There is nothing in my mini-fridge except a moldy carrot and cheese. Food for pigeons. I go downstairs and across to the Happy Café for a sticky bun and cup of tea.

"What would you like, miss?" asks Mrs. K. I look up, surprised. She is talking to me like a customer.

"The usual. Bun and tea, please," I say. "How are you?"

"Tea and bun. Very good," she says, ignoring my question as she sails back into the kitchen. *Oh dear.*

I get out my little notebook. Today, I start my list of Amsterdam tasks.

1. *Get Iggy to go.* I think about this one for a minute.

2. *Find Hans and ask about Sanja.* Would the UN keep track of its returned peacekeepers? Would they even tell Iggy, this fake Armenian? I realize I don't even know Hans's last name. My head starts to throb. Finding a red-haired Dutchman called Hans in Amsterdam may not be easy. But Iggy is good at hunting. If he is there for some days, he will find out something, even if it is just to come back with a better list. *He will go.* I will give it another day or two, and then—

Naveen comes in with my sticky bun and tea. His eyes are reproachful. He has no poker face. He thumps the tray down and turns to leave.

"Naveen! What's wrong?"

"Nothing," he says. "Do you need anything else?" So the whole family is annoyed with me.

"Yes!" I say. "I need a chat!" Resentment and joy battle it out in his face.

"What about?"

"About you! How's school?"

"All right," he mutters.

"Any new girlfriends?" He scowls. Usually I can tease him, but not today it seems. He turns to leave. "Naveen! I've been busy, all right?"

"Very busy," he mutters, giving me a quick side glance. It's been over a week—I used to come in almost every day.

"Don't be cheeky," I say sternly, and he can't help grinning a little. "I'm here now, aren't I? People have lives, Naveen."

"Been clubbing?" he asks.

"No, of course not. Why do you think I do that?"

A pause. "That lady's been looking for you."

"What lady?"

"That blonde one. She rang your doorbell. About six times. Mr. Patel shouted at her." I digest this. So Jody remembered where I lived and came back.

"When was this?"

"I dunno. Last week? Then after Mr. Patel shouted at her she came and sat in here. She was watching your place. It was creepy! But the light never came on. It's been dark for ages," he says, accusation creeping back in.

"Naveen. Have you been spying on me?" He blushes and scowls.

"Of course not! It's just, she came and sat here and we don't usually get . . . get people like her." He means English white people. "I thought she might be a stalker," he says hopefully.

"She's just a friend. I'm impressed by your spying abilities!"

"Well, *I'm* not," says Jamaal, walking in from the kitchen. He smiles at me—hooray, one person who is not cross with me! Jamaal's teeth are amazingly white. He is very handsome when he smiles, also when he is not gray under the eyes from shift work and his law classes. "Mum wants you in the kitchen, Naveen." Naveen pouts. "Now!" Naveen goes in, dragging leaden feet. "Sorry about him," says Jamaal. "We'll leave you in peace." And he closes the kitchen door behind them both.

I don't want peace. I want Mrs. K. to fuss over me and ask about Iggy, Naveen to keep bringing me tea and buns, and Jamaal to chat with me in his dry, funny way. But this is my punishment for vanishing, and I will have to woo them back. I wait for a while, but there is silence from the kitchen. So I finish my tea and leave some coins. I pay the regular price, not the waifs-and-strays discount. (Two can play at this chilly English politeness.)

But when I walk out, I don't know where to go. The day hangs empty before me. A solitary puff of wind stirs my hair, nudges an empty packet of crisps along the gutter. I am angry at Iggy all over again; I didn't feel lonely before him. Afraid, and worse, yes—but not this simple desire to be with someone. But so many people are annoyed with me. Mrs. K. Naveen. Jody . . . I climb back up my stairs, but I don't want to be home alone on a gloomy Saturday.

Well—not quite alone. The shiny white packet from Photo Lab pulses on the dresser. *Sanja's last photos*. No—*her most recent*, I correct myself, but it doesn't help. I am too afraid to open it. My gaze slides from the packet to her beaten old Nikon by the side of my bed. It pulls at me. I avoid the packet and pick up the camera instead. Its weight, its familiarity—it is like holding an old friend's hand.

For the first time ever, I take off the lens cap and look through the viewfinder. It takes a little while to find the focus, but then I work it out. I look in the giant mirror at the sky. I notice the telephone poles, the antennae and chimney pots on the crooked roofs that line the street. A plane flies far overhead, leaving a silvery line behind that feathers out and melts slowly back into cloud. Everything is both closer and farther away. I like this. This is how Sanja regards me, both close and far away, with that little smile. She is making a frame around me, around the window, around Alma and her peacekeeper.

A photo is not dead. It is a little thumbprint of life.

Suddenly, I know what I will do today.

■ ■ ■

An hour later, I push through the crowds and out the Camden Tube station. There are many exits and roads, and I am always turned around, until I see the flower stall, the World's End pub, the Costa. I take a moment to find my directions, then head to Boots, where I buy a roll of film. When I ask the girl at the counter how to put it in the camera, she looks at me strangely. But she shows me how, and where to count the number of pictures left on the roll.

"Don't open it before you're finished, whatever you do, or you'll waste the rest of the film," she says.

"Thank you."

"And don't take it to one of those bloody Photo Lab places, they charge like wounded bulls. Not worth it if you're just learning. Just drop it off here and we'll get your prints done for half the price." She smiles at me. Her hair is magenta like mine, tied up in ringlets with a scarf with little skulls on it, but the color looks much better against her brown skin.

I weave my way through the crowds, through patches of music and loud voices and flapping T-shirts and leather belts and bags. But somehow, just holding the camera helps to push back the chaos. I take some shots—I have no idea if they are in focus, or if what I see will be the photo. But it is absorbing: Here is the umbrella stall, with its silly cat-ear umbrellas in the front and a massed bat colony of black hanging behind it, ready to fly out into the rain. Here, a pile of ropes in the alley, both alive and dead in the way of snakes. There, the back of a man in leather, leaning over a pale-faced, wary boy. There, the hands of the woman counting change at the soap stall, *click click click*, the knuckles large and bony.

And then, around the next corner—there is Jody's stall. *Why am I here?* My feet have betrayed me. Her back is to me, her arms akimbo, as she adjusts the display—a billowing skirt-and-shirt outfit. Her fair plait is today wrapped round her head, and her boots come up to the thigh. I lift the camera to shoot, but I feel like a spy. I decide to run—but at that moment, Jody turns and sees me. We stare at each other like stupid statues. Her face has no expression at all. Feeling slightly sick, I put the camera in my bag and walk toward her.

"Well," she says. "Look what's turned up."

"Hello," I say, and I would say more, but Marla comes out of the back and stands behind her, arms folded over her chest, feet apart. "Stand down," says Jody to Marla. "It's okay."

"How's your boyfriend?" says Marla.

"He's not my— He is well, thank you," I say. "How are you?" Marla and Jody exchange glances.

"Why don't you ask her how *she* is?" says Marla. "She likes hanging round waiting for people. Specially queers in the closet. Nothing better to do in life."

After a confused pause, I say, "How are you, Jody?"

"Fuck, why do you bother with this one."

"Give it a break, Marls, she's not from here."

"Yeah, that's obvious." Marla stomps off, pulling out a cigarette.

"Jody," I say. "I am sorry I haven't been to drinks this week."

"Yeah, you've been busy." I look down. "Dinner was fun on my own, too. Drank the whole bottle of wine." Dinner? Suddenly a flare of memory heats my face.

"Oh no!" I say. "I forgot completely, I am really sorry."

She lights a cigarette, regards me. With my new lens-eye, I see: the cigarette, the camera. They both make a little distance.

"Jody," I say. "Life is a bit complex in the moment. Can I buy you another dinner? Tonight? To make this up?" She looks at me for several seconds. Takes another drag.

"Life's too short for bullshit, Nadia," she says.

"Yes, but sometimes there is bullshit anyway," I say. "The last week is completely full of this. I can explain something of it later." She laughs now, with big snorts of dragon smoke out her nose.

164

"All right. But it'll be expensive. Lord Stanley, five o'clock." Then she turns. I am dismissed. As I walk away, I feel Marla's grin biting through the back of my shirt.

"Camden institution," says Jody when she arrives. We squeeze into the last corner table. The place is jammed with locals, families, women reading the paper with a pint, blokes arguing over a sport event that is over. "So, what's up with the disappearing act?" she says. I go to speak, but before I can, she says, "Oh, and I don't give a shit about who you're screwing, I'm not the sex police. Just don't do this bullshit straight-girl act. Pretending you don't see me. What the fuck?"

My mouth is open, then it closes. "Jody," I say. "It's not—"

"Yeah, it is." She takes a gulp of beer, puts the glass down with a thump. "Don't want your boyfriend to know, is that it?"

"No, no, he's not—he's from my country, a soldier, I think he can help me find my— Jody, this girlfriend of mine, she disappeared. Yes, so many disappeared, my family, my—but Sanja, she looks like you, so I just, I got this big shock, I thought it was her, I just couldn't—"

Jody's mouth is tight. She wipes the beads of water from her glass. Then looks back up at me. Her eyes are dark, searching. Hurt. I feel naked, my own eyes blur, I look down.

"All right," she says. "I'll half buy that one. You're a mess, you know that?" Then her hand is over mine. I let it sit there, just for a second.

"One more round," I say, and push away back toward the bar.

■ ■ ■

Three hours later, the world is throbbing. Jody has given me half a white pill, just to get in the mood, she says, and now we are drinking water and dancing, dancing, laughing and dancing. We are at the Flamingo this time, and it is not just women.

Men with pretty red mouths, women with tight pants and bulges—there are shapeshifting parts and wholes, skin muscles bodies, everyone moving and pulsing, people twined in the doorway of the loos and thrusting in twos, threes, solos on the dance floor, I recognize some, Jody's tall friend with the muscles and shapes cut out in the hair, her eyes are glazed and she sways alone to some slow beat in her mind, the bleached-hair twins are here, too, boy-girls, why do they make my pulse race, they smell like men, rainbows flash round the room and drip from the walls, the floor thumps, sharp shards of light spike a throat, an arm, a naked belly over tight leather, I am spinning, laughing in the joy of—what is this feeling? *I'm home*, I shout. Jody throws her head back and laughs. Her throat is white and long, like a swan, and the green butterfly in her neck hollow dances, flaps its wings with her pulse. I spin around, soaking in everything, everyone.

There's Marla, dancing in a corner. She turns her back when I look toward her, but tonight I have X-ray vision; I can see through skulls to the cloud-clusters of thought underneath, Marla is the puppy kicked out into the dark, who has learned not to whine but to growl. There is dark around her, and a stubborn pulse in her that pushes it away, heartbeat by heartbeat. I've seen her on the streets back home, digging in for a fight, facing down the men with shaved heads and metal fists—but then one of the boy-girl twins moves in to Marla, unbuttoning her shirt; Marla's face brightens and I lose confidence, my X-ray vision flickers in a hellish strobe light—is this Marla or the past? Where am I? The room spins.

Jody reaches out and pulls me in, holds me tight. Life pulses through her belly, her hips, it fills me with warm liquid honey. This is real, her body is real, here-now, here-now, here-now . . . my heart thuds this song, she laughs a little bit, she feels it. Her breath is close on my cheek. Then she is kissing me and heat runs in bright copper lines to my crotch, I'm throbbing, *Let's get out of here*, she says, then we are in the shiny world of lights and cars and rain, silvery rain like the mirror rainbows inside, *Everything is rain*, I say, laughing, and we pile into a taxi and into the night.

My landlord, I whisper, so we take off our shoes to climb the flights of stairs, and then we are in my pink-eyeball room for the second time, but this time I will remember. I am printing every second into my skin. She is a flame I circle, then dive into—I fling my bag on the dresser, and then my clothes on top of that, so the white envelope from Photo Lab is buried.

But even through the next hours, deep in the skin and taste and touch of this beautiful not-Sanja, this Jody, I have the feeling that this envelope is watching, like a hidden shiny eyeball. If I learned nothing else from the war, I learned this: someone is always watching.

27

The weekend, without her. The futon's rolled up in the corner to make room for the drum kit. Your and Bibo's amps are sprouting leads, there's a mic stand set up, and the floor looks like electrical spaghetti, cords and leads everywhere. You're on your hands and knees with a roll of gaffer tape, trying to get some order into it before the others arrive and someone trips over and electrocutes you all.

You check out the window—ah, here they are, lit by those huge orange perimeter lights that never turn off. You can see them coming from about five minutes away, across the long exposed walk to the warehouse. Shooting meat. You calculate distance, speed, angle: you could take both of them easily. Two straight shots. Unlike the English, who wouldn't notice a ticking bomb in the middle of the pavement, they're aware of it. They're each scanning a different direction as they walk, ready to hit the ground or run.

This must be how Goran watched you, that first day. He trusts you by now, or what passes for it: he leaves you alone a lot. He's away on weekends, sometimes for whole weeks; never says where he's going or when he'll be back. You haven't exactly told him about the band; you don't know if he'd laugh, shrug, shout, or throw you out.

Glancing back out the window, you catch a glimpse of bodies on the ground, guitar cases cracked open, an ugly tangle of instruments and limbs in pools of blood. You shake it off. Get away from the window before they see you spying on them. Don't lurk behind the door. They have a key by now so they can let themselves in—now for that, Goran would kill you.

They're not terrible. Jablan's rock steady on drums, stays in his lane. Bibo's a bit frilly for a bass player. If he just sat in the groove with Jablan he'd be fine, but he's one of those bass players who got demoted from guitar and never got over it. Even so, once you get going, the sound starts to come together. You crank up your axe, try out a few power chords, settle into a riff with Bibo. It feels so good to make some noise. Hard to keep the rhythm tight because of the overwhelming echo—the space is the size of a railway yard, except mostly empty.

New song. Bibo starts a familiar riff, grinning at you—you cut it off.

"Nah. Not that shit."

"What's wrong with it?"

You shrug. He wants to play a nostalgic song by Bijelo Dugme, a huge stadium band that went mainstream a decade ago. These guys. No taste! You flash for a second on Stefan—his snarl, his edge. A monster, but one with taste. He loved Laibach—the menace, the uniforms, the proto-fascist symbols, the ironic military marching-band feel. You start up the opening riff to a Laibach classic, "Večno V Zvezi," instead. Bibo looks surly, but Jablan grins and joins in and after a moment, so does Bibo.

Drzava skrbi za zascito, dvig in izkoriscanje gozdov: You're bellowing into the mic and for a moment, it almost feels like a gig, the words washing back to you from the echo that could be a crowd. The power chords and crashing drums echo and build, louder, louder, drowning out the sneaky voice that wonders what she's doing right now, whether she misses you. You close your eyes and crank up the volume.

Midnight, you wrap up. Go downstairs, head outside, perch on milk crates where you smoke and share a bottle of Johnnie Walker. It's almost the best bit—just hanging out after a session. Bibo's grinning at you, already making plans.

"Next weekend, same time?"

You pause. "Maybe. Should be okay."

"Why, there's a problem?"

"Oh—it's my . . . This girl. She has this stupid idea I should go to Amsterdam. But I don't think so." They look at you like you're deranged.

"Everyone should go to Amsterdam!" says Jablan, miming a long toke of a joint.

"I should go to Amsterdam!"

"And the girls!"

"The girls! Yes! Go! Go! We can play here without you one week. What is your problem here?"

"Oh, she wants me to look for this girl."

"Another girl?" Bibo counts on his fingers. "How many girls is this now?"

Jablan joins in: "One . . . two . . ."

"Shut up. I mean, this girl that disappeared. From the war."

Now they're serious.

"Serbian girl?" asks Bibo. You shrug. "Do you have a lead? Address?" You shake your head. The others exchange glances. "Igi. How would you even . . ."

"Bibo, I know! I know!"

Jablan stubs out his smoke, reaches over, and grabs your shoulders.

"Igi, look at me. You should go. It's Amsterdam."

"Yes, but there's no way—"

"So you say you tried! And you have this great music and party weekend and then you are a hero for helping this girl, for looking everywhere. What's the problem?"

You can't think of the problem. But hidden in there somewhere, there is one. You shake your head again, like a dog clearing water. Now they're looking at you a little warily. Time to shut this down. You stand, pick up the half-empty bottle.

"Same time next week."

"Without you! Get on that plane!" You pretend you don't hear that.

"Great session, guys."

You close the door, shutting them outside. You don't even watch them leave.

28

The pigeons coo. Silvery light presses on my eyelids. Last night I was laughing, I was dancing . . . oh. *Jody.* I reach out, carefully, but my fingers find only sheets. I sit up and look around. She is gone. Then I see that she has written on the shiny envelope of Sanja's unopened photos. I don't like that she touched it. It says *xxx. Drinks Tuesday? P Island, 5:30.* No. Tuesday is only two days away. Too close. I remember Jody looking at me in the pub, the softness in her eyes, and a hard lump of fear forms in my belly. Nights could wash over into days, and then what? My feelings are on churn cycle. With Iggy I never close my eyes, we push each other until one falls, it's close to fighting, but with Jody, I blur and burn. I crave her so much, her tongue, her wetness, the strength of her arms, the way she takes charge, pushes me down, the release—but when she is gone, I push her out of my head, climb back into my own skin, and shut the door. Jody's world is too full of melting edges, these queer night people who strut around in the daylight. It tumbles me, makes me seasick. I try to remember ordinary happiness, but I can't.

The week crawls to the weekend on its hands and knees. The Baltic Bigwigs are not around, and neither is Charles. The whole office seems to have a hangover. Iggy and I do not speak together, and Maudie and Priya roll their eyes behind our backs. I type numbers. *Click, click.* There they go. They mean nothing, these numbers, they just float in space, in spreadsheets, ticking through time. Profit, loss, who cares. I sign in, I sign out. I am stuck in *True Crime,* with the other families who must wait. *I will make him go,* I tell myself, but I am afraid to use my last card.

Saturday comes again at last. I have finished my morning tea and sticky bun—at least things are now back to normal at the Happy Café. It took some repair work. I had dinner there three times this week, left the regular-customer price on the table, and also chopped onions, which I hate doing, for each dinner. Mrs. K. graciously allowed me to do this, to wash up each time and to scrub the floor once, and then after that I was invited back to the couch, and TV.

But now Naveen has gone off to play video games with his friends at the arcade. Jamaal has gone to bed so he can wake up in time for night shift at the cereal factory. Mrs. K. is doing the laundry and the ironing and has no more time to chat. Mr. K. has opened his newspaper, with a definite-sounding shake. There is that *eleven o'clock, time to get on with it* feeling. With the fight with Iggy dragging on, the day looks long and dull again. And the cursed envelope of Sanja's photos is still staring at me. I decide I will go to Camden again and make new photos. And maybe I will see Jody and we will devour again and I will feel better for one moment.

Sanja would love Camden. I imagine her shooting there, angling in on the punks, the shopping girls from Italy, the street kids. She is good with faces; she has no shame about pointing the camera at them. So far, I do not shoot people in their faces. Just clouds and umbrellas and pigeons and ropes. Maybe she would be selling her fashion designs. She makes everything more glamorous. If she is in Amsterdam, someone must have noticed her. They must have. Not possible she would blend in, anywhere.

Rage flames up my spine. Damn this *True Crime* waiting hell, Iggy could be looking for her right now! I will play my danger card. Before I can change my mind, I run to the corner phone box and call Iggy. He has a mobile phone, which he never answers—his friend's uncle gave it to him for the factory lookout work. But I know he checks messages. I tell him to meet me by the motorbikes at one o'clock for lunch. *Or else.* I don't say that part, but my voice is stern. He will know.

Outside the Tube, the wind is blustery and the sky keeps changing its mind. But I have purpose, a fizz in my stomach—the risk of Jody and Iggy meeting; the mission to push Iggy to Amsterdam—these little bits of danger have pushed away the dull, heavy feeling away. I push my way through the stalls and crowds, planning to shoot Jody without being seen—her beautiful neck, her hands, her stance with arms akimbo—but when I get near her stall, it's not there. An unpleasant sense of ambush prickles my neck, even as I remember in the same moment that she is at Notting Hill this week.

Rattled, I turn too fast, and there in my face is another surprise— the shabby man. He is with his son, in their matching glasses. The boy looks straight through me; the man is trying to remember me.

"Sorry," I mutter, and push past them. Mud, river, ruined shoes— I hate surprises.

"Excuse me!" the boy's voice calls out. I want to keep going, but he taps me on the back. "You dropped this," he says as I turn. He holds out my wallet.

"Oh. Okay. Good work," I say.

"Glad we could catch that for you," says his father, shambling up behind him. "Too many light fingers round here. Not the safest place to drop something."

"I am safe," I snap. He blinks, then steps back.

"Yes, of course, well, glad we could . . . Come on, Ernie." He tugs at his son's sleeve; the boy is still looking at me, waiting for something . . . what? But then they're walking away.

"Thank you!" I call out, too late, to their disappearing backs.

One twenty-five p.m. The weather has the jitters. It was sunny a moment ago, but now I'm chilled with cloud-shadow and wind, and my bottom is sore from the stone saddle of my motorbike. The remains of my samosa and peas are greasy on my paper plate. A thin, tall girl with lank hair, holding a fresh samosa, stands too close. She wants my seat. Well, she can wait another minute. I count to ten. No Iggy. I get up to leave but a familiar voice behind me says, "Nadija." I turn and it's him.

"Iggy," I say. Then, idiotically, "You came." He shrugs—*obviously*. I smile, but he does not smile back.

"What is it, Nadija?" He is not so stupid. I wait a moment. Then lift my chin and aim my words.

"You have to go. You have to look."

"Fuck. Not this again."

"There is only this. Until you go."

"What if I find nothing? Because there's nothing to find? How is that better?"

"It's better," I say.

"Why?"

"Because— Because then we tried." He looks at my face—and something softens in his look.

"It could be the worst," he says. A heartbeat passes. *Do it, do it now.*

"No, Iggy. The worst for you would be prison. Or deportation. This fake Armenian passport you have. Go to Amsterdam or I call the police. The anonymous tip line. For migrants, criminals."

He is stone. He is still. I have the sense of humming birds, of something flickering so fast in his thoughts that nothing shows movement. Then his face clears.

"You have no papers," he says. "No work permissions, with this asylum case. Only these fake Temp Angels papers."

"Same as you," I say. "I could lose my job. But you also have a fake passport; much worse problem. Use it for me or lose it." And now he looks at me, and something wary has fallen from his face. His eyes are electric, alive.

"I shoot, you shoot, is that it?"

I do not smile. "Yes," I say. "But if you don't go—I shoot first."

To my big surprise, now he is smiling. "Look at you! *U inat.* Mad girl!" But I still do not smile. I stare, chin up, and wait. "All right, you win," he says. "On Monday. I will go, take the week. But Nadija, don't hope for—"

He will go! Fierce triumph floods me, washes away this moment of danger, this feeling of *too easy.* And then, most of all—hope. Hope for my Sanja! I can't help laughing. He picks me up and swirls me round. My flying feet knock over a trash can and bump the thin, tall girl, still waiting with her samosa for my seat. She yells at us, but I don't care. The sun comes back out. We kiss.

After a while I say, "What about work? Will they let you go?"

"I will do drinks tomorrow. With just Roger. He will take care of it; they can get Elsie back for a few days." I raise an eyebrow, but he chooses not to see it. Iggy can be very charming. I can imagine Roger fluffing his feathers, Iggy laughing at his jokes.

"We have so much to do!" I say. "Maps! A guidebook!"

"Slow down! I know my way round, I've been there before."

"Yes, but we—"

"Saw Nick Cave play the Paradiso there once. Total legend!"

He's full of energy now, bouncing along. He plays a few bars of air guitar. He fits right in; he and Sanja would both thrive here. They would both be dealing and making plans—Sanja with her fashion stall or art shop, her camera, her prints. Iggy is more the back-alley-deal type. They are both magnets to the eye. Sanja is a bare light-bulb, white-hot and flickering. Iggy wastes no movement, but you still have to watch, because danger swirls in his shadow. I am happy again, walking with both of them through Camden, even though only Iggy is truly here.

The sun dips under the buildings, bringing a little chill. We swing into the World's End for dinner and a pint, and after half a beer, the world looks rosy. It swirls around me in all the languages of London. Iggy swigs back his beer and turns to the jukebox, fishing around in his pocket for coins. I see him pull out the glass button, then shove it hastily back in, hoping I didn't see. I blink and ignore it; I will not think about this now. He chooses a song. I expect it to be raw, the Raincoats or Ian Drury or ska, but instead, a cheesy Top 40–type song floats out. It's one of those that everyone knows but no one can remember. *All night long,* sings the chorus. *All night long . . .* "What is this?" I say.

"Lionel Richie. Music for exits," says Iggy with a grin. But when I press, he won't explain. "Private joke," is all he says.

29

When I get to work on Monday morning, I discover that the spider plant is gone. In its place is a plump, smug-looking peace lily. It's as if someone died and nobody thought to tell me. How could it just be gone? I find Mrs. McGinley.

"The spider plant," I say.

"Well, good morning to you too, Nadia."

"Where is it?"

"It was looking a bit sick, so Elsie threw it out. She bought the new one for the office."

Rage fills me. How dare this Elsie throw it out?

"Where did she throw it?"

"What's got into you?" says Maudie, always the bloodhound on the scent of discord.

"My spider plant!"

By now Mrs. McGinley's eyebrows are almost swallowed in her hairline, but Maudie jerks her head toward the bin under the sink. I run over and retrieve it. It is broken almost in half, but not dead yet. I scoop the earth that's fallen out back into the pot, and whisper to it. I break off the top half, which cannot be repaired, and take it back to the desk.

"I thought you hated that plant," says Maudie.

"No, it just—" I can't explain it to them.

"Iggy problems," Priya stage-whispers to Mrs. McGinley behind my back.

"I thought you'd be pleased, young lady," says Mrs. McGinley. "You're always shoving that plant out of the sunlight." I put it back in its rightful spot. It actually stands up better without that long, trailing top half. The peace lily I put firmly on Iggy's desk—Elsie's for this week, while he is in Amsterdam—where there is no sun at all. Peace lilies are dull; every office has one. They thrive in low light, like slugs.

Just then Elsie comes in with coffee for everyone. "Oh! Didn't you like . . . ?"

"No," I say. "It lives here. For longer than me, and than you especially."

"Can everyone get back to it?" calls out Roger from his corner. "We're not a bloody flower shop."

This begins a tricky week. I am rattling with everyone, I snap at Elsie because she is not Iggy, and then she wilts like the spider plant. I don't joke with Roger or the others. At lunch, I walk as fast as I can until the hour is over. I am like one of those wind-up toys that doesn't run down, and all the time in the back corner of my mind is Iggy. *What will he find out?* I want to know, but I dread it too. I want the week to end but also not.

Finally, Priya corners me in the loo. "Nadia, love. Are you in trouble?"

"A little bit," I say.

"Well, if you need—I can help you."

"How do you mean?"

"If you need a doctor. A nice one, no questions asked." A pause. Then I work it out.

"Oh no, it is not that. No."

"So, what's the matter, love?" Priya's eyes are soft. It is not just the gossip she wants. So I tell her—some of it, anyway. That my friend is missing, maybe in Amsterdam, and Iggy has gone to find her. "Oh, Nadia," she says. Then she surprises me and hugs me. I feel tears come but I push them away.

"He might find her," I say.

"He might," she says. She does not believe this. I feel worse than before. "Come down the pub tonight, we've missed you," she says.

And indeed, since Iggy and Jody, I have neglected them. The pub is the last thing I want. I want to chew my fingers to the elbow thinking about Iggy and Sanja, as if by force of will I could make him find her. But I smile and say yes.

At five fifteen, then, we're all in the Hag and Crow. Helen is at the bar, in a fluorescent pink tank top. She lifts her chin in welcome as we come in. Her hair is a new shade, somewhere between blue and green, it matches her lovely tattoos. Lines of men push at the bar, her arm snakes out rhythmically to keep them watered, the hum and shout of voices rises and soaks into the velvety purple wallpaper, and for just this moment, the world is in its right order. It's almost like old time.

"Old times, not time," says Roger.

"Pedant," says Maudie.

"Just trying to be helpful," says Roger.

"Helpful—yeah, that's your middle name, Rog," says Maudie. Priya smiles sideways at Maudie. They are getting on better again, perhaps because Oleg is out of town.

Maudie looks serious, though. "All right, you lot. I've heard something," she says. "About the Baltic Bigwigs." Priya stops smiling.

"Dish!" says Roger.

"It's not great news." Maudie draws circles on her coaster with her finger.

"Come on, Mauds, don't keep us in suspense," says Roger.

"Well then. Some bloke at the dock opened up one of their containers, random check, apparently," says Maudie.

"They always do that, it's routine," says Priya. "Shipping 101."

"Yeah, but they weren't supposed to, not with ours," says Maudie. She's not looking at Priya. "And that's why the deal's gone south."

"What's gone south?" says Priya.

"Fuck," says Roger.

"Come on, Priya," says Maudie. "Seen Oleg lately? Or Charles, for that matter?" As I said, Maudie is clever.

"What are you talking about?" says Priya.

"We all heard Mrs. M. and Charles shouting, right? So I did a bit of digging. The last three shipments didn't go through. Held up at the wharf for inspection. And the payments stopped too."

"Bloody bureaucracy," says Priya.

"Yeah, but here's the thing. There's a line item in the budget for a recurring payment. No name, just 'Oversight Services,'" says Maudie. "I think it's some bloke on the docks or in the warehouse. Looking after our shipments."

"What do you mean?" says Priya.

"Someone's getting paid off," says Maudie patiently. "To game the timing, or look the other way when the Baltic boxes come in. Not all of them. Just to make sure the special ones don't get inspected."

"Special, how?" says Priya. Her refusal to understand is impressive. Maudie puts a finger on one side of her nose and snorts theatrically.

"God! Or even worse!" says Roger. "Guns. Girls. They ferry Eastern European girls over in shipping containers—sorry, Nadia, but they do. A whole container of them were found dead a few months ago."

"That's ridiculous!" says Priya. "Oleg would never do that. This is all—how do you know any of this is true?"

"I don't," says Maudie. She looks very tired. "I'm just following the bread crumbs."

"You just can't stand it when I'm happy, can you," says Priya. "You're always finding fault, sticking your long nose in—"

"Priya, love," says Maudie. It is worse by far than if she was angry.

"Don't 'Priya, love' me!"

"It's a smoking gun. I wish it wasn't . . ."

"Actually, you wish it was. So you can shoot down whatever I get that you don't," says Priya, and with that, she picks up her jacket and leaves.

We all look down into our drinks. There is a buzzing silence. I have been much distracted with love problems and Sanja, but now the last few weeks' events click into place. The rush of work. Then how it stops. Charles's urgent calls with Oleg. The shouting. Mrs. McGinley looking as if she had been hit. Then all of us just in limbo, doing our usual not-very-much, finishing reports for minor clients, while we wait for the next big shipping job. But there is no next big job.

"There's one more thing," says Maudie.

We don't want to hear one more thing.

"What?" says Roger.

"Your agency, Nadia. Yours and Iggy's."

"Temp Angels?" I say.

"You two are great, nothing against you. But the 'Oversight Services' pay line. The one that doesn't track to a person. It's routed through them."

We drink our beer. We have never been so quiet. Temp Angels offers a simple deal: an office job in exchange for a pirate's slice of the paycheck. A short-term solution for the shadow people like Iggy and me. But maybe that is only the surface—until a shadow business needs a short-term solution too. And then they have some workers in place who can turn away when a gray-market box comes in, or adjust the spreadsheets for that shipment. Someone like Iggy.

We might not be an office. We might be a pipeline and a money laundry.

"Well, this is a pile of shite," says Roger eventually. He has been seeing his own version of the jigsaw. Maudie, of course, is seeing it all week. She looks ten years older.

What does Iggy know? I can't ask him, he's in Amsterdam.

30

Beneath the funky cool, the hundreds of bars and tourists and street people and the scent of pot hanging over everything, Amsterdam's a clean, orderly kind of place. Easy to get around. But by now your head and feet are aching and your tourist map is folded up wrong and starting to tear. You've slogged across endless bridges and cobblestones, through hordes of cyclists, through the red-light district, shopping arcades, looking for council offices, a town hall, any kind of government-looking place. The town hall is closed for repairs. Another official-looking place just does local shit—parking permits, AA meetings, bicycle registrations. So many bicycles.

The old guy at the counter looks you up and down, tells you to try the main library. Of course it's way across town, back the way you came. When you get there, the polite and patronizing librarian tells you in her excellent English that the UN, and anything to do with peacekeeping, is in Den Haag, not Amsterdam. You can't just walk in either, she'd said, just to rub it in: you'll need an appointment and a reason. And they won't just give out NATO peacekeepers' addresses.

At that point, you admit what you've known all along: You're not trekking out to Den Haag, where right now the generals from your country are being torn to pieces in the courts. You're in Amsterdam, not far from the legendary Paradiso, with a different lineup playing every night. Nadia's friend is gone. Jablan's right: you can say you've tried.

The hostel's not bad. You're in a share room but the other guys moved out yesterday, so you have it to yourself. Across the way are four American girls jammed into a two-bunk room. You have no idea why they're there. One of them's cute, dark hair, long legs.

"Hi, I'm Jessica," she'd said in the kitchen. "What are you up to, here on your own?"

"Not so much. I look for an old friend, hear some music."

"Anything good on?"

"Yes, actually. The Ex is playing Paradiso tonight."

She looks at you, for a moment too long. Appraising. You look back. This girl can handle herself—she's a bit less of a constant smiler than the others. They all have those astonishing white American teeth. "You will come?"

And now she does smile. "Yes, I will come."

■ ■ ■

Sweat, thumping bass, the magnet eyes of women, sweet clouds of hashish smoke, the lights flashing on the huge stage, the air hung with melted smoke and the band on fire: at last, at last, you're home. Now the lead singer's ripping open his shirt, snake tattoo up his torso. He picks up his axe and shreds it with a shrieking solo, rising then exploding in a blizzard of notes, the crowd howls and he howls back, throws the guitar down, letting it smash, and dives into the crowd. The band thrashes on as he surfs, almost dipping then rising, then he's flipped back up on the stage, squats there panting and laughing, staring into the crowd with pure desire and they love it, they roar, back goes his head and he roars too.

So do you, bound with the crowd to this mad guy, the smoking-hot band, the American girl sweating and dance-sliding alongside you. But something's wrong with your ears, there's a loud whining, building like a feedback loop. It's bad. It's coming from you. You press your fist to your mouth. Gotta get out.

You bend and use your elbows, your boots, and finally your fists, and a path through the sweaty bodies opens and closes behind you like a surprised mouth. You're getting kicked back and pushed now, bent down like this—don't fall or you'll never get up, and for a moment you almost let it happen, the drowning. Then you push up and out, toppling someone else over, a small woman, she goes down, disappears. The crowd's pumping, no one sees the woman vanish, no one hears you or sees your face streaming, but who would care anyway, all your friends are dead.

Outside, leaning against the graffiti-covered wall, you slide to the ground. That singer. He could have been Stefan, reborn in a Dutch alt-rock band. A beast in full: on stage, at war. The war's over, but Stefan will never see the stage again, never see the world beyond the fucked-up ruin of your country. Because you killed him in a shitty rape hotel. For what, for nothing: the hotel girl and Milan are dead now too. The girl had no chance, but Stefan and Milan could have got out, if not for you.

Like a hellish slideshow, there it is, clicking behind your eyes: The Life Before. The grimy rehearsal corner in the old barn, now forever cursed—you hope someone's burned it down by now. Here's Stefan scowling with concentration, figuring out a solo. Milan laughing at his own dumb jokes, practicing weak drum fills, always a bit behind the beat—but not in the good way. Then the gig in a dingy pub two hours' drive from the village, with an audience of five, not counting the town drunk, Stefan's cousin, and a dog pissing in the corner. You relive your gigs for weeks. Work the orchards, fix cars, all the while figuring out new guitar riffs in your head. Before rifles, before bullshit uniforms and patrols, before turbo-folk killed the real music, young people's music, replaced it with crappy anthems of past glory and marched the country to its grave.

You put your head in your hands, press hard into the dark. Push on your eyeballs till colors explode. If you didn't have to breathe. If you could just crouch here, a gargoyle, till the end of time, till stone turns back to flesh, till the band can get back together—you push harder.

"Iggy."

A soft hand on your shoulder. "Iggy."

You don't want to respond, but now someone's shaking you, and louder in your ear with your name. Now they're standing up: "Ambulance! Help!"

That snaps you out of it. You unbend. It's the American girl, looking at you with worried blue eyes.

"Are you all right?"

"Just dizzy for a moment. Yes."

She looks around, makes some decision. Long legs, denim shorts. She's about to take charge. In three years, she'll be running some fat senator's office in Washington.

"Come on. Let's get you back to the hostel."

She heaves you up and starts walking you back.

"I'm not sick. Let me go."

Now you're staring at each other. On a seesaw. Tip, tip. This way or that way? You could still get off it. You could turn away.

But instead, you say, "I have a better idea. Let's go to the pub round the corner. Meet up with the others." A moment; that cool stare you're starting to like, then she grins.

"You're on."

31

The blue glowing clock by my bed says four a.m. Cockroach time. I am staring at the ceiling. It is lit with ugly orange flickers from the streetlight outside—as ugly as my night thoughts. They crawl out between midnight and dawn to conduct their interrogation. Tonight, they chew away at my mind. What is Iggy's real job, at this warehouse where he is keeping the eye out for these boxes? Maybe boxes with guns or drugs. Maybe just the cheap bootleg electronics or goods sneaking past the import taxes. We both know the kinds of men who do this work. Baltic Bigwigs men.

But it could be nothing. It could just be this friend's uncle helping him with connections. *Possible.* I think of my tata's tunnel under the airport. Yes, food came in, and medicine; also guns and knives and ammunition and Johnnie Walker whiskey—every branch of the gray market connects to another. But some are clean, some dirty. Which is Iggy's? Maybe innocent, like he says. But now he is away while there are these problems at work, and suspicions, and that is a coincidence. Not a good one. They almost never are.

These thoughts give me a bad feeling in my stomach. I writhe, I can't lie still. There's so much I don't know. Before the thought forms, I get up. I put on my dark jeans, black woolen hat, and hoodie. The batteries are nearly dead in my small torch, but I slip it into my backpack. I check that Sanja's Nikon still has my film in it, with pictures left to shoot—yes—add it to my gear, and slip down the stairs in my socks, holding my boots. I lace them up quickly on the front porch—good, no one is around.

The streetlights are dim; half are broken. I can make out a few faint stars. The moon is a tired yellow lozenge, about to be swallowed by a row of houses. A white cat slinks along the gutter, looking for scraps. I settle in for a very long walk. But after ten minutes, headlights push long shadows along the road—good luck, an early bus. I run for the stop and fling myself on, puffing. The driver scowls at me. Two weary-looking women sit up front. They are probably in the gray market too, cleaning warehouses before the workers arrive. They doze, jerking awake as the bus goes over bumps in the worsening road toward the docks. Me, I am wide awake. I am the last one off the bus, near the end of the line. The driver gives me a strange look as I wait to climb down. "Sure this is your stop?" she asks.

It does look desolate. There are just barbed-wire fences, yards filled with big trucks and tractors, and big brick storehouses. No houses, no people, just the giant dinosaur bones of cranes stark against the coming dawn. "Early start," I say, which is not really an answer, and jump off.

I walk along the road until the bus is out of sight, in case she is watching in the rearview mirror. Then I crawl through the fence and round the back of the weedy block, to face the little metal door that is our secret entrance. It's been drizzling out here, and my shoes sink into the mud. Now I am cold, and my courage has ebbed away slowly on the bus. The pointlessness of the trip has sunk in—what can I even see, before sunrise, from the outside of the building? What am I doing here? *Hunting for clues*, I tell myself firmly. Hunters have to wait in the dark, and watch, often for nothing. . . . And there is never the opportunity when Iggy is here.

Iggy—what is he finding in Amsterdam? My mind whirls with dread, a feeling of floating over dark water. I squat against the fence post. The solid cold metal against my back steadies me. I take out Sanja's camera and attach the zoom lens—this too is calming. I will just look. I will just see if there is any movement, perhaps walk around the perimeter and mark the entrances and exits. Maybe, if nothing else, I can be a spy for Maudie's investigation. Then everyone will buy me drinks and cheer me at the pub.

I turn the lens. Through the viewfinder, the building jiggles, then suddenly the small door Iggy and I use is right up close. I sharpen focus. It is metal, purple, with gray graffiti. The red of brick above it and the dull of the door make a harsh poem and I focus, trying to get the texture of brick. . . . I hear a faint clink behind me, and I jump and spin round. My heart thunders, but it's just a Coke can; the breeze rolled it into the fence. *Idiot! Focus, chick!* I am not here to make artistic photos, but to spy.

I settle back down and start to lift the camera again, but before I can look through the lens, the door swings open, and a figure is silhouetted in the doorway. The figure looks around, then the door closes, slowly. After a moment, a light goes on in the upstairs window. The world spins, then shudders. This sick thud—this is the seesaw landing back down. *Stupid, stupid*, I whisper.

I am very alert now, and cold. I lift the camera and focus the zoom lens. The window is bright, and nothing moves at first. But I wait. And then, a man's back appears. Who is this? I never saw another human at Iggy's place. He is talking to someone I cannot see. A second man appears, thin-faced, young. Grimy T-shirt. He faces the first. They are joking around. I take the photo. *Click, click.* Another. Another. Then the men move, and the light in the window goes off. After a moment, the small purple door opens again. *Click. Click.* But all I see is the shadows of men, monster shapes elongated in the square of light flung from the door.

Run, bitch! shouts Sanja, but I am rooted like a tree. Light flares, there are silhouettes and laughing voices, but no one comes outside. Perhaps they are smoking and just opened the little door for the air—Iggy would do this. Sounds float through the still air toward me. Someone is telling a joke, about a deer and a girl. It's only after a minute that I realize it's in our language. They reach the end, and laugh. Then there's the clink of bottles.

"One more round," says the joke man. "You're the host tonight." And I hear shoving and joking.

"Nope, your turn. Get off your fat arse and get it yourself. The good stuff."

"What, Iggy's stash?"

"Ah, he won't care. He's getting drunk in Amsterdam—"

"On his mission to find a girl!" They both laugh.

"So many girls in Amsterdam, how will he choose?"

"Yeah, what a problem. Come on, let's drink." The shadows move away, still bantering, but now I can't make out their words.

I scuttle back through the fence into brambles and bad-smelling wet soil—my life as a cockroach, always hiding in the dark. After a moment, I hear the little door slam. And the night silence is ripped open by a sudden howl. Electric guitar, the thump of drums. It stops after a few bars, then starts up again. A riff comes in—oh—I know this song—everyone does. Happy lyrics pour from my memory, mocking me: *Lipe cvatu, sve je isto k'o i lani. . . . Linden trees are in bloom / Everything's just like it used to be.*

I run crouched over until my lungs burn, back through the fence, and then I walk, faster than my thoughts can catch me, along the empty road and scrubby wasteland that leads from Iggy's house of lies toward my home. When a bus finally comes along, I sit down in the back and scowl.

I have the whole back of the bus to myself. Everyone carefully sits up front and not-sees me, and probably not-smells me, too, in my stinking, mud-covered jeans. They must think I'm homeless.

It's nine by the time I finally get back to Mr. Patel's. I really hope Mrs. K. doesn't see me. There are bad sides to a neighborhood where everyone watches the street. I stop at the phone box on the corner to call in sick to work, then tiptoe up the stairs. *Home.*

Once I'm inside my door, I am suddenly bone-tired. I drop my filthy clothes near the door and fill the shallow bath, easing into it as soon as there are a few inches. The water rises slowly, taking grime with it. I exhale and lie back, sloshing the water around. Light dances on its surface; the outline of my body also dances, still visible through the reflections. In the rippling motion, I see Sanja's hands. She is holding tongs in her bathroom lab, where sheets of shiny white paper lie exposed in a bath of chemicals. *Exposed.* Bad for humans, necessary for film.

Pictures are made from darkness; I know that much. But why did Iggy keep this warehouse band hidden from me, lie to me that he saw no one from before? Slowly a pattern, an image forms. White is the empty beginning; darkness writes the picture. I close my eyes, willing myself to see in the dark, to find this picture, but nothing is there but buzzing red.

32

Morning crawls in like a dog through the window. You roll over, turning your back to the light, back toward dreamless green, but bump into something warm. It's the American girl, jammed into the skinny bunk bed between you and the wall. You think about slinking out with your gear, not coming back, but your cock's already hard and she's stirring against you, awake. Too late.

Patches of memory float back on a tide of whiskey. The bar, all stained glass and old wood, jammed with a Russian folk-music group, locals selling hash to hippies, Spanish tourists, and the American girls. They dominate the room, loud and clueless as babies. Two of them are wearing baseball hats indoors. You're all playing some balancing game, crawling under a bar backward. Every time you lose, you have to take a shot. Limbo, that's the game. Perfect name for this place between drunk and hell, hovering near oblivion but never quite getting there. Shiny patches of beer on the floor, grinning mouths above you. You're good at the game—the last man standing—the girls are all round you looking down, cheering you under the bar, so close to the ground. You get cocky and wave at them, then land flat on your back.

Shot! Shot! Shot! Shot! they're yelling now, the whole bar's yelling, the girls triumphant and raucous as a tree full of parrots. You sit up and take a shot, then another, stand up, then fall over and you can't get up. Jessica drags you up, they're all laughing their heads off. She manages to half drag, half steer you back to the hostel, and the night air revives you just enough. Her long legs, those shorts you'd wanted to pull down all night—the speed, the roughness of it against the wall, how wet and loud she was. You come too fast, regret it before you've even pulled out, and then you're both laughing again which might as well be howling, collapse toward the bed, wallop your head hard on the bunk above, pass out.

Now, as if on cue, your head starts up like a bass drum. Welcome to limbo. Your eyeballs ache. You slide yourself upright, wait for the dizziness and nausea to pass, grab a towel and head out for the bathroom down the hall. You hope none of the other girls are around to see you, clumsily tenting the towel over your hard-on. Once you get to the loo, it takes a long time to settle down and piss. Once you start you don't want it to stop. Let it all wash away, the sickness, the whiskey, the dirty morning. The band.

When you get back, Jessica's up and dressed in last night's clothes. Apart from the black mascara smears under her eyes, she looks undented. She would be the one to organize the family photo album, coordinate calendars for Christmas get-togethers. Her children will always have matching socks.

She smiles at you, a bit tentative, and suddenly you're ashamed of putting her in this box.

"Hey, big boy."

"Hi."

And then there's nothing. She tries again:

"How long are you here for?"

"I will go back today. I must work."

"Oh, sad! Work sucks." Another pause. "Far to go? Where did you say you're from?"

"Yugoslavia," you say, surprising yourself. Then, louder: "From Bosnia. The north. But I'm Serbian."

"Oh, okay! Wow, that's a lot—a lot of places. I'm from Ohio." Of course she is.

"Dayton?" You're almost sneering.

"No, Columbus. Why?"

You just look at her. It takes a moment. Then she gets it. "Oh, the Bosnian thing—the Dayton Peace Accords . . . right! No, Dayton's kind of a dump. Columbus is cool, everyone looks down on Ohio, like we're all corn farmers, but that's just a stereotype. . . ." She trails off into your chilly silence. "It was terrible, right? The war. It sounded terrible."

"The music was bad." She starts to laugh, then sees you're serious. A pause, and then she starts again, tries to get her expression right. Earnest, humble, caring.

"I mean, it was just so confusing. . . . Like, you have history, like real history, going way back, all those ancient grudges, neighbors killing neighbors, that sounded so awful—we don't get it, we're a new country, well, compared to Europe, we just don't have history like that." She smiles, but it seems your gargoyle wish has come true. You're stone. "It's just, hard to understand from the outside, that's all, it's . . ." Of course she doesn't understand. She never will. When Nadia looks at you—she knows. Suddenly you ache for Nadia with every bone in your body.

"I have to get to the plane." Even as the words leave your mouth, you're aware of how churlish they sound.

"Right. Okay." Her lips tight, she looks round for her bag and shoes and in one stride is at the door. "See ya."

The door closes. You weren't even worth a slam.

■ ■ ■

On the bus to the airport, you're the only one with a seat to yourself. Elderly couples in matching polo shirts, a harried family with two toddlers and a giant pram, glum business men, the inevitable back-pack crowd—everyone's jammed in, but some force field of repulsion keeps them from your seat. As it should be. The sun falls in flickering tiger-slats through the fences, the houses, the trees, the telegraph poles. The land's so flat, it could have been laid with a ruler. What kind of country doesn't have a single hill?

After a while, the wheels turning, the hum of the bus, the rhythm of sun and shadow through the window make a music with the churn of your guts. Round and round it goes. This Ohio girl, dumb as a frog; the tourists, the loud Americans, the useless Dutch who went to keep the peace when there was none; they all float through life, unanchored to truth: death is in every shadow, every corner.

Every shadow, every corner hums the bus. And yet, still there is life. Life after the death of others. There is all this time stretching out before you where the future used to be. No one can walk it but you.

You sit up straighter. Yes. It is time to take an axe to all this useless past. Why drag the dead along? Nadia knows this; she has no ties, no Yugoslav friends. Except for this one lost girl she made you hunt for on this stupid trip. But you will fix that for her. After last night, you see it: Not only Stefan and Milan, but all the old songs you played are dead. You and Bibo's guys, playing songs from a dead country in a London warehouse: No. You'll cut them away. Find other musicians, English, French, African, who cares. Play different music, play in English like Black Tooth, with people from across the world. New city, new soundtrack. If you feed ghosts, the present starves and with it, this possibility of the future.

The future. For the first time, you imagine it: you and Nadia. You will cut away this lost girl for Nadia too. Then it could be more than just this sexy game tangled up in the pain of memory. It could be real.

There is Goran and the warehouse to manage, but the side job is not so much—and soon you will have saved enough to move out. Leave all this old-country business behind. No more gray-market boxes, no more bands from history. You can get a new job. Rent a room. Maybe a whole flat. Maybe even with Nadia.

By the time you're buckled into your plane seat, you find yourself smiling. You feel for the glass button in your pocket, rub it between your fingers. Your frozen flower. Your lucky charm.

33

Monday. On the Tube into work, dressed for war. High boots, tight shiny shirt, miniskirt, green eye shadow. I have chewed my mind to pieces all weekend. Jody was out of town with her stall at a stupid English folk fair, where they camp in the mud and listen to music. She invited me—or left a pause for me to say I would come—but I don't need more mud, and besides, I wanted to think about Iggy.

I replay my warehouse spying visit over and over. This song I heard. It belongs to this huge band that moved to Belgrade, played stadium gigs. And Iggy's group plays it now. He told me nothing, nothing about this group, except this lie that he sees no one from the past. Because he ran from the war and they are dangerous to him. But is this a lie too?

Here is my stop. One hundred and eighteen steps to the office. Twenty-two up the stairs. The creak of the hinge. I unlock. I am early again; I want to be ready. I water the spider plant, push the peace lily farther into the darkest corner of Iggy's desk. Boot up. I am over by the coffee, filling the pot, when the door creaks open to the sound of voices and laughing—it's Roger and Maudie.

"Nadia! Well, well, early bird!" says Roger. "You feeling all right, pet?"

"She's finally getting enough sleep with Iggy away, isn't that right, Nads—"

"Good morning, how was your weekend?" I say primly, and make a show of setting out the cups. No one answers, and when I turn to look, their faces look strained, as if joking was an effort. And I remember the office also has these new problems.

We settle into our desks. The clock ticks. Priya comes in ten minutes late, scowls at Maudie, and plants herself in her cubicle. Still no Iggy. In this gloomy, nervous silence, my data entry sounds like faraway machine-gun fire. It's hard to sit still with my back to the door. I stand to pour my third cup of coffee in an hour, when finally Priya calls me.

"Nadia. For you. Putting it through."

I pick up the phone on the desk, and Iggy's voice says, "Nadija." Blood thuds in my ears. "Hello?"

Focus, chick. "Where are you?"

"Gatwick. Plane was late. Meet you after work—Purple Crown?" He wants to avoid the Hag and Crow, the inquisitive ears of the others.

"Did you find anything?"

"Five thirty. We will talk," he says, and hangs up.

I stare at the mossy wall. I have missed today's sun altogether. But the spider plant bristles with energy; a new leaf is coming out, after it was chopped nearly in half. *What doesn't kill you makes you stronger,* Maudie says. Well, nothing has killed me yet. But I am sick with hope and fear.

The eternal day grinds to a close. Priya slings on her purple jacket at the stroke of five p.m. and strides out, not looking at Maudie. Maudie shrugs and rolls her eyes, but I can tell she is hurt by her mouth pressed tight. Life is unfair. It is hard to be the one who sees.

We say our subdued goodbyes, and I walk toward my Tube stop, just in case anyone is watching—my old habits are back. Then I circle back through Soho's narrow alleys toward the waterfront, and in ten minutes, I am at the Purple Crown. I stand across the street to watch. The sun is setting earlier now, and long shadows fill the courtyard, which is bulging with people in suits, ties loosened, voices loud, clutching beers and blowing smoke upward above their neighbors' heads.

It is almost a train station of a pub—not cozy, just close to the Embankment for all these workers to gather, like bees on clover, before lifting off again into the Tube, the bus home, the night out. Big enough to be anonymous, too loud for couples. You could have a fight here, or get stabbed to death in the toilets, and nobody would notice unless you crashed into them and spilled their jug of beer.

I watch and wait, but Iggy doesn't arrive. He is probably already inside, with a dark corner staked out like a spider spinning its web. I wait one more heartbeat. Yes, I am calm. I am ready. Okay. I cross the street and push my way in. He is at the bar, looking at the door. I smile and wave through the forest of bodies, and he gestures to a high corner table, where his coat has claimed space with a full jug of beer and two glasses. When we get there, his back is to the wall, and my chair faces only him. I move it to the side, so I can see the room too, and stand. For a second, I am floating above us, looking down. I squeeze my eyes shut and force myself back. Smile.

He kisses my cheeks. I kiss him back, one, two. I speak in English, our neutral zone.

"What happened?"

"Beer?" I nod. He pours. His face is in shadow.

"Tell me."

"How was your week? I missed you."

"I will say later. Tell me now."

"It's— Nadija. It's not good." I look at him blankly. "Shall we walk? By the river? It's loud in here."

"No, we will stay," I say. Alone by the river at night—no. Too easy to be pushed, slip under the dark water, disappear. I don't know what is truth and what is lies any more. I want people around. He glances at me quickly, from the side, then back down into his beer.

"Tell me. Please."

He takes a breath. Then, in our language, like a speech he has practiced for school:

"It took a few days to track down Hans. The UNHCR didn't know anything about peacekeepers, they said I'd have to search the asylum seeker lists for her, and they didn't give those out to just anyone. So that was useless, then I tried the UN branch office, they just said, forget it, we don't release details of postings to unaffiliated people,

I was going to give up but there was this secretary . . . it happened that her dad was from near my village, married a Dutch woman in the sixties. So I talked to her and it took a little while, but she helped me find this Hans."

He flicks his eyes up to me, then back down into the beer. I see him through a mental viewfinder now, a little more clear and cold than life. I zoom in on the coffee-cream skin; there is pencil-gray under the eyes. A day's stubble. His fingers rub to and fro on his glass, wiping away the steam.

"Hans," I say.

"It happened there were twelve Hanses, but only one has red hair and was stationed in Sarajevo that last February. So we went to see him." *We.*

"And what. What did he say?"

Iggy breathes in. Flicks a look at me. Then he looks back down at the table.

"He didn't want to talk to us at first. But then I showed him the photo you gave me and he recognized her. He said yes, he was helping her sometimes, but then she just stopped showing up. He looked around for her but never saw her. This was winter. Then one day his friend, a peacekeeper from Tunisia, told him she had been shot."

"Shot? Who by? Shot dead?"

His mouth is grim, lips pressed. He glances across at me, looks down again. Rubs his jaw, as if to loosen it. "That's all I know, but he said the guy was sure. That she . . . she didn't survive."

I can't move. The room roars around us, life is everywhere, but in our little corner I am frozen under glass.

"I'm sorry, I'm sorry," he says, reaching for my hand. I pull it away. "I hate war. All wars," he says softly. There are tears in his eyes.

But he is so good at lying. How can I know, how can I ever know? Terror floods me. My body propels me upright, pushes through the people and vomits me out into the street. Plan abandoned, I run.

"Nadija!" he calls out, but I have surprise, and a start, and I have run like this for years. I weave into an alley, then another, crouching, darting from doorway to shadow, until even I have lost track of where I am.

The clatter of running boots melds with the banging of sledge-hammers, the *rat-a-tat* of machine guns. Huge shadows loom as a monster red bus careens through the narrow street. Yellow light slices from doorways, a woman shouts "Hey!" as I bang into her and keep running. Tall buildings shudder and blur, melting into bullet-scarred concrete, dull plastic windows. I run past the library, I smell smoke, it is about to burn, my tata is laughing grimly as cinders float through the darkness in dreamy winks of light. The shell of a burned-out tram marks the road to the airport, the red and green lights of tracer bullets curve overhead.

A helicopter *thud-thud*s overhead and lights sway wildly, I dash for the shadows, there is the scream of brakes and someone is shout-ing, there is salt on my lips and something warm running into my eye, it's itchy, I can't see properly, the world spins and shudders and I careen into something shiny and slide down the glass and keep sliding, there is no ground, I am falling, back, back, back in the mar-ket, where I can never escape, running from stall to stall, *Where is she?*

Dread. Terror. Cold to the bone. Why did I wait, why did I sit for three days with my stupid book, waiting for you to come crawling back, but you didn't, and now there is no one on the street, no peace-keeper on our corner, just a terrible silence, Hans is gone, so here I am at the market where there are people, *Have you seen her? Tall, green dress, an attitude*—head shakes, nothing, my gut churns with terror, there's ice on the ground, nothing in the stalls except a few lemons, some weevilly rice, some UNHRC plastic to cover the windows, *What can I do,* I turn to go home and the world explodes, the blast knocks me off my feet, my brain thumps in my skull as my head hits the cobblestones and then everything slows. I hear shrieks and moans. Smoke curls lazily upward. One stall, oddly still standing, collapses in slow motion, and a few potatoes roll into the carnage. A child's bloodstained pink backpack with a Disney princess on it lies on the road. Two teenage boys, one with a rifle, run past me, going back to help. A middle-aged woman runs along behind them.

I'm such a coward, I want to run the other way, but I'm dizzy, I can't stand up, there's something warm and wet touching my face, *Sanja?* but there is just this rubbing and snuffling—what?

I open my eyes to a long, wrinkled face and the licking tongue of a dog. I push at it and it sits back, wet brown eyes reproachful, tail still wagging.

"Sorry, sorry," says a man's voice. "Come on, Rufus." The dog is pulled away, but a pair of shiny black shoes stays. "Hey—are you all right?"

I sit up. "Few too many," I mumble to the trouser legs above the shoes.

"Okay then, if you're sure . . . ?"

"I'm fine," I say. A silence. Then a hand is pulling me up.

"Steady—steady on." A sad beagle face, the mirror of the dog's, gazes at me through thick glasses. The rumpled suit tells me, *English*— they have the style of potato sacks, these English men.

"You've cut your head," he says, as if I did it on purpose.

"Sorry," I say. We stand awkwardly. Rufus's tail bangs against my leg. I would walk away, but my balance is not excellent.

"Far to go home?" he offers. This question is too hard. My eyes blur.

"Okay, okay," he says. "Where— Look, how about we get you a taxi." His voice brightens. He is relieved to have solved the problem, which is me.

I nod my head like a little girl whose lip wobbles, and Beagle Man takes my elbow and we walk with Rufus to the main street. Beagle Man waves and a taxi pulls up, and then he helps me in, pushing a twenty-pound note into my hand at the last moment and slamming the door before I can protest or thank him. I tell the driver the address, then sink back as the taxi moves through London, calm and sure, like a slow-cruising black shark in a sea of flashing, swishing fish.

■ ■ ■

My blood-speckled shirt, my war clothes, are in a pile on the floor. The taxi has long since driven away. Outside, the evening sounds of laughter and chatter float up through my window from the Happy Café. The door swings open and closed. Smells of cooking, of incense, of the slightly ripe rubbish bins in the alley swirl, all speak of late-summer warmth. But I am cold, so cold. The bathwater has scalded me pink, mist and steam fills the room, but still I shiver.

I close my eyes and slip under, as far as I can, until finally my body unclenches. I float gently up, above the bathtub, and look down. This pale body, its outline shaky from water ripples. What is one more girl, anyway? We are always disappearing. Into white vans, rivers, bombed buildings, unmarked graves. I stare at the ceiling and the mist thins and the bath cools.

After a while my eyes adjust, and I see myself sitting in the window. Here I could die fast, from a bullet, or slow from hunger. For a second, I am both places, here and there, the shiny reflection in the window, the ripples on the bathroom ceiling . . . and then the cold steals softly inward from my hands and feet to my belly, my lungs, and I am back where I always am.

My head aches from falling over in the bombing. I am alone in our freezing, lightless apartment. Tata is gone. Sanja is gone. Hans is gone. The streets are empty. The market is destroyed. Days, nights, awake, asleep—at last, at last the quiet darkness of sleep pulls me, and I start to feel warm again. It's beautiful. I close my eyes. But then a sharp tug to the back of my hair jerks me awake. *Wake up, chick!*

I try to turn around to see her, but her grip is tight and won't let me. She pulls my hair, really hard. It hurts. *Ow! Get up*, she says, in that voice you can't argue with. *It's time. Get your books.*

I get my books.

Good. In the stove.

I want to protest, but before I say a word, there's that sharp pain at the back of my head, right where I banged it on the street. I wriggle but she won't let go. Why is she so cruel?

Now, bitch!

I stack them in the iron stove.

Not like that. Fan the pages.

I hate even creasing the spines of new books, so it's very hard to turn them upside down, to open the pages. And I can't move easily because of her steel grip on my neck. But I do it.

Matches. Strike.

At first the fire is reluctant, blue and sluggish. But then it gets a taste, gets hungry. Leaps up. Andrić. Kiš. Pavić. Selimović. All these, my oldest friends. And my precious translations: Dostoyevsky. Bulgakov. Shakespeare. Woolf. Joyce. My first ever book, *Peter Pan*, a gift from my mother. Letters, whole sentences, glow brilliant, then blacken and burst into flame.

Go get warm. That bullying hand on my neck pushes me forward. I kneel by my books. The heat spreads, the room grows lighter. I stare at the flames, my mind gone somewhere I can never find again.

Eventually I realize the grip on my neck has loosened, has gone. *Sanja*, I say, with everything in my heart.

Little baldie, she whispers behind my ear. *You're such an idiot.*

I spin round, ready to laugh, to hug her and never let go, to tell her—but no one is there.

■ ■ ■

Someone is crying. *Who is it?* I turn my head and water sloshes. Ripples reflect on the ceiling, merging with the streetlights' orange glow, the flickering of headlights outside the window.

I am here. In London. In the bath.

I get out of the bath, like the living do. I dry myself. I put on all my clothes and huddle on the bed, where the sky flows through the mirror and I can look out, and up. *What doesn't kill you makes you stronger.* Well then. It is time to think, not die. *What do I know?* My mind rolls it around like a pebble.

One: Iggy is a liar. Maybe worse; he plays with this group now, people he swears to me he will avoid. They were near his age, spoke his dialect—probably fighters too. Killers, maybe.

Two: He knows what Sanja looks like. *How?* Maybe from this photo, like he says. Maybe from watching us in the siege.

Three: He tells me he saw Hans, that this Hans knows Sanja is dead. Why does he say this? *Because she is,* says a cold voice. I brush it away. *No.* This Hans explanation— Iggy never talks this way, like a police report. With no pauses. Some days, he will not even do a whole sentence. So he wants her to be dead, or dead in my mind. Is he still playing war games? Now my head is hurting.

Four: Iggy is my only link left to Sanja. Maybe he did see her. After all, he found this button, found me. How can I make him tell me what he knows? A picture rushes to my mind, very satisfying: I am holding a gun at his head, he is on his knees, begging. . . . *Get real.* I am small and he is a trained soldier. What weapons do I have? *Help me, Sanja,* I beg, but nothing. Silence. Then I think of Maudie and these boxes.

I stand. I look out the window at the dark, which is smudged with orange from the streetlights and the rhythmic stripes of car head-lights. The street blurs; we are standing at the window, looking out at a different street. Here comes Alma, red mouth, high heels. Sanja smiles, she lifts her camera. . . . And the saying floats into my mind: *Why would you use poison when you can kill with honey.* And in one moment, the plan is formed.

34

The next day, I call in sick for work. Over my tea and sticky bun, Mrs. K. tut-tuts over the cut over my eye.

"It is nothing," I say. "I tripped."

"Drunk again, Nadia?" says Naveen, who is hanging round the door as usual.

"Don't be cheeky," I say. And Mrs. K. glares until he disappears.

"Is everything all right, my girl?" I look up at her. It is a real question.

"It will be. But I might— Will Jamaal be home tonight?" She looks at me, lips pressed, eyebrows raised. Her son is out of bounds.

"This Iggy. There are problems, I need to talk to him. And you told me I should have people around, so . . ." She is frowning.

"Is this trouble, Nadia?"

"No," I say, but I feel the sting of guilt. Mrs. K. and Mr. Patel hate trouble. They are the secret police of our street, to keep the real police away from their brown sons. Stephen Lawrence's photo is everywhere in the news; he was murdered by white boys, and the police did nothing.

She is still frowning. She needs more.

"I am finding out where is my friend, the one who went missing. It may be a bad conversation, so I thought here, with the family around . . ." And now she is smiling as she fusses with my teacup.

A picture flashes into my mind: a poster on a Soho council office door I walk past. It's a circle, yellow on top, gray underneath. The writing says *Help Is the Sunny Side of Control*. But trouble, real trouble, cannot always be controlled.

■ ■ ■

Evening comes. I dress carefully. Gone are the tarty secretary clothes: the short skirt, the tight little shirts. Instead, I take a dress from the back of the closet, untouched since I got here. My honey-poison dress, with the roses shaped like the imprints of mortars on the street. *Sarajevo roses*, we called these. Then I take Sanja's butterfly brooch and pin it to the bodice. Put up my hair. Add red lipstick. I look at this girl in the mirror. Yes. She's worked for me before. She'll do.

Just before five, I go back to the phone box and call the office again. I really hope it is Priya, and not Mrs. McGinley, who will answer.

"Global Flow Solutions," says Priya. I am in luck.

"Priya, it's Nadia. Don't tell," I say. A pause.

"How can I help you?" she says, in her best office voice.

"Put me through to Iggy?"

"Very good, putting you through," she says. The phone rings once, twice, and then Iggy says hello.

"Don't say anything, I'm supposed to be sick." A sharp inhale from his end, then silence. "Meet me at the Happy Café at six," I say, and give him the address. Before he can say anything else, I hang up.

By six p.m., I am ready. I have brushed my hair again and redone my lipstick. I watch the door of the Happy Café from my window, waiting for Iggy. 6:02 . . . 6:03. . . . Will he come? The café door swings, my heart thumps, but it is just Mr. Patel's daughter coming out. I close my eyes. She crosses the alley and I hear her feet on the stairs. When I look again, a slim, dark figure appears across the road. Iggy walks past the café casually, pauses on the corner, then turns, crosses, and walks in. I know so well this caution, this checking.

A heartbeat . . . two . . . then I walk down the stairs and down the alley, doubling round the back so I come in from the other direction than my home, and walk in. He looks up, face carefully blank, waiting for my cue. Time slows. I wonder if he does this always, if everything is calibrated as my echo.

"Iggy, thank you for this." And I smile and I kiss him on both cheeks.

"Pretty dress," he says.

Even before I sit, Naveen is there. "Here's a menu," he says, eyes down, and hands it to us, then retreats to lurk by the door.

"We'll just have chai," I say. When he doesn't move, I say, "That's all in this moment."

"Naveen!" Mrs. K. calls from the kitchen, and he retreats, but not before widening his eyes at me, as if to say *What*. Iggy sees this, of course.

"Boys," I say, with a little laugh.

"How do you feel?" says Iggy with a smile. "Still 'sick'?"

"Ah, much better," I say. He waits. "Iggy. I'm sorry I ran, I was just— it totally stumbled me, what you said."

"I understand. Of course." Naveen is back now, with chai, also a pad and pencil. He is impersonating being a waiter. Now I raise my eyebrows, but only a little.

"Anything to eat?"

"Maybe later," I say. "But we will call you."

"Very good," he says, and retreats. The door swings closed. I give it a few seconds, for Mrs. K. to drag Naveen away from spying. I look down and draw circles on the table with my finger. I let the silence grow.

"Travel is tiring, isn't it," I say.

"It can be," says Iggy. A pause.

"Has Amsterdam changed much?" I ask.

"Yes and no," he says. A longer pause.

"Tell me again," I say. "What did this Hans say? Was he really sure?"

"Nadija—"

"I must know," I say. Iggy sighs and looks down into his chai.

"Yes. He was sure. He said he . . . He knew your friend well. And this Tunisian, he and Hans worked next to each other. So the Tunisian saw her sometimes, when she visited Hans—high boots, tall, long blonde plait, string bag. On this corner, across the river from the library."

I feel sick. Sanja's yellow string bag—it is not in any photo I have. And this is Hans's corner. But then, many people had string bags, blonde hair . . . Iggy glances at me quickly, then continues.

"He told Hans he saw her . . . get shot, running across the street. This very cold February day. Near the end of the siege, right before the bombing of the market." A pause. He doesn't look up. "I'm so sorry," he says quietly. "All the wrong people die."

My mind scrambles. How much did I tell him, how much is he inventing from my own stories? I did not tell him where is the peace-keeper corner. But maybe he saw Sanja on the street with Hans. Did we talk about the Markale bombing? That she disappeared three days before this?

Naveen comes back with the fake-waiter writing pad. He is unstoppable.

"Two samosas, please," I say.

"Very good," says Naveen. He writes something down and retreats.

"Iggy. Thank you for hunting this Hans for me," I say.

"You had to know, I know this," he says.

"Is there anything else to tell?" I say.

"Like what?" I look at him. He returns my gaze, guileless as a saint. Naveen returns with samosas. I give a little nod, wait until the door closes behind him.

"About the warehouse." I sense Iggy's muscles coiling. The lights shut out in his face. He says nothing. He just waits. This enrages me. "You have this Serbian rock band." He is surprised, then starts laughing.

"This is nothing! This was just, just some guys I met at a bar when you and me were—" Suddenly serious: "How do you know about this?"

"I saw. I was there."

"What? You are spying on me now?"

"You lied to me! You said you see no one from before—they are dangerous to you—but now you play music with killers—"

"They're not killers! Just guys from—"

"So maybe you didn't run from this war, maybe you hide something, something bad. How can I believe anything? This story about Hans. I don't believe."

He puts down his chai carefully. He does not deny, he is thinking. "Why not?"

"So smooth, so bullshit—how do you know how Sanja looks? I never showed you this photo! You saw her on the street! Tell me!"

"Nadija, she is gone! What does it matter—"

"It matters to me! To me! Why do you kill her in this story with Hans? To torture me, to—"

"No! No! The opposite of this, to stop this torture in your head, always this thinking, *what if, what if*—"

"So, you admit it. This lie."

The silence hovers, sharp as knives. Under the fluorescent lights, Iggy's skin is waxy, almost green.

"Iggy, now you will tell me. What you know about Sanja, anything, everything. All of it. Or I will call this tip line for criminals. I will tell about the fake passport, I will tell Maudie where you live. These boxes. This gray-market-uncle man."

"What? What are you talking— Crazy talk!"

"I have photos." My face must be strange. Now he is staring at me.

"What photos," he says, very quietly. My skin prickles.

"I took them. The band. Then inside, of these special boxes."

"Bullshit. You have no camera—"

"It's Sanja's. From before."

The moment stretches, unreal, flat. I suddenly see the old man he will be, all bones and crags, eyes sunk to pinpoints of black. This wild swinging lie of mine, this boxes-photo story, has hit a target. Maudie was right.

"This story was only to save you pain," he says eventually. "But

Nadija, she is gone. This one night, all the women were . . . were taken. I think . . . I think I saw something . . . but I can't be sure it was her." The room spins in sick circles, then steadies. I grip the table with both hands.

"Tell me. Tell me now. Now!" I shout, and bang the table, and instantly the kitchen door opens and Jamaal is there, Mrs. K. behind him, and Naveen crowding behind them.

"Is everything all right?" asks Jamaal. One hand is in his pocket. Iggy's eyes flick quickly over the Kapils, registering the instant response, the tension in Jamaal's body. Then in one movement, he is standing, his coat is on—

"Tomorrow," he says, and slips quickly out the door.

■ ■ ■

It's time for work. If the office is even open. Everything is eggshells. Jamaal makes me take one of the blue bricklike mobile phones from the shop. He says cornered rats are dangerous. I wish now I had said nothing to them, met Iggy in some anonymous pub. Now this sickness from the past leaks into my home.

Time for the Tube. I am dressed back in my librarian clothes. Or not quite; my hair is still magenta, after all. I don't need the tarty Camden clothes any more. But they have infected my look a little bit—or London has—because my shirt is a bit tighter, I am keeping my purple platform shoes for the height, and my skirts are these days higher than my knees. Sanja would approve. *Sanja.* Rage floods my body again, but I tamp it down. I need to be cool.

I walk in prepared: I will say hello to everyone, smile a nothing smile at Iggy, then sit down to type. But I have barely opened the door when I see my plan is derailed. I scan the room in vivid, hyper-clear slow motion. Not only is Iggy gone, but his desk is cleared, empty. His blue cup is washed and in the rack. His jacket is gone from the back of his chair.

Solid desks, shabby green-gray room, fraying partitions. The window and the brick wall view. The struggling spider plant I rescued from the bin. All it wants is some sun. Twelve steps from my desk to the coffee machine. Nine to the door. Seven to Priya and Maudie's nest where Maudie, Priya, and Roger are clustered. Maudie's pretending to type; her long, lilac-painted fingernails tap at the keyboard. Roger tugs at his too-tight shirt, smooths the gingery hair that won't lie flat. Only Priya looks up at me, with that melancholy fierceness that hides pity.

"Where is he?" I say. Priya and Maudie exchange a glance. And I know—they're wondering how to break it to me.

The three of them silently decide it's Roger's job, because then he says, "He's gone, love."

"What do you mean?" I say stupidly, but of course I know.

In the silence, Priya and Maudie jump in together: "It's not you, it's him," says Maudie.

"Got another assignment, he said," says Priya.

"More fish in the sea, love," says Roger.

"Oh well, easy go and come," I hear myself say from far away.

"Easy come, easy go," says Maudie.

I make coffee mechanically, sit, type. I have no idea what numbers flow through my fingers, how the day passes. But eventually, Roger calls out, "Time for a drink, what do we think, girls?"

It's only four o'clock—too early for drinks—but who is to stop us? Mrs. McGinley hasn't come in at all today and Charles is away on yet another trip. Everything is upside down, and not just with me. After all, we might be a money laundry, not an office. Any day could be our last, working here. Already Priya and Maudie are laughing together, jostling toward the door. They seem to be friends again. Perhaps my misfortune has brought them together.

"Earth to Nadia—Hag and Crow? Come on, my shout," says Roger.

And before I can form another thought, Priya grabs my jacket and handbag. Maudie logs out my computer and they swirl around me and half carry me down the stairs toward beer and chips and salvation. Already the three-way gossip machine is revving up as we hit the street—they're talking and laughing, bundling me along. I struggle to understand, to get a word in. But as we near the corner, I glance back to the dark, empty office. A single light turns on as I look. I see the silhouette of a sniper. *Hey!* I yell to the others, but no one's listening, and when I turn back to the window there is nothing. My head spins, back in the strobe-light world: *Here, gone. Here, gone.*

"Come on, Nads, don't go weird again," says Priya, grabbing my arm firmly, and we barrel around the corner and into the pub.

■ ■ ■

"Have some more," says Mrs. K, heaping rice on my plate with a frown. "You are not eating." The two of us are in the kitchen, eating lamb curry. It is delicious, but I can't taste it, not really. Everything is a little far away. "So, my girl," says Mrs. K. "So, he is gone. Good riddance." I poke at the rice with my fork.

"I don't know. I thought I saw—"

"What?" She is glaring at me. Her kind heart holds her hostage, and this annoys her.

I decide not to tell her about this sniper at the window—it was just a glimpse, it could have been a trick of the sun—and I have dragged them too far in already.

"Nothing. You're right," I say. "It's just—he is the only one who knows what happened to her."

She snorts. "Rubbish. He has this whole story, took this trip—why would he do this if he knows? How do you know it's not true?"

"Because he lied about other things. This band, these secret friends."

"Oh, and you never lie? No secret friends?" She smiles sideways at me. She is not stupid; she has seen Jody—I feel heat rise up from my neck.

"That's different, she's a girl, she's English, it doesn't . . ." I trail off in confusion.

"Doesn't what? Doesn't count?" She is laughing at me, but I just stare at the tablecloth; my whole face is hot. "Anyway, he's gone. Good. Let it be, Nadia. Life is too short."

"I know," I say, and shovel some rice mechanically into my mouth. But I will not live in *True Crime*. I will find Iggy and make him tell me. Mrs. K. is still looking at me, as if waiting for something more. There is no more. I will keep them out of all this. "The curry is lovely. Thank you," I say.

Mrs. K. snorts. We wash up in silence. When Jamaal and Naveen clatter in from their errands, lugging large sacks of lentils, rice, and a parcel that smells like hot, damp earth, I slip out, unnoticed. I am turning into a shade.

I walk around the block, wait to check that no one has moved to the front room of the café, then sidle back to the phone box on the corner. A thin, dark woman is on the phone, balancing a little notebook and pen as she scrunches the phone to her ear, writing something down. Soon she hangs up and leaves, trailing clouds of worry. I dig out my coins and dial. The phone rings and rings, until the tone changes. I hang up, collect my coins, and dial again. I am about to hang up, when the phone stops ringing. I feel someone listening. The softest whisper of air, or static electricity, moves through the line. I breathe. He breathes.

"I have to know," I say.

Silence.

"Please."

Silence.

"I will give you the photos. The negatives. Just tell me what you know."

Silence.

"I will be there," I tell him. "Your place. Before dawn."

Silence. Then a *click*. Still I wait. I can hear the faint sound of the sea, the crackling of millions of miles of cables, of humans talking to each other across time zones, war zones, along the thinnest of wires . . . *don't go yet I miss you* and *how was your day* and *what time is it there* and *your mother is dead* and . . . A banging startles me.

"You done yet?" says the man waiting outside. He is scowling, and I realize I have been standing immobile, silent receiver jammed to my head—just another of the lost bodies who haunt phone boxes.

"Sorry," I mutter—if you have only one English word, it should be this—and slink out, and upstairs to my attic, where the enormous mirror reflects the gloom of the darkening sky.

I crouch on my bed for a long time. Then I check Sanja's camera and set it on the little chair by the door. I put on my black clothes in readiness for the night, set the alarm for two a.m., and crawl into bed.

35

You hang up. The click echoes in the cavernous space. At the far end of the warehouse, all is motion, bustle. But you are still. Very still.

You think for a moment. She can't come over tonight. Too much going on, could get messy. It's all action, now that the game's up at the office. Goran's skeleton crew is setting up already: positioning forklifts for the boxes, making sure the short-notice emergency guys are on board for tomorrow. Checking that the trucks are fueled up and ready to go at dawn. The setup crew should be gone in an hour, but who knows.

Still, you do need to see her. You have one big card left to play. You find your backpack, check supplies, and slip out. You hope no one notices. You'll be back before the early-morning crew arrives.

36

Nadija . . . Someone is whispering my name. I can't reply, though, because I am buried in the earth, under spadefuls of soil and leaves, and I cannot move. *Nadija!* It's louder this time but I can't breathe. Earth is in my eyes, my nose. Maybe I am dead, someone has flung me in a shallow grave—I fight for air, there is scrabbling, a patch of light, hands at my mouth, choking me—I jerk awake and scream but nothing comes out because there is a hand over my mouth, and a voice says, *Shh . . . shhhh.* Hot electricity runs up to my scalp. I know this voice, this body, this scent. We both breathe.

Then he says quietly, in our language, *I won't hurt you. Just don't scream, okay?* After a moment, I realize he's waiting, and I nod. He releases my mouth and switches on the lamp by the bed. I leap up and move to the door—he moves fast and catches me by the arm, hard. "Sit," he says.

"No," I say. We stare at each other. He looks thin and grimy. "Why are you here? To kill the next one?" I can still taste earth in my mouth. He looks at me with those black eyes. They show nothing.

"No," he says. "Of course, not this." I have the sensation of looking through a tunnel, as if he were very far away. But I can hear his breath, see the pulse in the side of his neck, close as my own heartbeat. *Thud. Thud.* Hunter and hunted.

I shake my head a little, as if water were in my ears. The room settles into its familiar shape.

"Tell me what you know," I say. He is still. Then he nods.

"Please. Sit," he says. Instead, I cross to the window, as far away as I can get. We stare at each other across the bed that fills the room.

Everything is very sharp and clear. The small stain on his dark shirt. The work boots, the black jeans. Dressed for dirty work. The grime under his nails, the gray under his eyes. He is almost as tall as the doorframe behind him.

"No more lies," I say.

"I saw something. But I can't be sure," he says. My mouth is dry as chalk.

"What do you know," I say. "Everything."

"I told you. We did see some girls—"

"Through your guns—"

"—but it was far. Hard to tell faces. Maybe you two; maybe not. And only once. I stopped Stefan, he would have shot." His foot is tapping. His hands are curled, almost fists. "Then came this night. February, very cold. They paid off the peacekeepers, swept the streets for women. Before the Markale bombing."

Then he tells me. His voice is flat and cold. The hotel. The women in the rooms, the soldiers lining up. My face is wet, but I make no sound.

"They'd kept her ready for us—no one had . . . But I can't be sure." Now his words tumble. As if a pipe rusted shut had burst open and red water gushed. "The light was low, she looked older than us—but the face was bruised, so— And she was—I don't know what she'd been wearing, before they— But she was blonde, I'm pretty sure. And this string bag was on the chair, with tomatoes, some cans."

He takes a breath, and his voice flattens out again.

"They made us go to her. Milan first. To rape. He pretended—but then he shot her instead. Then he shot Stefan too, and we ran, but they caught Milan and killed him." His face is gray stone, all angles and shadows. "So. That night, any woman out on the streets—bad odds. All I can tell you is, this one was brave. Still fighting. And no rape. Milan saved her that. And then he paid the price. I couldn't save him. Them."

I cannot move. I cannot breathe.

"This is all I have. I don't know if this was your friend. But Nadija, she is gone. I'm sorry." There is silence. I don't know how long it lasts—seconds, hours.

Then he looks up at me, and his eyes shine. "Come to Berlin with me."

"What?" My ears must be broken. I cannot be hearing this. But still, he is talking, fast now—

"There are so many dead—I know, I know how it is—in Amsterdam, I thought I saw Stefan, it nearly broke me. But you have to cut them, or you go crazy. London is over now, okay. But Goran knows this guy for passports, so we could—new city, Nadija, we could . . ." A pause, then softly, looking to my face, "We're still alive."

In the mirror, I see it is raining. Soft drops run down the window. Faces, bodies, buildings flicker before my eyes, flicker out. Stone time, ice time, passes. Sanja says nothing, but she is here, waiting. What can I do, what can I give her? I am still, but my mind clicks like the wheel-running rat. This glass button Iggy carries—I see it now. It is hope. Iggy wants me to give him this future, stolen from all the dead and the missing. From my city and all the other towns and villages. Srebrenica. Mostar. Gorazde. From my tata. My Sanja.

No. This is my revenge for Sanja.

"Killer. Chetnik pig. Fucking murderers, all of you," I say. And I spit on the floor. He looks down, but I catch a flicker across his face. *Yes.* I hit target. Five seconds. Ten. When he speaks again, his eyes are dark, his face is cold.

"Little Turkish bitch." He leans forward slightly. There is a glint of metal.

"Do it. What's one more dead girl?"

But then he glances sideways. Grabs Sanja's camera from the chair and runs out the door.

A second. Two. Then I unfreeze, scramble over the bed, out the door, scream *Stop*, I'm running, faster, faster, trying to catch up to his clattering footsteps, but I trip and fall hard down the last few stairs. I get up to chase, but the front door swings open, I collide hard with a body and fall again. Now Naveen is looking down at me, eyes white around the edges like a frightened colt, yelling "Mum!" Mr. Patel is thumping down the stairs, the daughter's baby is screaming, and by the time I can stand again, there are more people: Mrs. K, Jamaal, the daughter, her husband, everyone is shouting, and when finally, I shove my way through them, the street is empty in both directions.

Iggy and the camera are gone.

37

It's still night by the time you get back, but barely; there's a yellowish tinge to the eastern sky. The extra trucks are parked round the back, the lights are off inside— Good, they're all gone for now. But not long till dawn; not long to get it all done. You go in, head straight to the band corner where you rip out the leads, fold down the mic stand, unplug the amps and instruments. Lug them downstairs and dump them outside—it takes several trips. By the time you've finished, you're sweating but your mind remains robot-cold, ticking off tasks. Next: Call Bibo.

The phone rings for a long time; finally he answers, voice furry with sleep.

"Come and get your shit."

"What?"

"It's outside. You have to get it this morning. The warehouse is done."

"What? Iggy, man, what's—"

You hang up. The guys nearly cleaned you out, but there's half a bottle of Johnnie Walker left. It'll do. Enough to keep you numb. You drink straight from the bottle. One swig, two. Welcome to limbo. You cough, then keep drinking. Once the bottle's empty, you grab the bag and head out across the wide concrete space toward the waterfront. By now, an egg-yolk yellow is staining the sky but you're not too drunk to make yourself walk slowly; though the rain has stopped, the concrete docks are slick with oil and moisture.

You reach the concrete lip of the dock where the boats tie up. Nice hard surface. Take out the camera out, place it down. Pick up a brick from the pile nearby— No. One more task first. You open the camera, remove and pocket the roll of film, then close it up again.

Now the whiskey fire rises as you lift the brick and smash the camera, once, twice—it breaks too fast, almost straightaway. The ease of it enrages you. You lift, smash, lift, smash until your breath is ragged and your arm aches and the thing that was a camera is just a pile of shards and broken glass. *Fuck you*, you mutter, and then you're howling, *fuck you fuck you bitch*, kicking the pieces, again and again, they fly into the air and then the water. Most of them sink, but a few bits of plastic float, then swirl away. A fairy dust of pulverized glass remains, clinging to the dock.

Far above you, the tops of the giant cranes glow spectral orange and yellow in the first rays of sun. You steady your breath, let your heart settle. Goran's full cleanup crew will arrive soon. You're the whistleblower; they'll be expecting you to help.

You walk almost steadily back inside and put the essentials in your backpack. Take one last look around, inhaling the phantom scents of coffee, sex, cigarettes. Then, before the sun can claw down and dispel the shadows, you slip out into the last of the night and you're gone.

38

There is in English this word, "gutted." It means the feeling when the middle is scraped out but you are still standing.

During the siege, many buildings were gutted. They were wounded on the outside by bullets and shell, and on the inside by fire, mortars, the loss of water and power. We fought against this *gutting* with everything we had. We had hunting rifles; they had mortars, jets, assault weapons. We had parties, dance bands, art in the streets, in cellars, in burned-out offices. We had a film festival. When a journalist—oh, these journalists, these intellectuals, who would visit us, wring their hands, then fly out—when she asked, *Why do you hold a film festival during a war?* the director blew out smoke, thought a moment, then said, *Why do they hold a war during our film festival?*

We even had a beauty contest. Usually, Sanja and I hated those things—"cow parades," she called them—but we were there with my tata and Emir and the other men from the tunnel, cheering and clapping as our teenagers put on bikinis and showed off their skinny siege-fed ribs, their smiles, their *fuck you* to the war. Miss Besieged Sarajevo, 1993. The banner they held up together said *DON'T LET THEM KILL US.*

But then. After one winter, then another. After yet another bombing and children's deaths. After we understood that yes, they would let them kill us, while they watched it all on TV. After leaving family lying dead on the street until night came and they could be retrieved—after all this, some eyes went dark and dull, like the windows in the gutted buildings.

■ ■ ■

Somehow, the days pass. I go to work. I come home. The spider plant is parched but I do not water it. I just watch it shrivel a little every day, until finally Priya stomps over to give it water, staring at me with those big brown eyes. But I say nothing. I am gutted.

The office is very quiet. Charles has disappeared. "Probably in Argentina by now," says Maudie. And Mrs. McGinley has taken a couple of days off to "look into things." So we drift.

There are no numbers to enter; we have no new accounts to work on. We just do "busy work," as Priya calls it: tidying files, updating the calendar, cleaning out the kitchen, ordering more coffee and envelopes. Roger and Maudie whisper in corners. I don't care about their secrets, but even I notice that they are serious, worried—not the usual gossip. Priya floats in her own sad cloud, missing Oleg, but nobody even teases her about it.

Finally, Maudie corners me beside the photocopier. Her usual sarcastic expression is gone; there are worry lines round her mouth, and her hair roots need touching up. She looks at me in sharp little glances. She says she told Mrs. McGinley what she found—the "Oversight Services" line from Temp Angels; the boxes that didn't come.

"To show we're good little soldiers," she says. "The shit's going to hit the fan with the audit, might as well be on the right side of it. But, Nadia, we don't know what'll happen to the office. So—"

"So, what."

"Just—we don't know, so— Be prepared." She is frowning at me, waiting for me to understand. I just shrug and return to my desk, where there is no sun and no new numbers to type, and stare out at the wall. There are two new patches of moss, and a little bit of orange lichen. The wall and I are close these days.

On Thursday, Mrs. McGinley returns, and it's as if someone turned the lights back on. Her heels are higher, her hair is lacquered into a bombproof bun, her lipstick is burgundy to match her jacket, and she carries a new shiny black bag with a metal clasp. In her wake slides a neat little man so professionally faded, I cannot remember his face or clothes the second I look away. *The auditor*, says Maudie.

"Good morning, everyone," says Mrs. McGinley. "Thanks for holding the fort." She has her professional face on, the one she wore to fire Elsie. There is good news and bad news, she says. The bad is that Charles and the Baltic Bigwigs cannot be found. The good is that, thanks to Maudie's detective work, we could freeze the accounts in time, so there is still money in the bank. So the office will stay open; there is still "legitimate business to get on with."

But then she says, "I'm sorry, Nadia. It's the agency— We can give you till Friday."

My perfect job. Of course it couldn't last. I have this feeling of standing on a boat, watching the others grow smaller on the shore. Nobody looks to my eyes. Mrs. McGinley is still talking, but it is only later that I grasp that Temp Angels has closed, leaving no trace, taking my fake work permission with them.

■ ■ ■

I am at the Hag and Crow, as I am most evenings now. It's dark outside; Roger and Priya have just left. Already things are strained between us; they still have jobs. But Maudie is still here, her blue eyes worried underneath their spiky mascara. She is talking; I am not listening. I am looking at Helen. The tattooed serpents twine around her strong arms, the bar lights glint on her chopped, newly orange hair. She pours drinks. People drink them. So simple and perfect. I want to live and die here, in the velvet cocoon of the bar. Why not; the world is full of shadows like me. Old men who sit in bars, washed up from some war no one recalls; women on park benches, clutching plastic bags full of bread crumbs. Other people flow past them, over them, through them.

Maudie clicks her fingers under my nose. "Nadia! Snap out of it, I'm talking to you!" I look up, frowning.

"What."

"The bloody brochures. Take them!"

"I don't want," I say. "Why would I study."

"Oh, for fuck's sake, we just went through all this. Okay, you can't work with a pending asylum case. But you could do a course. I looked it up. Get an allowance, take their money, screw those Home Office bastards!"

I shrug. My English is bad, how could I write essays? My books have burned to ashes. Sanja is gone; Iggy has stolen the last piece of her. Maudie is talking again but I am not listening. I am looking at Helen pouring a Guinness. The foam takes a long time to clear, and she must do it slowly, bit by bit. She has marvelous control.

Maudie's chair scrapes. She is getting up to leave. I look at her; she is sick of me, I can tell. Words are still coming from her mouth: ". . . or catering, or even bloody art school, it doesn't matter, it's people, company, a bit of money, they pay you to paint or take photos or learn cooking, pottery, there's loads of bullshit degrees in here. Just take a look." Her eyebrows are scrunched in crossly toward her nose. She gives the brochures a final shove toward me.

"All right," I say, to stop this glaring at me. "I'll take a look. Thank you, Maudie." She waits, as if to speak, then just pushes her eyebrows back up, too high, nods, and leaves.

"And don't just sit there till bloody closing time," she says over her shoulder.

Why not. I turn back toward the bar, but now Helen is packing up, and a pimply young man is serving instead. All the charm has left the bar. Where will I go? Then I remember. It's Tuesday. Paradise Island night. Images of dancing flesh, of the butterfly in Jody's neck, her soft skin, flicker in my mind. I drain my third glass and head out. In less than a week, I will have no income. Might as well spend what's left in bars.

A bass beat is already thumping up from the club as I walk down the steps. Smoke twines up from the door; two women are pressed against each other in the entrance, murmuring. I squeeze inside. It's after nine; everyone is dancing. At first there are just shadowy forms, silhouettes flecked with diamonds of light from the mirror ball. But as my eyes adjust, I make out familiar shapes. Marla, at the bar as always, shoulders half-hunched away from the action. The boyish twins in jeans and leather jackets, circling a short brown woman with jeweled nose and bleached blonde hair. I am a shadow, invisible, so I can stare.

Then I see her. A tall, fair woman, her plait swinging behind her, long neck stretched up as she laughs. But her arms are solid, and her face is pinky-freckled. With my new ghost eyes, I see nothing, nothing of Sanja here. The glamour is gone; this is just a market girl with outdoor skin. But still, she is pretty, why not . . . I start to move, but then the music slows, and she pulls a body toward her out of the darkness. A small one, brown hair, short skirt and tank top. A bit like me.

I watch as they sway, and in this light, I could be looking at Jody and me. Or Sanja and me. Or shades of people I will never meet, all replaceable, a little more faded with each copy, each twin, each shadow. Except for the originals, who are forever gone.

I slip out; nobody even turns to look.

■ ■ ■

It's late by the time I get home. I creep up the stairs, sit on my bed in the dark, and watch the clouds move in the mirror for a long time. All the light in the world is outside. It pulls me. I stand and push the window up, up, open wide. I slide one leg out, then the other, until I am sitting on the windowsill. Above me, the patchy orange night sky of London. Below, a long way down, the alley with its rubbish bins and rats. I am weightless, perfectly balanced. I rock a little. It would be so easy to rock just a little more forward.

I look along the alley one way, then the other. Once again. If a light goes on, or someone walks by, or a cat slinks past, or a bird flies . . .

even a rat . . . I wait, but there is nothing. Nothing at all. The world is an empty frame. The sky pulls at me, harder. I am already so light, the wind could take me away. I rock back, forward—but something tugs at me. A prickling on the back of my neck. It bothers me. I rub at my neck to get rid of it. But instead, it gets stronger. It won't leave me alone.

I am being watched.

I turn back to the room, ghost-gray in the dark. *Who is it?* I scan the room, but of course there is no one. Perhaps the clouds drifting across the mirror caught my eye. I wait. *Stupid.* Nothing is here. Still I wait. Now the sky is impatient. It pulls at me, harder and harder. *All right!* I turn, finally, toward the window—but there's a sudden flash of white at the far edge of my vision. And this time, I see. Staring at me from the dresser is the shiny envelope of Sanja's photos.

I stare back for one second—then fling myself inside. *What was I thinking*— I am shaking. I close the window and lock it shut. Turn on the light and, before I lose courage, tear open the envelope.

I place the photos blank side up on the bed, like a deck of cards, leaving the negative strip in the envelope. I will see them one by one. If I spread them all out together, my heart might explode.

I turn over the first picture. Black and white. There is a sweep of light, something moving fast. Knees bent in a crouch, a girl is spinning, on roller skates. She is laughing, her hair flung out as she spins. Defiant. Joyful. *Besima.* Shot dead in the street. The image shudders, vibrates.

I put her back under the pile.

Next photo. The man's coat is still on, his hand behind him is a blur pushing the door closed. He is very thin, and tiredness is in his shoulders. There are crinkles round his eyes, and he smiles mostly on one side of his face, with an eyebrow and a little grin. He is so alive, so *there*, I can feel the chilly wind swirl in behind him. My tata, coming home.

After this picture, I have to wait a moment until my eyes clear.

Next, a more formal picture, shot from above. A pretty girl approaches a soldier, who is about to light a cigarette. She is loose, smiling. He has stopped midgesture, suspicious. Suddenly the scene floods back to me: Alma bargains for food; we are the hidden watchers, Sanja is shooting, I am frowning, Sanja leans out our window with the camera, ignoring me. The scent of her forgotten cigarette smolders in the ashtray, she pushes back a long loose strand of her hair, her chipped nails adjust the focus—I could almost touch her.

Bolder now, I turn over the next pictures.

Second shot: The girl plucks the cigarette from the soldier's hand.

Third shot: Like a forties movie star she stands, chin lifted, waiting for him to light it.

Fourth shot: He is laughing a little bit. She smiles.

Fifth shot: He lights the cigarette. This one is a clever picture, romantic like the World War II victory shot of the soldier kissing a woman on the street. He is handsome; they are in soft-shadow light. The line of her neck and hand are elegant. The flame of the match centers the picture and lights their faces with a glow.

Sanja is so good at this. Deception, citation, irony—I see this scene more sharply now, through the photo. See her sideways glance to me, the lift of the eyebrow. I can't help smiling back.

Sixth shot: They are holding hands, turning the corner.

Seventh shot: It is later; there are long shadows. Alma is alone. She looks haunted, tired. Her lipstick is smeared, her stockings torn. She holds a string bag holding cheese, some tomatoes, some cans. She is walking fast, head down.

I have to put them down again. She just started earlier than we did.

Next photo: Here is a young woman, framed in the window seat, absorbed in her novel. She wears an old wool cardigan with glass buttons; one of them has fallen off. She twirls her hair absently. The shadow on her face is soft but her eyes are bright. All the life in this picture shines in the eyes. It is a picture of my soul.

But the final picture is strange, blurred. An angry face, a hand lifted—I am running, arm raised. Just before I struck the camera from her hand, in these terrible last days. Her camera, her life. *No.* I shut my eyes, then force myself to look again. *Yes.* It hurts me. But it's true.

My Sanja. You never blinked. You kept looking and you never turned away. And me? I shut my eyes. Shut you out. And then I ran like a rat.

■ ■ ■

I set out to find you again. I do. But walking is harder than I remember since I hit my head. A light snow dusts the streets. One block. Two. No shelling yet. I brace myself, smile and walk around the corner. But Hans isn't there. And then I look up and see that the building he'd been stationed outside has no glass in the windows. The front door is nailed shut.

I stand there like a winter tree. I have no other ideas. But then sudden hope blossoms—if he's gone, maybe he's taken you! You joked about this future for Alma—maybe it comes true. I see postcard pictures of you in Amsterdam, laughing, riding a bike among tulips— *Get real, chick*, you say. *Focus. Heat, food.*

I go back home and burn the last shelf of books. When they go out, the room grows cold. Now there is no food and no heat. If I stay here I will die.

I look for other exits, my Sanja, but there is only one. So. I brush my hair and clean my teeth, for the first time in a week. Wipe what I can of the stink from my body. Put on my tight pretty dress, the one with the roses. Open your huge makeup box, nearly empty now, and put on your red lipstick and butterfly brooch. Butterflies don't last long, but they are so beautiful. Like flames. Like books burning— *Stop this shit. Get real.*

I get real. There are several peacekeepers toward the south, right on the enemy line, where Sanja used to live. Very dangerous, but so are starving and freezing. Two ways to die—fast or slow. *Fast is better*, you drawl. I gather myself. One—two—heartbeats. I walk to the door—but then, a banging stops me. I can't comprehend this sound. Then it comes again. The door opens, and there is Emir, with a bag of supplies. Some sticks for the fire. We stand like gaping cows.

"Well? May I come in?"

"Of course! Please do."

You'd laugh at our absurd manners. Emir walks in and dumps the bag on the table. His black eyes dart round the room from inside a nest of grimy wrinkles. Remember he used to have that hard little tummy? Not anymore. His clothes hang off him.

"Sorry we couldn't do more. Milk, cheese, crackers, Valium. Antiseptic ointment. That's it for this week. They tried to bring a goat through, but she panicked and wouldn't go in."

My mouth floods, smelling the cheese, but I don't move. "Thank you, but."

"But what? It's food! Take it!"

"Everyone has gone. I'm here on my own," I say, and my lip trembles.

"Is that so," he says, and something in his voice changes. "You wouldn't have to be."

His eyes have that slightly shifty look now. And I remember I am wearing the rose dress, the lipstick. Dressed as peacekeeper bait. And—joke—here is Emir instead! One of our own! He moves toward me. I step back, I can't help it. His wife and my stepmother were friends. We'd all gone to his son's funeral.

"Think you're too good for me? Miss University."

"No, no, no, I just—" *Get real. Eyes on the prize.* I smile, and say, "You just . . . surprised me."

He moves closer. I look down again, shyly. *That works.* The quiet but sexy librarian. I run my fingers along his arm. And the ugly little fish is hooked.

Emir is not the kind to force me, not yet, he is vain, in the way of small men. He wants to believe this is my desire. So I wait for you, Sanja. I do. I tease, flirt, demur, for as long as I can. Give him a little bit, push him away, in case you walk back in. Or someone finds you. But the days pass, every day the bombing is worse, there is talk of having to close the tunnel. And every day there is nothing.

I wait five days. And then I make the deal: If he agrees to get me out, I am his. He takes the deal. But somehow, it's never the right time to leave. *Too many patrols today. The tram isn't running. Rumors of bombing raids. The tunnel is booked up.* I have to do something.

On the ninth day, Emir arrives and hands me a box of Cadbury chocolate. No one has chocolate.

"Hello, my little rose," he says, beaming with his cleverness.

"Our deal," I say. I do not smile—and I always smile.

"It's not safe today," he says. "Another few days."

"Now," I say.

"Why so cross today?" he says, moving toward me.

I fling the precious chocolate box on the floor and stamp on it. It cracks open, loud as a gunshot. Emir raises his arm, then stops, makes himself smile.

"It's not safe outside, bad things could happen."

I say nothing, and his words echo in the room. I look at him until he has to look away. Then I grab the knife from where I have placed it by the sink and hold it against my neck, close to the artery.

"Emir," I say. "I will leave or die, now. Which do you think my tata would want?"

And that is how, on February fourteenth, day of lovers, I abandoned you, my Sanja. Left our city, the lost, the living and the dead, to hide like a rat under a stinking sack in the trolley. And the man I fucked to pay for my escape pushed me eight hundred meters through the tunnel that my father had built and died in, and out the other side.

After I tell you this, I sit on the bed for a long time. Slowly, the light softens toward dawn. I spread out your photos, face up, in front of me. I don't look at them, but I feel them there. Keeping watch. Keeping me company.

39

You stare into your coffee, head still pounding from last night's after-party. Brutal, but worth it. Across the café, two pretty blonde girls—everyone in this city is blonde—are whispering and giggling. One is egging the other on. In a moment, she'll walk over to you; all you have to do is look up. You don't look up. Instead, you pull out the big envelope you picked up this morning, rip it open, and go through the prints.

Half the roll came out black. Shot in the dark, most likely. The rest are just ordinary street scenes, Camden market pictures, most of them out of focus. Some pigeons, seen flying in her big mirror; those were pretty. But no warehouse pictures, no boxes. She was bluffing. *Nadija, je težak inadžija!* Mad girl! You almost laugh out loud, but the thudding in your head stops you.

You remove the strip of negatives, reseal the envelope, drain your cup. Places to go, people to do. One last disposal job first. You walk round the corner into the nearest alley, check both ways: no one around but a sleeping drunk in a doorway. The prints are harmless, but still—there will be no more. Enough of this story. You pull out your cigarette lighter and hold it to the strip. It crackles and burns; in the daylight, the flame's just a shimmer in the air. In seconds the fragile plastic is ashes; you blow at them and they're gone.

Two blocks farther, the Central Post Office is crowded from the after-work rush. Good—gives you time to lift some Bubble Wrap, tape, and a box. No one notices; they never do. Brian Eno's *Music for Airports* plays at subliminal volume; the patient Dutch wait in line, like cows in a landscape painting. You pull the brand-new Nikon F90 out of your backpack, wrap it, and put it in the box. You flash briefly on the one you smashed—maybe bits of it have floated out to sea. Or just sunk into the mud of the Thames, become part of the city's bones.

Someone coughs, politely—you're holding up the line. You shuffle forward, add the envelope of prints to the box. Write her name and the address on the side. Go to seal it up, hesitate—then shove an old-fashioned glass button into the box too. By now you're at the register. You pay the international postage and lift the box toward the counter.

For just one moment, it's hard to let it go.

But then you do and you're out the door. You don't look back to watch the postal worker stick a stamp on the box and toss it into the giant sack behind her, to join the endless flow of stuff moving between buildings, vans, boats, planes, countries.

Train to Berlin leaves in two hours. *New city, new soundtrack.* Time to get moving yourself.

40

Two months go past. Autumn finally comes. The leaves are brown and yellow, people wear coats and walk more briskly. The tourist hordes have thinned out. The city seems to have shaken itself and gone back to work. Not me. But I did finally look at Maudie's brochures. And I got into photography school.

"'Course you did," said Maudie. "They love that war porn stuff." Yes, I used Sanja's prints to get in. She would have laughed.

■ ■ ■

London Bridge shudders as a bus chugs past behind me, and I clutch at the railing for a moment. Then I look down. A long, long way down. Below me, tugboats, ferries, big flat barges loaded up with coal and shiny boats screaming *money* jostle for space. They churn the water behind them to a foamy coffee. Lines from their passing crisscross, slap each other, subside.

I look up. Above me, the vapor trails of planes stitch the space between clouds, form a moving, melting map. *Amsterdam. Paris. Brussels. Berlin. Moscow. Damascus. Cairo. Bangkok.* Not Sarajevo, not yet. One day, maybe. *Home.*

A breeze whispers on the back of my neck, plays with a loose strand of hair, but nobody is there. It's just air. It dances over the water, scattering diamonds of light.

I will never forget, I tell her.

A shaft of reflected sun stabs my eyes. I blink, hard. Then I lift the new Nikon. I am still getting used to its lightness, its shiny sides. Through the lens everything is closer, more lovely. This light.

This London afternoon. This small breeze stroking the skin of the Thames, sliding toward an unseen ocean.

Focus, chick. I know how to do this now.

I slow my heartbeat. I watch, and wait. . . . Above me, a departing plane traces a sharp line upward. I look down, way down, to find its silvery twin reflected in the water. There! And now here comes the plane's shadow, flicking quickly over the river. The reflection and the shadow approach each other . . . close . . . closer—*now!* I take the shot. *Yes.* I know I've nailed it.

Then the lens shuts again, and just for a microsecond, everything goes dark.

ACKNOWLEDGMENTS

So many people helped bring *Nadia* to life. I will never be able to thank them enough.

This book would not exist without Linsey Pollak having persuaded me, in my early twenties, to visit Macedonia and Bulgaria. Our (sometimes hair-raising) travels sparked my long relationship with the wider region—with lifelong gratitude for the hospitality and musical brilliance of the Destanovski family and their community. My visit to their home in the Berovo mountains inspired my love of Romany and Balkan music, first as a musician, then as a writer.

Fast-forward a decade later to 1999: I met Dijana Milošević, Sanja Krsmanović Tasić, and Maja Mitić (then the core artists of Belgrade-based Dah Teatar) at a Magdalena conference in Cardiff, Wales. Their work as wartime theater artists and peace activists, and their amazing hospitality, began another connection that has continued for more than twenty years. I'm especially grateful to Dijana for hospitality, stories, introductions in Sarajevo, artistic collaboration, time at the splav, and, of course, the parties.

Duca Knežević advised me on queer life in former Yugoslavia and, along with Dragan Todorović, gave essential editorial notes on cultural-historical details. Dragan was a gold mine of information on rock and indie music of the era. Dženana Hozić kindly shared stories from her experience as a refugee in 1990s London and inspired the camera's role in the story. Jennifer Fink gave invaluable writerly feedback and insight into queer culture in the nineties. Any errors or misrepresentations of those elements are entirely my own.

Nadia herself first appeared as a ghost character, played by Kathreen Khavari in my play *You Are Dead. You Are Here.* During our trio's long collaboration, director Joseph Megel and media designer Jared Mezzocchi showed me that Nadia needed a bigger story; now she has it. Thank you to the whole team who made this piece with me— it's one of my core artistic experiences.

Thanks to Sarah Cypher for the Threepenny Editor Novel prize and for the exceptionally astute first-draft edit that it came with; to Caroline Leavitt and Mary Kay Zuravleff; and to fellow writers Arifa Akbar, Rachael Blok, Katherine Vaz, and Laura Zam for feedback and camaraderie. To Curtis Brown Creative, Anna Davis, and my London novel-writing group. To Liz and Tim Evans and extended family; and to Liane Laing, Stacia Saint Owens, and Hanna Berrigan, for their kindness and hospitality in London.

I'm grateful for the time and space to write provided by the Rocke-feller Foundation at Bellagio, MacDowell, the Virginia Center for the Creative Arts, DC Writers Room, the Porches and Trudy Hale, and a Georgetown University Junior Faculty Research Fellowship.

Thanks to China Miéville, for the magical pen when I needed it most. To beloved friends, sisters, and traveling companions: Renée Calarco, Rosalba Clemente, Gail Evans, Jenny Evans, Vanessa Gilbert, Holly Laws, Nadia Mahdi, Charlotte Meehan, Carole Sargent, Mary-Lou Stephens, and Ciella Williams. To Pat and Ernie Evans and all my extended family, for their love and support.

Thanks to my wonderful agent, Jennifer Thompson, who never gives up. To James McCoy for that one crucial note that changed the book; to Amy Schneider for astute copyediting; and to Susan Hill Newton and the whole team at the press: Meghan Anderson, Amy Benfer, Karen Copp, Danielle Johnsen, Allison Means, and Margaret Yapp.

And lastly to my love, Rick Massimo, for everything.